SECRET SANTA

Kati Wilde

SECRET SANTA

She's always been on the outside of love, looking in…

After years of struggling to make ends meet, Emma Williams finally lands a job that suits her perfectly—she enjoys her work, likes her new boss, and especially loves knowing her first paycheck is coming just after Christmas. That is, if she lasts that long. Because Logan Crenshaw, the creative force behind the company, doesn't seem to want her there.

Not being wanted is nothing new for Emma…but she doesn't know what she's done to make Logan stalk around the office, growling every command as if her very presence infuriates him. She can't afford to lose this job, so her plan is to keep her head down and try to avoid any contact with him—no matter how big and sexy and unavoidable he is.

But a Santa hat full of names, an office gift exchange, and one unexpected knock at her door are about to shake up all of her plans…

Warning: This super-hot holiday romance contains Santa hats, red satin blindfolds, and an obsessed alpha male who knows exactly what to do with his big hands. Lots of swearing. No cheating, no cliffhangers.

KATI WILDE

SECRET SANTA

SECRET SANTA &
ALL HE WANTS FOR CHRISTMAS

Also by Kati Wilde

The Hellfire Riders MC Romance
(Discreet Cover Editions)
SAXON

BLOWBACK

GUNNER

BULL & DUKE

STONE

(Original Covers & Ebooks)
THE HELLFIRE RIDERS: SAXON & JENNY

THE HELLFIRE RIDERS: JACK & LILY

BREAKING IT ALL

GIVING IT ALL

CRAVING IT ALL

FAKING IT ALL

LOSING IT ALL

Contemporary Holiday Romances
(Discreet Cover Editions)
SECRET SANTA & ALL HE WANTS FOR CHRISTMAS

THE WEDDING NIGHT BEFORE CHRISTMAS

(Original Covers & Ebooks)
SECRET SANTA

ALL HE WANTS FOR CHRISTMAS

THE WEDDING NIGHT

The Dead Lands
(Discreet Cover Editions)
THE MIDWINTER BRIDE
(MORE DISCREET COVERS COMING SOON)
(Original Covers & Ebooks)
THE MIDWINTER MAIL-ORDER BRIDE
THE MIDNIGHT BRIDE
PRETTY BRIDE
THE MIDSUMMER BRIDE
(COMING SOON)

Wolfkin & Berserkers
BEAUTY IN SPRING
HIGH MOON
TEACHER'S PET WOLF
SHERIFF'S BAD BEAR
(COMING SOON)

Contemporary Romance
GOING NOWHERE FAST[1]
THE KING'S HORRIBLE BRIDE

Fantasy Romance
EVIL TWIN[2]

---

[1] Includes cameos by the Hellfire Riders
[2] Set in the same world as the Dead Lands

SECRET SANTA

EMMA

"Well, look at that." My new boss's bemused voice pulls my attention from the spreadsheet laid out on my computer screen. He's standing by the Christmas tree in front of the big window overlooking the office parking lot, his ever-present *World's #1 Dad* mug in hand. "It's snowing."

Dread tightens my stomach as I look out into the dark. It's the middle of December, so night comes early, and huge flakes are swirling through the halos of the streetlights. The pavement in the lot is already covered in white.

"Isn't that lovely!" Her huge belly leading the way, Marianne bustles in carrying a bright red Santa hat.

"We might have a white Christmas after all."

A white, *freezing* Christmas. Oh joy.

"Maybe you better hold off on hoping for that," my boss says with a significant glance at her stomach. "You don't want to be driving to the hospital in a blizzard."

"And that's just like him, Emma." Marianne's pretty face is wreathed in a smile as she turns in my direction, so I drum up a weak smile in answer. "You'll say 'snow,' and a moment later, Bruce'll be thinking 'blizzard.' Or we'll run out of coffee pods, and a moment later he's dying of thirst. So you keep his head out of the doomsday clouds and you'll get on just fine."

My smile becomes more genuine then. I've only been working for Bruce Crenshaw for two weeks, but I've seen the older man's tendency to leap from the mundane to the dramatic in the space of a breath.

He winks at me, his faded blue eyes twinkling. "You'll notice that even though she's leaving me, I'm not crying that the sky is falling."

Marianne harrumphs. "You should have seen him last month, worrying we weren't ever going to find someone to fill my shoes. Yet here you are, Emma, and doing just...*oooh boy*."

Flattening her hand to her stomach, she purses her lips and draws in a long, slow breath.

Bruce's face goes pale. "Did your water break?"

"Her tiny feet just gave my lungs a good kick." Rubbing her belly, Marianne awkwardly lowers into the seat facing my desk. "Maybe I shouldn't head over to the workshop right away, though. Do you mind running out there before you head to the bank, Emma?"

"Not at all." Pushing back my chair, I reach for my coat. It's only a denim jacket, hardly warm enough for the weather, but the dress code at this job runs to jeans and flannel so I've got a hoodie layered beneath it. "What do you need me to do?"

I'm being trained to step into Marianne's position as general office manager for Crenshaw's Custom Woodworks, which means that I'll pay the bills, take care of the payroll, and answer the phones. I won't have much reason to leave the small main office, and in the past two weeks I've only been to the workshop once—during the tour of the company on my first day, when the builders were out on a home installation.

Which is fine by me. Because one of the men in the shop unsettles my composure so badly, I'd rather avoid him.

Not that I have to put in much effort, since it seems as if he'd rather do anything than talk to me.

"Secret Santa," Marianne says, holding up the fuzzy red hat. "The guys each need to pick out a name. We'll be doing the gift exchange at the Christmas party."

Which is scheduled for next week—on the day before Christmas Eve, which is also Marianne's last day of work. I can't imagine how much of a party it will be, considering that only three people work in the office and four more in the shop, but if free food's available, I'm all in.

At the window, Bruce says, "Actually, Emma, it looks like my son's about to save you a trip. He's probably coming in to look over those new estimates. Marianne, will you sit in with us while we go over them? And when Logan heads back to the shop, he can take the Santa hat with him."

Nodding, she begins pushing up out of her chair. They start off toward Bruce's office, and for a long second I'm rooted to the spot, looking out the window at the man coming from the workshop on the opposite side of the parking lot.

Logan Crenshaw doesn't move like he's in a hurry, but his long strides are eating up the distance. Snowflakes glitter in his dark hair and dust his wide shoulders. He's not wearing a coat, just a faded red T-shirt that clings to his thick arms and broad chest, along with black jeans and steel-toed boots, but he doesn't seem to mind the cold, anyway. His face lifts to the sky as he walks, and through the dark his white grin flashes—as if in sheer pleasure at the sensation of the snowflakes drifting across his skin.

The sight of that grin sears something deep and unnamed inside me. Chest hurting, I turn away from the window and look blindly down at my desk.

I don't know why Logan Crenshaw affects me like he does. Well, part of it, I know. He's gorgeous. Rugged and masculine, with cheekbones as sharp as a knife's edge that could have been honed on the chiseled stone of his jaw. But whenever Logan comes into the office, he barely does more than grunt and growl his responses. And he looks at me as if… as if…

The truth is, I don't really know what to think of the way he looks at me, because I've never seen anything like it before.

He's got his dad's light blue eyes, but they're icier—and more intense. When he turns that glacial stare in my direction, I feel like the smallest, insignificant idiot who ever walked the earth. My tongue tangles up and internally I shrink like a mouse cornered by a snow leopard. A giant, gorgeous snow leopard.

But a mouse is *not* what I am. Not usually. It's just that when Logan's around, I can barely even squeak. And when Logan looks at me, he never grins—with pleasure or otherwise.

I think a part of me would give anything to be the one who made him smile like that.

It won't be today. Whatever enjoyment he found in the falling snow has darkened into a scowl by the time the office door swings open.

I catch that forbidding expression with a quick glance. And there goes the mouse inside me again, shriveling up into a tiny ball. My gaze immediately drops to the deposit slip on my desk, but I'm aware of Logan's every step as he comes closer. Neck aching with tension, I wait for him to pass by on the way to his dad's office.

But he stops in front of my desk. Heart thundering, I look up.

God, he's so big. The reception area where my desk sits isn't small, yet he threatens to overwhelm the space simply by standing there. It's not just his height—his dad is almost as tall—or the strength in his thick muscles, but the sheer *presence* of him. As if there's so much more to Logan than what I can see, and the magnitude of that unseen portion takes up all the room.

With snow melting in his dark hair, he stares down at me with that intense, unreadable gaze.

I'm not a mouse. I'm *not*. Forcing steel into my spine, I tell him, "Mr. Crenshaw is expecting you in his office."

Beneath straight black brows, those icy blue eyes narrow. His voice is a deep growl as he echoes, "'Mr. Crenshaw?'"

My cheeks heat. Now I sound like an uptight, mousy idiot. No one in this office is so formal. "Your dad."

Still scowling, he watches me for another long second, gaze slipping over my face. A muscle works in his jaw. Finally he nods and, without another word, heads for Bruce's office.

Immediately the tension gripping my body loosens, and I draw in a deep, shuddering breath. Every inch of my skin feels prickly, tight—and covered in gooseflesh as if I'd been running naked out in the snow.

As if I were cold. But I'm not. I'm burning, and my

panties are so wet that if there was ever any ice inside me, it's long since melted.

Which is why Logan Crenshaw unsettles me so badly. Around him, I don't just transform into a tongue-tied little mouse. I become a tongue-tied little mouse with a drenched pussy.

I've never responded to *any* man this way—which is the reason I'm still a virgin at the age of twenty two. It's not that I've never noticed men, or never found them attractive. But from the moment I graduated high school and left my last foster home, trying to make a living always took priority, and I was too occupied with getting by to give more than a fleeting thought to sex.

I shouldn't be thinking of sex now, either. My priorities haven't changed. After being laid off from my last job and months of unemployment, I'm still just getting by. My overdue rent, my electric bill, my dying car—those are what I should be prioritizing. My body just hasn't gotten the message. Either that, or it's sending a message of its own.

Time to get laid, girly. Too bad it chose someone who scowls and growls at me instead of smiling and flirting.

Then again, maybe it's for the best. Screwing around isn't going to pay the bills. Neither is sitting here in sopping wet panties and staring blankly at a deposit slip, as if the form will fill itself out. With a sigh, I force myself to focus on work, and try to pretend that every cell within my body isn't attuned to the man sitting in

Bruce's office.

I almost manage to convince myself. Still, when four-thirty rolls around and it's time to head to the bank, I drag my feet while collecting my coat and car keys. I need to knock on the office door to let them know I'm going. But poking my head in means Logan will probably scowl at me again, and then I'll be obsessing over his reaction all weekend—wondering what I ever did to deserve that response…and wondering why it hurts so much.

Too late, though. Because I've only just picked up my purse when the office door bangs open and Logan strides through, his icy gaze fixed on me.

He's looking pissed again, as if seeing me standing here irritates the hell out of him.

Why? What did I ever do?

My throat tight, I tear my gaze from his face and scoop up the deposit envelope. Marianne's right behind him, so even though my chest is aching, I force a chirpy, "I'm heading to the bank, unless there's anything else I need to do before taking off for the weekend."

Logan's deep growl answers me. "Have you picked a name yet?"

"A name?" I echo stupidly, because he's stopped right beside me. So close, I can smell him—the warm scent of pine and sawdust, deeper and warmer than the fragrance of the office's Christmas tree.

In response, he shoves the Santa hat under my nose.

For the Secret Santa gift exchange. Oh shit. My gaze darts past him to Marianne. "I'm not part of that this year, am I?"

"Of course you are, honey," she says brightly. "You're an employee of Crenshaw Woodworks now, aren't you?"

"So you already put my name in the hat?"

"I did."

"But…" I scramble for an excuse, trying not to stare at the steely tendons flexing in Logan's forearm or his strong fingers crushing the hat's fuzzy white brim as he continues holding it out to me. "I barely know the other employees. I wouldn't know what anyone likes."

"Oh, everyone's easy. If you pick one of the guys' names, you just bring them a six pack of beer or make some cupcakes. Just something to celebrate the spirit of the season—and there's a ten-dollar limit, so no one's expecting anything fancy."

Except I don't have ten dollars to spare. I don't get my first paycheck until the thirty-first. Ten dollars means choosing between gas money or grocery money the last week of December. It means choosing between driving or eating.

And I need this job, so I'd probably choose driving.

Feeling sick to my stomach, I meet Logan's icy gaze—and only feel shittier when he grinds out, "I'm not going to bite you." He gives the hat a shake and the dangling white puffball swings wildly back and forth. "Just pick a fucking name."

Why is he so angry with me? Sparked by raging frustration, the timid mouse inside me burns to a crisp. I hiss at him, "I'm glad to see the spirit of the season has infused you with so much fucking patience" as I reach into the damn hat.

And oh my god. I thought his stare was intense before? I was wrong. *Now* the look he gives me pierces straight through my skin and sears me with a promise of…something.

Something that leaves me utterly frozen and helpless, tension riding my every muscle, my nerves on fire.

His gaze holding mine, Logan steps closer. His voice is a low rumble of gravel as he tells me, "You think I'm impatient, Emma? You have *no fucking idea* how patient I've been with you."

Why? What have I done? I search his face, but don't find an answer. My hand is buried in the velvet hat between us, and as he steps even closer, my senses are overwhelmed by his woodsy scent, his dominating size. Liquid desire pools deep inside me. If I don't get out of here, I'm going to dissolve into a puddle of arousal at his big, booted feet…where he would probably just scowl down at me.

I snatch a slip of paper out of the hat and flee.

LOGAN

I THINK IT'S REAL DAMN FUNNY THAT EMMA WIL-liams calls me impatient. She obviously doesn't know what the hell impatience looks like.

Is she sprawled across her desk with my face buried between her long, long legs?

No.

Is she on her knees with her golden hair tangled in my fist and with her pink lips wrapped around my thick cock?

No.

Is she crying out my name while I'm fucking her hard and deep? Is her hot pussy squeezing my dick when she comes all over me?

No.

None of that's happened yet. Even though there's been nothing else in my head since I first laid eyes on her. So it seems to me I've been *real* fucking patient.

But my patience is coming to an end.

And it's all I can do not to tear after her when she races out the door. For some reason, she's been terrified of me since day one. At first I wondered if she was shy, but Emma doesn't have trouble meeting anyone else's eyes. She doesn't refuse to speak more than a few words to them. She doesn't tremble and blush when anyone else stands close to her. So it's me that's making her skittish, and chasing after her now won't help settle her down.

Hell if I'm not going to try changing that, though. Especially after she snapped at me, called me impatient. Whatever I'm doing that's scaring her, that flash of temper says she's starting to push back.

So I can finally push a bit harder.

Beginning with this. I shove my hand into the Santa hat and grab all the remaining names. Dumping the slips of paper onto the coffee table in the reception area, I shuffle through them. There's four names left. My dad, Marianne, and two guys from the shop—Patrick and Tyrone.

Shit. I look up. "Did you get Emma?"

Marianne stops fussing with the decorations on the Christmas tree and raises her brows at me. "If I tell you, it's not a *secret* Santa."

"Did you get her name?" Each word drops like a stone.

A lot of people scramble to fall in line when I use that tone. Not Marianne. Her amused gaze skims the table, where the slips of paper are scattered around. "That's not how you're supposed to pick a name. You're supposed to trust in the magic of Christmas."

I do. But I also trust in the magic of capitalism. "I'll trade you a crib for Emma's name."

Which doesn't sound like much, except that Marianne knows I'm not talking about a crib that comes out of Babies"R"Us. My dad built a solid cabinetry and furniture business years ago, but in the past decade it's been my work that's put us on the map. Any custom piece I design and make, she can eventually sell for a small fortune or give to her kid as an heirloom.

A short battle plays out on her face. Finally she sighs, a sound filled with deep regret. "I can't trade hers because I got someone else's name."

Which leaves only two people who might have gotten Emma's. "You think she picked out her own?"

And ran off before she even looked at it.

Lips pursed, Marianne regards me silently for a long second—then gives a small shake of her head.

So my dad got Emma's name. Fuck yeah. I can work with that.

I pocket Marianne's name and sweep the others back into the hat. And because she looks so damn disappointed, I tell her, "Don't you give up hope on that crib."

Especially considering I've got a completed nursery set sitting in my workshop at home—a present to Marianne from me and my dad, for putting up with us the past ten years.

Laughing, she wags an admonishing finger at me. "Don't you ruin my holiday surprise, Logan Crenshaw."

"I won't." But maybe she'll be willing to trade something else—such as information. "Did Emma say anything that explains why she's so damn scared of me?"

Marianne doesn't even blink, or try to claim that Emma isn't afraid. So she's noticed it, too. But she shakes her head. "Not a word."

Fuck.

So what is it, then? Is it my that size terrifies her? I'm a big man, but that's not going to change anytime soon.

And when I get her tight little body under mine, she's going to love how big I am.

If I get her under me. Frustrated as hell, I rake a hand through my hair. It's a bit long. I don't bother shaving every day so my jaw's got some scruff. Not enough to scare off a woman, I don't think. It never has before. But that was then, and none of those women matter now.

Only Emma does.

"Although…" Marianne draws out the word as far as it can go before continuing, "It might be the way you look at her."

I frown. "How do I look at her?"

"Like you're a raging bull moose in rutting season."

That's pretty fucking accurate. But I didn't realize it showed.

Marianne isn't done, though. "And when you look at her, the air around you is combustible. I sometimes think the only reason everyone in the vicinity doesn't spontaneously become pregnant is because they're all men. And because my husband already knocked me up."

Shit. So Emma probably sees that I'm a walking hard-on. But what am I supposed to do different? *Not* looking at her isn't an option. Neither is toning it down.

Hell, I thought I *was* toning it down.

But it doesn't matter. Failing isn't an option, either. "All right. Thanks. I'll work it out."

"Well, hurry up about it," is her cheeky reply. "Because I want to see this happen before I'm gone."

I do, too.

Santa hat in hand, I head outside. The snow's still falling. Everything's quiet in parking lot. Only a single set of footprints are visible through the snow. Emma's. My gaze follows them to the spot by the fence, where she's been parking her ancient Toyota. Her car should be gone.

It's not.

The streetlight's shining through her windshield, giving me a good look inside Emma's car. She's leaning forward in the driver's seat with her elbows braced against her steering wheel and her face buried in her hands.

I know that posture. It's the universal sign for *'Why the hell won't my stupid fucking engine start?'*

Bad luck for her. Merry Christmas to me.

Boots crunching in the snow, I stalk across the lot. She doesn't look up until I rap my knuckles against her window. Her head jerks back and her gaze flies to mine.

And a second later I'm laid out, just fucking laid out. Physically still standing upright, but internally flattened by a one-two punch.

The first blow comes when I see the glitter of tears in her big brown eyes, glistening drops that magnify a soul-deep despair.

But it's the second blow that's the hardest. Because in the next moment she blinks and a smile curves her full lips. And although her eyes are still overly bright, there's barely a sign that anything's wrong as she begins cranking down the window.

Beautiful though it is, that smile's all wrong—because she's never aimed one at me before. And her tears squeeze at my chest, but this brave face she puts up is a kick to my heart. Because that brave face…that's armor.

This woman's a fighter. Someone who's been knocked down—maybe more than once. But who always gets up, straps on her shields, and keeps going.

And I wanted Emma before this moment. From the day I first met her, I wanted her in my bed, and a whole lot more.

Now I'm sure I *need* her.

She's still wearing that friendly, bright smile as the window comes down. Her cheeks and nose are pink from the cold or from crying. "Do you need help with something?"

"By the looks of it, I'm not the one who needs help." My voice is rougher than I intend, but this woman just knocked something loose in me. Though I'm dying to know what's hurting her—dying to fix it and take that hurt away—she obviously doesn't want to expose her vulnerabilities. Demanding answers might make her more scared of me than she already is. "Did you leave your headlights on?"

"No. My battery just doesn't like the cold." As if the gesture's part of the explanation, she waves a hand toward the passenger side, where a pair of jumper cables lies coiled on the seat.

I frown. That's not where people usually store their jumper cables. "This happens often?"

She shrugs. "I usually just have to get a jump from my neighbor in the mornings. Then in the afternoon it starts okay. Except for today."

Because the temperature dropped. But it's not getting warmer anytime soon. "Sounds like you need a new battery."

"I guess I do." Her smile becomes brighter, tighter—as if she's putting up another layer of armor between me and whatever put those tears of despair in her eyes earlier. "Do you mind giving me a jump so I can get to the bank before it closes?"

"I could, but unless you're driving for a while, a jump will only get you as far as the next time you turn off the car."

"That's fine. The bank has a drive-thru. I won't need to stop until I get home."

"And if your engine stalls? You'll be sitting dead. So I've got a better idea." One that'll keep her near me for a while. "I'll get Patrick out here to hook up the battery charger that's sitting in the shop, then I'll give you a ride to the bank in my rig. By the time we come back, you should have enough juice for a couple of starts."

Tonight, at least. Most likely it'll be dead again by morning. But I'll take care of that soon enough.

She hesitates, her gaze searching my face before looking past me—toward the office. Weighing her fear of me against the fear of making a bad impression at her new job, I'm guessing.

Neither my dad nor Marianne would give a shit if she didn't make that deposit until Monday. I won't point that out, though.

"You don't mind?" she finally asks.

Mind helping her out? That doesn't even merit an answer.

"Pop your hood so Patrick can connect the charger," I tell her. "I'll bring my truck around."

A few minutes later, I've got Emma Williams sitting in my cab, holding out her ungloved hands to the blast of the heater. She's withdrawn into herself again, avoiding my eyes—maybe afraid that I'll drag her across the bench seat and fuck her hard and deep.

But I won't do that. I'm just thinking it.

The doing can come later.

"Thank you again," she says softly.

"Yup."

A short answer, but I'm trying hard not to fall into rutting bull moose mode. Not easy, considering that my cock's a steel spike lodged behind my zipper—and considering that Emma's only an arm's length away, eyes bright and her armor in place. Christ, but she's a sight. That long, just-been-fucked blond hair. Those big brown eyes and a sweet short nose over succulent pink lips that have featured in every fantasy since I've met her. Those lips and those legs. They're a mile-fucking-long, though she's not that tall. Average height, maybe. She's wearing jeans now, denim hugging her sweet thighs and calves and cupping her ass the way I'd love to. First time I saw her, she was wearing a short pleated skirt over dark tights, and I've been picturing those leanly muscled legs wrapped around my waist ever since.

Around my waist, or around my head. Don't much care as long as her thighs are squeezing me tight as she comes.

But I keep the rutting bull reined in, even though I can feel her stealing glances in my direction. I'm guessing she won't look at me if I'm looking back so I keep my eyes on the road, instead.

But it's killing me not to see her pretty face. At the first intersection, I glance over. She's watching me, her plump bottom lip trapped between her teeth as if she's got something to ask but uncertain whether she should.

Emma Williams shouldn't ever feel uncertain around me.

I narrow my eyes. "What?"

Maybe that was too blunt, because her hesitation seems to deepen. But only for a second.

Then her eyes narrow right back. "Did you really drop out of high school when you were fifteen?"

There's no question where she got that. "You read that piece in *Northwest Quarterly*?"

A regional magazine, which currently has my face staring out from the cover in the checkout aisle of every local grocery store. It's not the first time I've been featured in industry and small business magazines, and probably won't be the last. Because as much as I hate those interviews, they're good for the company. In this latest one, the photographer posed me in front of a black walnut armoire I'd just finished, then caught me grinning at some point during the shoot, and the overall effect could be called *Smug Dickhead in a Flannel Shirt*.

Then the headline reads, "At fifteen, he's a high school dropout; at twenty six, he's schooling the woodworking masters."

Which is bullshit. I've done well for the company, made a name for myself. But I'm sure as hell not schooling any masters.

It's all right if Emma thinks I am, though. And I especially like the thought of her being curious enough to read about me. God knows if she was on the cover of a magazine, I'd snatch up any information I could about her.

Then stroke my cock raw while looking at her photo.

But she shakes her head. "I only saw the cover when I was at the library. Someone else was reading the magazine, though, so I didn't get a chance to look at the article."

"Ask Dad or Marianne for a copy. There should be a couple lying around." Because my dad bought a whole stack of them when the edition first came out in November—and the more Emma knows about me, the faster she'll realize she doesn't need to be afraid. And I still haven't answered her question. "Anyway, it's true. I left school early. But what the article doesn't say is that it was done with state approval, as kind of a homeschool arrangement. I spent the next year in apprenticeships and got my GED as soon as I could test for it. Those write-ups always use the dropout angle, though."

They have since the beginning—which was when

HGTV produced a season-long show following a celebrity renovating her house. They added segments featuring the architects, the construction crews, and the artisans involved, so when they discovered the actress picked out a dining set that was designed and built by a teenager, they were all over it. We got fifteen minutes of national airtime, complete with a heart-tugging interview with my dad, tears in his eyes and choking up while he talked about how we lost my mom in a car accident when I was eight. By the end of it, they had me looking like a woodworking prodigy who'd arisen from the ashes of tragedy.

As slanted as it all was, I'm not complaining. After that show aired, we could barely keep up with the orders. Now we have two sides to the business: the custom shop, that's me and the guys. And my dad's side, which is the production of our catalog items—all off site and basically like a furniture assembly line.

That original story slanted every interview afterward, though, and the dropout label is brought up every time. But I get it. A 'loser makes good' headline probably sells more copies than 'asshole studies his craft and works his ass off—and is lucky enough to sell a piece to a high-profile buyer and capitalize on the wave of publicity that follows—then over the course of ten years takes his dad's already solid business to the next level.'

Emma's eyes are alight with interest. "So you didn't flunk out. It was more like you weren't going to waste your time doing anything else."

"That's exactly what it was like." I practically grew up in my dad's shop. Officially I wasn't an employee until I was sixteen, but I was in there designing and building long before that. I didn't see any reason to spend more time in school when the stuff I wanted to learn was outside of it.

"You were that sure at fifteen?"

"I was that sure at five."

Her dark blond eyebrows arch in disbelief.

It's true, though. "When something's right for me, I know it," I tell her.

The same way I know Emma's right for me.

I don't think she's ready to hear that, though. And maybe it's the way I'm looking at her, but she bites her lip again and averts her face, squirming in her seat as if she's itching to escape.

So I ease up. "But it wasn't just me. You've probably seen already how my dad always jumps right to the worst, yeah? He worries about everything." At her nod, I continue, "When I told him that I wanted to leave school, he didn't have a single doubt. He knew it was right for me, too. And he says I get that certainty from my mom, because she was the same way. She knew exactly what she wanted and she didn't waste time pursuing it."

Her career, my dad. My mom proposed to him a week after meeting him, so I'm already trailing behind her. I don't suppose my dad was afraid of her, though.

Not considering that I was born nine months after they met.

Chances are I won't move as fast as she did with a kid, either. I'd like a few years with Emma to myself.

And although I'm glad she asked about me, I'm ready to talk about her. "What about you?"

She shrugs. "I finished high school."

Then went to the local community college to study business and accounting, all the while working part time as a bank teller and part time as a file clerk at an accounting firm. She got her associates degree and started a full time job bookkeeping at a construction firm, until it went under a while back.

"I've seen your résumé," I tell her, but I don't add that I only pulled it out of the filing cabinet after I met her. My dad and Marianne handled the hiring. "I'm asking whether managing an office is always what you wanted to do."

"Oh." She blinks. "Yes, it is. I didn't imagine Crenshaw's, specifically, but this kind of work."

I love that answer. Not sure I believe it, but I love it. Because I don't want her moving on to another job anytime soon. "Really?"

She nods. "Maybe not the part where I answer phones, but the accounting part of it."

Marianne's the opposite. She puts up with the bookkeeping because it's part of the job. But she loves interacting with people.

"So you like the numbers?"

"Not the numbers themselves, exactly, but the way they add up in a ledger. The way they all make sense." Her voice softens with a note of utter satisfaction, just as I imagine her sighs might sound when she's lying against me, sweaty and exhausted and her pussy juices still coating my dick. "I love how the assets and the liabilities equal each other, and that, no matter how many expenses go out and how much income comes in, there's always a credit for every debit—and a debit for every credit. The way it all fits together just…appeals to me on every level."

"I've never heard anyone talk about accounting like that." Jesus. It's sexy as fuck.

So is the blush that climbs her cheeks. "It's just that balance sheets are simple," she says, "no matter how complicated the accounting itself gets. And the math is never as complicated as people are."

"People are simple."

She gives me a look that says I'm crazy.

"Take me, for example," I tell her. "All I want out of life is football in the winter, barbecues in the summer— and beer to drink with both. Add in work for my hands and the love of a good woman, and I'm set for life."

And if I could only have one, I'd take the woman and give up everything else.

But only if that woman is Emma.

A little smile curves her lips. "All right," she concedes.

"Maybe I said it wrong. *People* can be simple. But the relationships between them usually aren't."

I won't argue with that. Though it makes me wonder how complicated her relationships have been that she takes such pleasure in a balance sheet. It also might explain why she's so damn scared of me—maybe she senses what I want from her isn't simple at all.

Aside from when we're fucking. That'll be real simple. So I'll start with sex before easing her into the complicated shit, like living together and marriage and babies.

Except she's fidgeting again, face averted and squirming a little in her seat, so I'll have to hold off on the fucking, too. Until she's not so jumpy around me.

And start with something even simpler. "What do you want for your Secret Santa gift?"

Her head swings around, that long golden hair tumbling over her shoulder in thick waves, her eyes wide. "You picked my name? Well, I'm easy. Just don't get me anything."

Like that'll happen. "I didn't get your name. My dad did."

"Tell him the same thing, then. Tell him he doesn't need to get me anything."

"Yeah, you don't know my dad. If he gets you nothing—or the wrong thing—he'll spend the next few months worrying that you're offended and planning to quit."

Her brow furrows. "I wouldn't do that."

"Try telling him that," I say dryly. "He'll worry anyway. But if I mention to him that I overheard you saying that you want…?" I leave that open, hoping she'll fill that in. But when she remains quiet, I continue, "If I can tell him what to get you, he'll stop worrying that he'll give the wrong thing."

"Oh," she says softly.

"So what do you want? If you could have anything."

My answer's easy. I want Emma.

It's apparently a harder question for her. She bites her lip again, and I glimpse naked yearning in her eyes before she faces forward, looking out the windshield.

After a long minute she says slowly, "Maybe a pair of pine scented candles? The tree in the office smells so good. It'd be nice to smell that at my apartment, too."

The bank's coming up across the street. I slow the truck and wait for a break in traffic. "Because you've got one of those artificial trees?"

"I don't have any tree," she says, and as a wood man, I can't decide if that's better or worse than having an artificial one. "It's just me at home."

It's just me at home, too, but I've got two trees—one in my bedroom and one downstairs—and both are fully decked out.

I enjoy the hell out of Christmas. Hell, being the simple man that I am, I enjoy *every* day. But especially this one, since Emma ended up in my truck.

I cross the lane, pulling into the bank's lot. "So I

should tell him that you want your place to smell like a Christmas tree."

"Yes." She hands over the deposit envelope as I drive up to the teller window, then a moment later she's looking past me with a gorgeous smile widening her lips. "Hey, Traci."

"Emma!" The teller on the opposite side of the window clunks open the metal drawer. "How are you doing, girl?"

"Good." Emma glances at me. "I finally got a new job."

"Mmm-hmm," is the skeptical reply through the speaker. "Well, he does look like a lot of work."

Emma's cheeks burst with color, but her laugh is light and easy. "No, really. Logan Crenshaw, this is Traci. We used to work here together when I was a teller. Traci, Logan is one of my new bosses."

Oh *hell* no. If I'm Emma's boss, then everything I plan to do to her becomes some fucked up sexual harassment shit. She likes things to be simple and that would *not* be simple. Or ethical.

Frowning, I shake my head. "Not a boss. Just an employee. My dad owns the place. I don't."

Emma looks at Traci again and they exchange one of those glances that women do, a flaring of their eyes that seems to contain an entire conversation.

Then Emma says, "How are your boys?"

"Texting complaints every minute since it began

snowing."

A little frown pleats her brow. "But don't they like the snow?"

"They love it. They're just upset because it started after school let out. So they're complaining that the universe cheated them out of a snow day." Traci huffs out a laugh, her long nails tapping rapidly at her keyboard. "And me, I'm thinking, 'Hallelujah!' No need to arrange for a sitter."

"A Christmas miracle just for you." Emma grins. "Are you doing anything special for the holiday?"

"Not a thing. Just my parents and my sister coming over. You?"

Emma shakes her head.

"Well, give me a call if you want to join us. You know there's always a seat at our table for you. And here's your receipt, Mr. Bossman."

"Thanks," I say gruffly and reach for the slip. "Nice meeting you, Traci."

"You, too." She looks past me at Emma and winks. "Enjoy your new job, hon. And every time you make a deposit, make sure you come to my window to tell me about it."

"I will." Emma's face is pink again. "I'll see you soon."

She falls quiet as I drive forward, my jaw clenched against boiling frustration. Because she claims relationships are difficult and she prefers balance sheets to personal interactions. Yet here she is, sweet and funny and obviously on easy and friendly terms with this woman. Just as I've seen her be with Marianne and my dad.

But not me.

I feel her studying my profile, and there's another of those maddening hesitations before she says, "Traci didn't mean anything by any of that, you know."

I shoot her a sharp glance. "Any of what?"

"Nothing," she whispers and turns her face away from me again.

Goddammit. "Why are you so fucking scared of me?"

Her head whips around, eyes wide. "What?"

"You. Scared." My fingers tighten on the steering wheel. "Of me."

"I'm not!"

"Bullshit. Then why are you always shrinking away from me?"

"Because you're always growling at me!" she shoots back. "And I don't know what I did to piss you off!"

That surprises the shit out of me. "You think I'm angry?"

Her eyebrows abruptly draw together, as if she's as surprised as I am. "Aren't you?"

"No."

She eyes me warily. "You look like you are."

"That's just my face." My *I'm going to fuck you good and hard* face. Which she ought to get used to, since I'm not sure I can look at her any other way. "I'm not pissed."

"Oh." It's a soft realization, and I see some of the

tension in her posture fade as her gaze searches mine—as if recalibrating what she thought my expression meant.

And she thought I was angry. All this time. Marianne saw a rutting bull moose, but she knows me well. Emma doesn't.

But now we can start over. "All right?"

"Yeah." Then her brows arch and she gives me a little smile. "Though now I'd hate to see how scary you look when you *are* angry."

"It doesn't happen a lot." Frustrated, yes. Angry, no. And this time with her is too damn short. We're only a few minutes away from the office and I'm not ready to give her up yet. "Is there anywhere else you need to stop before we head back to your car?"

Pressing her lips together, she shakes her head.

Shit. "The longer your battery is hooked up, the more it'll charge."

"That's okay. I just need it to start."

"We could stop at Murphy's, kill some time over a few drinks."

She hesitates again, but this time I know fear of me isn't causing that uncertainty. And that sweet yearning touches her face, as if she'd like to go.

But she says, "I shouldn't."

"You got something better to do? You said you were heading straight home."

"I am."

"So you've got someone coming over or picking you up for a date?" It's Friday night. No way she made it through this week without someone asking her out.

Shaking her head, she laughs as if me asking that was a joke instead of the deadly serious question I meant it as.

"Then come out with me," I tell her.

Again that yearning. Again she shakes her head. "I really can't."

"Why?" I'm pushing hard, I know it. Maybe too hard. Because I can see that armor go up.

Tearing her gaze from mine, she slowly says, "Well, I've got a new battery to buy."

Ah. Little Miss Balance Sheet. I bet she budgets every expense for months—and she was out of work for a while, so her budget probably looks pretty damn thin.

"My treat," I tell her.

Still she shakes her head. "I don't know when I can pay you back."

"Pay me back?" That frustration rears up hot and hard again. "A treat doesn't go into a balance sheet."

The look she gives me says she doesn't believe that for a second.

And then there's nothing left to say. Because she's withdrawing again, going quiet in the passenger seat. Not in fear, but just…pulling away from me.

Fuck.

If I push now, she's just going to withdraw further.

So I'll back off tonight. But I'm not giving up. I'll simply find another way to get beneath her armor. I just need an *in*.

And thanks to a name and a Santa hat, I've already got one.

EMMA

SATURDAY MORNING, I WAKE UP BURIED UNDER my mound of blankets and lie there for a while, my mood strangely buoyant. I don't realize why until after my quick shower, when I'm scrubbing a towel over my shivering skin.

The heavy knot of anxiety in my stomach is gone.

It shouldn't be. My apartment's freezing because I've been staying one partial payment ahead of the electric company's cutoff notice for months, and to keep the bill manageable I don't set the thermostat above fifty five. And last night after I drove home, I added the expense of a car battery to the spreadsheet I use to calculate my budget. When I was hired at Crenshaw's, putting in my anticipated income was an enormous relief, but many of the columns still remained in the red until June. With the purchase of a battery, the red will creep into July.

But Logan Crenshaw isn't angry with me.

When I head outside, my car doesn't start. I don't expect it to, really, but last night in the parking lot when I turned the key and my dash indicators didn't even light up, months of despair and worry crashed in on me in an overwhelming rush. This morning, that dead battery doesn't seem so dire. It just needs to last two more weeks, and jumping it each morning has worked well so far. When I'm at work, I can ask them to hook up that charger again. That'll get me to and from the office until the end of the month.

And Logan's not angry. He just looks that way.

That shouldn't matter so much. When I weigh Logan's not-anger against those red columns, that anxiety should still be chewing at my gut.

It's not, though. Instead I feel hopeful as I start off through the snow. The best thing about my apartment—aside from my awesome landlord who let me pay only half my rent this month on the promise to settle the balance out of my first paycheck—is that the location is within walking distance of everything I need. So I spend a few hours at the wonderfully heated library, then walk to the grocery store armed with its weekly ad flyer. I don't buy anything. Instead I head to the bakery aisle and try to figure out how I'm going to afford a dozen cupcakes.

I work it all out back at home, sitting on my sofa wearing a stocking cap, fingerless gloves, my heaviest sweater, and a blanket tucked around my legs. My back is wedged up against the sofa arm, because my ancient laptop battery doesn't hold a charge any better than my car battery does, and whoever designed this apartment put only one outlet in the living room—and in the most inconvenient possible spot—so I've got my adaptor cord strung across the floor in a taut line from outlet to couch. But I'm cozy warm because the laptop is like a heating pad on my thighs, I've got a peanut butter sandwich filling my stomach, and I'm no longer dreading the gift exchange so much.

This Secret Santa thing might turn out okay, after all.

Buying store-made cupcakes would be cheaper than making them—only five dollars versus eight dollars for a cake mix, chocolate frosting, a dozen eggs, and cupcake liners. But the mix only calls for three eggs, which means I'd have nine left at home. Plus it yields two dozen cupcakes, so after giving half away, I could eat the remaining cupcakes for breakfast or lunch. Add a bag of potatoes and I'm set for next week.

Not exactly healthy, but I can make up for that when all those red columns are in the black.

I'm already dreaming of hashbrowns and eggs on Christmas morning as I put away my laptop and grab one of the paperbacks I picked up at the library—*The*

Martian. It's a re-read, my third time through in as many years, because its such ridiculous fun.

And compared to growing potatoes in human feces while stranded on an alien planet, those red columns don't seem so bad.

That red won't last forever, either. Only seven more months of pinching every single penny and barely keeping my head above water. Then I'll catch up on all of my payments and those columns will be in the black.

And Logan isn't angry. He's just absurdly sexy.

Maybe next time—when those columns are in the black—I can go out for that drink. If there is a next time. He's not angry, but my answer yesterday didn't make him happy, either. So maybe he won't ever suggest it again.

My chest suddenly aching, I settle deeper into my sofa cushions—then almost jump out of my skin when someone pounds on my front door.

Holy crap. Someone's got a huge fist. And I'm not expecting anyone—I rarely have visitors—but I suppose it's not too late for a delivery. Not that I've ordered anything. But I can't imagine any of my neighbors or friends banging on the door like that. The UPS guy, though, maybe he would.

I throw the blanket from my lap and the skin on my thighs immediately goosebumps in the cold air. I'm not completely bare, though—I've got on flannel sleep shorts and striped knee-high socks—and my sweater is long enough that I could belt it and wear it as a dress.

With my hat and gloves, I probably look like a complete dork, but…that's pretty accurate. And I'm sure the UPS guy won't care.

Book still in hand, I go up on tiptoe to look through the peephole.

No one's there.

My apartment building is basically two buildings separated by a breezeway that leads to the parking lot. Through the fisheye lens I can see the unit doors across from mine, along with most of the breezeway. It's all empty. With my security chain connected, I open the door.

A small white gift box sits on my step, topped by an envelope with **OPEN ME NOW, EMMA** scrawled across the front in thick black marker.

Weird. But okay.

The box is light. I rip open the envelope. There's a typed note inside—on Crenshaw Woodwork's letterhead. So this isn't some random gift drop. It's starting to make more sense. But only a little. Because the message is:

> **Open the box and find your first gift. Put it on.**
> **Unlock your door and wait.**
> **Don't remove your gift until I'm gone.**
> **Signed,**
> **YOUR SECRET SANTA**

The signature is scrawled in the same thick marker. Then there's another little handwritten note, a **TRUST**

ME, EMMA with an arrow pointing to the logo on the letterhead.

Because I'll be unlocking my door so that someone can come in. He's trying to reassure me that I'll be safe.

He won't be a stranger. I know my Secret Santa is Bruce Crenshaw. Logan told me he was.

Logan was also supposed to tell his dad to give me pine-scented candles…and the gift exchange is supposed to take place during the Christmas party. We're not at the Christmas party, and the gift isn't heavy enough to be candles. Unless they're tea lights.

My breath stops when I open the little box.

A blindfold. Or more accurately, a sleep mask—one that Santa might wear, made from red satin and trimmed with white fur. But since I won't be sleeping, the intended purpose is the same as a blindfold's.

So I'm supposed to cover my eyes and let Bruce come in? The note seems to suggest he'll quickly go, and the blindfold is just so that I won't know who he is.

So he must be bringing something in, then leaving it here. And although I'm hesitant…I'm also *so* curious. I'm charmed by all of it, too. I like Bruce. He's so sweet—and he's apparently taking this Secret Santa thing to another level. And no one's *ever* put this much effort into a gift for me before.

And, okay—this is the most exciting thing that's happened to me in a very long time. Which is sad. But there it is.

I leave the door open a few inches. Backing up against the wall so I'm out of the way, I take a deep breath.

And put on the mask.

I have to pull off my stocking cap to fit the elastic strap over my head. As soon as I tug the satin into place, every sensation seems to sharpen.

The prickle of the cold against my thighs. The softness of the mask's furred trim against my cheeks. The rapid thundering of my heart.

And from the breezeway, the approaching tread of boots on concrete.

A shiver works over my skin. Not cold. Not really. It's just that my head is trying to make up for the blindfold, and I'm imagining what I can't see.

But I'm not imagining Bruce. I'm imagining Logan.

It's because of that tread. The unhurried pace of it. Logan moves like that, his stride slow and long, as if he's never in a rush to do anything. I've noticed it so many times.

Maybe Bruce does, too, though. My impression is that when he walks, he's quicker and more focused. But the truth is…I haven't paid as much attention to Bruce as I have his son.

So I try to adjust my mental picture. I try to imagine Bruce's lean height and his salt-and-pepper hair and his easy smile.

But when my hinges softly squeak, I imagine Logan's dark scowl, instead. I imagine his broad frame filling my open door. I imagine him spotting me standing here, my back pressed against the wall, my hair in a thick messy braid, wearing a satin mask and knee-high socks and with my breath skimming quickly through my parted lips.

He wouldn't be able to see the hardening of my nipples through my thick sweater. He wouldn't be able to see my pussy flooding my panties.

Oh my god. I'm so turned on.

My face heats. Beneath the mask, I squeeze my eyes tightly closed, as if to shut out the mental picture of Logan watching me with that icy gaze. But it's not Logan, it's his dad. I'm getting hot while my poor unsuspecting boss is standing right there.

Luckily, Bruce can't see my arousal. He has no idea what's going on in my head.

And I have no idea what he's bringing in. There's a strange brushing sound, as if he swept the stiff bristles of a huge broom across the side of the door frame.

I'm still puzzling over that noise as he takes the first few steps inside, then the strong scent of fresh pine hits me and all at once I know what the sound was.

Branches. From a Christmas tree.

A *real* Christmas tree.

A burning lump fills my throat. Behind the mask, my eyes squeeze shut again, trying to stop the tears that threaten to burst free, but I can't stop the soft sobbing breath that shudders from my chest.

I don't think he hears it. His boots are still crossing the room, then he pauses for a moment. Maybe deciding where to put it. Maybe looking for an outlet so that I can plug in the lights.

I don't have lights. But it doesn't matter. Already my apartment smells *so* good, and this is going to be the best Christmas ever.

My throat aching with sweet tears, I whisper, "The outlet's over in that wall nook," and point a trembling finger in that direction. "Just follow the computer cord."

A moment later comes a soft *thunk* as he sets the tree down. I think he fiddles with its position a couple of times, because I hear the scrape of pine needles against coarse fabric, as if he's reaching in between the branches to adjust the rotation of the trunk.

Finally he starts heading back my way. Leaving.

"Thank you." My voice is thick. "You must have spent much more than a Secret Santa was supposed to, but—"

"You're going to take it anyway."

My breath stops. That gravelly voice doesn't belong to Bruce.

It belongs to his son.

And Logan's not heading for the door. Everything inside me draws up tight and hot as his footsteps come nearer. I can't see him, but I know he's right in front of me. I can feel his warmth and his breath, and there's a soft thump against the wall—as if he's braced his hands beside my head so that he can lean in, and I think our gazes would be level if a mask wasn't covering my eyes.

"You're going to take it, Emma." Low and rough, he moves in closer, until his mouth can't be more than a few inches from mine. "Aren't you?"

I am. He'd have to fight me to get that tree out of my apartment again. Even though— "I shouldn't. It's too much. We have a ten-dollar limit."

His growl deepens. "Didn't your parents ever teach you not to haggle over the cost of a gift?"

"No," I respond breathlessly, my heart racing. "They dumped me on the front steps of a church just after I was born."

Utter silence.

Then he says, "You ever shove your foot so deep into your mouth that you can just about feel your toes tickle your prostate?"

Giggling, I shake my head.

"Well, my foot's that deep right now. I'm sorry, Emma. I didn't know."

"It's okay." It really is. I never knew my parents, so I can miss the *idea* of them, but I don't miss them. Whereas Logan lost a mother he knew and loved. "Probably better to be raised in foster care the way I was than by someone who couldn't keep me."

"I don't know about that." His voice is a low rumble again, but lighter. Teasing. "Because your foster parents didn't teach you that you're supposed to accept a gift without questioning the cost."

"Yeah," I sigh. "Some of my foster families made certain I was aware of *exactly* how much a gift costs."

"So they put them on a balance sheet." Not so teasing now.

I shrug. "I can't complain. They mostly all treated me well."

There's a long pause, filled with his heavy exhalation, as if he's struggling to control his reaction to that. Maybe it's a response to the *mostly*.

Or maybe he doesn't like the balance sheet. He didn't yesterday when I turned him down for that drink. But it helps me make certain I'm not asking too much of anyone—or leeching off anyone. And when it comes to money and friends, I *really* don't like it when my columns are in the red.

I don't know if Logan is a friend. But I absolutely do not want to start off in the red with him.

"I just like it equal," I whisper when his silence continues. "And with the Secret Santa, that dollar limit makes it all equal."

Or as much as it can be. Some gifts are more thoughtful, chosen with the specific person in mind. Some people spend more time on theirs, decorating or creating their gift. But in monetary value, at least, they're fairly even.

"All right," he says gruffly. "So you're fretting over the difference between ten dollars and the cost of that tree. Well, then—you just make up the difference."

Familiar anxiety knots my gut. "Okay. But it'll take

me a little while to pay you back."

"I didn't say it'd be with money."

That makes no sense. "Logan—"

"Who the hell is this *Logan* asshole?" His voice is low and amused. "I'm your Secret Santa. Call me Santa."

I can't stop another giggle. "Santa."

"See? You don't owe *Logan* anything. But Santa's wondering how many kisses it will take to make up that difference."

My heart stutters. "Kisses?"

"The long and deep kind." It's a guttural confirmation. "As if my mouth's slowly fucking yours."

His mouth fucking mine.

Slowly.

Oh god. Everything inside me is shaking, my brain barely functioning. I feel him shift closer, as if he's no longer leaning over me with his hands braced against the wall, but as if he's straightened again and the entire length of his body is only inches from mine.

Big, warm palms cup my jaw and gently tilt my head back, as if he's looking down at my face. Callused thumbs slide along the bottom edge of the mask. "How many kisses, Emma?"

My body trembling, I manage to stumble into an answer. "I–It depends on what value you'd assign to a kiss."

I'd give mine for free and never make up the difference.

Voice pure gravel, he replies, "Emma Williams, I'd

bring you a thousand trees for just one taste of your lips."

A nervous huff of laughter escapes me, though he didn't say anything funny. It's just that what he *did* say has my mind spinning and my synapses misfiring and I can't control anything coming out of my mouth. "Then I suppose the tree you brought is worth one thousandth of one kiss. So I could make up the difference with a little peck."

"A little peck? Fuck that math," he growls, sounding like every time I thought he was angry with me. Hard and rough and abrupt.

But it's not anger.

Instead it's sweet and hot. And so soft, when his firm lips settle against mine. Lightly he teases the width of my upper lip with butterfly kisses before catching my bottom lip gently between his teeth. Erotic delight shivers through me. My mouth opens on a shuddering breath and he licks his way inside, his tongue tasting mine in a leisurely, sensual slide.

And slowly, so slowly, his mouth begins fucking mine.

There's no other word for what he's doing. I've never fucked anyone, and I've only kissed a few people, but those kisses were nothing like this. With every slow thrust of his tongue, Logan takes complete possession of my lips, his big hands cradling my cheeks as he angles me for a deeper taste, his chin rasping lightly against mine. His jaw is smooth, smoother than my mind pictured when I imagined him coming through the door, because only yesterday thick stubble shadowed his face.

As if he shaved just before coming. As if he had every intention of kissing me when he got here and didn't want to rip up my skin.

And the thought that this was part of a plan—that he made this effort just to kiss me—makes it all even hotter.

On a soft moan, I rise up higher on my toes, my arms wreathing his neck. The fingers of my left hand are still wedged between the pages of my book, my stocking cap dangling from my right hand. I drop the cap so I can bury my fingers in his thick hair, which is as soft and silky as his kiss.

When my fingers tighten, a growl sounds deep in his throat. It's the hottest noise I've ever heard, almost as hot as the way his big hands slide down to grip my ass through the thick sweater and lift me higher against the wall. Without hesitation he pushes into the cradle of my thighs. My inner muscles clench with aching need when the hardness of his cock wedges against the soft melting heat of my pussy.

Too many clothes separate us. Desperately, I rock my hips against his, needing that thickness to fill me, needing his entire body to fuck me like his mouth is fucking me.

Except his mouth's not doing that anymore. Abruptly he breaks the kiss and buries his face in my neck, his chest heaving against mine.

Oh god no. He can't stop. In the grip of frenzied arousal, I grind against his heavy erection. "Please."

His tortured groan rumbles against my throat. Strong fingers tighten on my hips to halt my frantic motions.

My next breath is a shuddering plea. "Logan, *please.*"

His big body presses closer, trapping me against the wall, forcing me to stop moving by the sheer weight of his length against mine.

His mouth opens against my throat, leaving a soft hot kiss against my skin before he lifts his head.

"Not Logan," is his gruff reminder. "I'm your Secret Santa. And there's nothing I want more than to finish this, baby. But when I fuck you, it won't be part of an exchange."

My breath catches. "When you do?"

"Yeah. *When.*" Slowly he sets me down, my back sliding against the wall and my pussy dragging over the long length of his erection before my feet hit the floor. "So you tell me, Emma—if I show up tomorrow, there'll be no gifts to put on a balance sheet. I'll just be coming to fuck you. Are you going to open your door?"

I don't hesitate. "Yes."

The swiftness of my reply seems to amuse him. "You don't want to think about it for a minute?"

"No." Though I should. We work together and I desperately need this job. Sleeping with Logan could be the biggest mistake I ever make.

It doesn't feel like a mistake, though. It feels…right.

Or maybe I just *want* it to feel right.

"All right, then." Big hands still gripping my ass through the thick sweater, he gives my butt a squeeze, then lets loose a half laugh, half groan. "You feel so damn good. I better get out of here before my control snaps and I screw you right up against this wall."

"You should anyway," I tempt him with a saucy grin.

This time his response is pure groan. "You're so fucking beautiful. You smile at me and I might do anything. But right now"—his grip tightens on my bottom—"I've got another quick exchange in mind. You figure that mask costs about as much as your panties?"

A naughty little thrill ripples through me. "Maybe about the same."

"You wearing some under this sweater?"

"Yes." It's a breathless reply. "And my pajama shorts."

"I don't want you freezing under there, so I'll just be taking your panties. Are they your favorites?"

I shake my head.

"Good thing. Because after all the unholy things I'll be doing to them tonight, you probably won't want them back."

I'd rather he did those unholy things to *me*.

Though this might be close enough. With the mask covering my eyes, I can't see him sink in front of me. I don't know if he's crouching or on his knees. I just know that his shoulders are somewhere on level with my waist, because my arms looped around his neck are much lower now.

Then I lose even that contact, when he grips my wrists and brings my arms back to my sides. Pausing for a moment, he angles the book I'm still holding, as if to read the cover, then says softly, "Is this what you were doing in here before I showed up—you were curled up under that blanket on your couch, reading?"

"My exciting Saturday night," I say wryly. "Me and a stack of library books."

"Smart is exciting. And it's sexy as hell." Long fingers skim up the back of my calves. "So are these striped stockings. Fuck. I'll spend the rest of my life picturing you wearing these while I've got your feet up on my shoulders and I'm burying my cock inside your sweet pussy as deep as I can get."

Need crashes through me at the onslaught of images those words paint, my inner muscles clenching painfully hard. Softly I whimper, my thighs tensing under his fingers.

A deep chuckle reaches my ears. "You like me saying I'm going to fill up your pussy with my thick cock? You like that dirty talk?"

I guess I do. Cheeks suddenly hot, I nod in response—unable to speak, because my entire body is trembling with tension as his fingers reach the hem of my shorts.

"These first." His voice is rougher now, his big hands reaching beneath my long sweater to grip the elasticized waistband. "Go ahead and step out of them."

The flannel is a soft whisper down my legs. Obediently I lift my right foot, followed by my left.

"Hold onto these." He curls the fingers of my left hand around flannel. "I'm going in again for my prize."

And he's taking the long way up, his palms sliding up the sides of my calves, long fingers brushing the backs of my knees, smoothing over the bare skin of my thighs. Then higher, curving up over my hips, and the cool air inside the room slips beneath the sweater, like an icy breath against the wetness slicking my inner thighs.

"You're shaking, Emma." Callused fingers trace the lacy edge of my waistband. "You all right?"

Dying. But better than I've ever been.

I nod, then clench my teeth against a tortured moan as he begins dragging my panties down my legs. My sweater's too long for him to see anything, but I feel so bare, so exposed.

And so aroused.

His breathing is harsh and slow. "Now step out—"

Abruptly his hands stop, my panties just above my knees.

"They're soaked." His voice is thick and guttural. "Your panties are just fucking soaked."

I knew they were wet but that sounds as if they're far wetter than they should be. My face burning, I awkwardly try to press my thighs together, to trap and hide the offending garment—and freeze when he growls.

"Don't you fucking dare." Roughly he shoves my long

sweater up to my waist, then a deep groan rips from his chest. "Your pretty little cunt's dripping with your sweet juices, baby. God help me. I tried. I was going to leave without taking more. But I can't leave you like this."

Scorching heat suddenly engulfs my pussy. My breath explodes from my lungs, my body stiffening with shock.

Logan's mouth.

That's Logan's *mouth*.

And his tongue, roughly stroking my clit. I cry out, my book dropping from nerveless fingers, my knees almost folding—but Logan's strong hands pin my hips against the wall. His ravenous growl reverberates over my sensitive flesh, and this is what I thought his kiss would be, but that was tender and sweet and slow, and this is ravaging, devouring. His hard fingers drag my panties the rest of the way down my legs, then he grips my left thigh and hooks my knee over his shoulder, opening me wider to the fierce hunger of his mouth.

Breath coming in sobbing little pants, I fist my fingers in his hair, and I can't stop the mindless rocking of my pussy against his face. The ruthless assault of his lips and tongue has completely shattered my control—if I ever had any.

With Logan, I don't think I do. There's just need and pleasure like I *never* imagined.

He lifts away from me just long enough to murmur harshly, "You taste so fucking good, Emma. So sweet and hot. I'll never get enough of this pussy."

My pussy won't ever get enough of *him*. My hips buck uncontrollably against his grip, desire spiraling tighter and tighter with every devastating lick, each one hotter, wetter.

Back arching, I cry out again when his firm lips close around my clit and he begins sucking on that sensitive bud, tongue flicking relentlessly. An orgasm approaches, but it's nothing like the ones I've given myself with my fingers before, that sweet shaking release that ends with a soft pulse through my inner flesh and a contented sigh. This bears down on me like a freight train, hard and fast and unstoppable. A ragged scream rips from my throat when it hits, my entire body clenching as convulsions rhythmically squeeze my inner muscles.

"Fuck, yes." Logan backs off my painfully sensitive clit, groaning hungrily as his broad tongue glides up the length of my slit. "Give me all your sweet cum, baby."

My body still shaking with aftershocks, I collapse back against the wall, moaning softly as Logan slowly licks through the saturated folds of my pussy, his tongue dipping past my untouched entrance as if he won't be satisfied until he's lapped up every creamy drop.

Except his mouth only makes me wet again. And if he intends to continue licking, then I have no intention of stopping him.

Though maybe I should have. Because he works me right up to the edge before suddenly slipping my knee off his shoulder and rising to his feet.

A deep chuckle against my mouth is followed by a light kiss. "That'll keep you going until tomorrow."

Oh my god. He's going to leave me like this? "You're an evil Santa."

"An evil Santa with a big dick." He kisses me again, then lifts his head with a soft reluctant groan. "A dick that'll be aching all damn night. I'm going now while I can. You keep that mask on until I shut that door behind me. You all right?"

Never better. "Yes."

"Tomorrow, then." His mouth covers mine again, hard and possessive, and while I'm reeling from the erotic taste of my arousal on his tongue, he pulls away.

I'm still panting against the wall when the door snaps shut. Heart racing, I push the mask up and stare at the tree across the room. There's a cardboard box on the floor beside it—I didn't realize he carried that in, too. Colorful, unwrapped packages are piled inside.

Christmas lights, I realize. Ornaments.

Logan knew I didn't have a tree. So he must have guessed I wouldn't have decorations, either. Tears burn my eyes, and I stand there for a long minute with a thick knot in my throat, wondering how my life changed so suddenly and so completely with one knock at my door. I don't know what to expect now.

Except I can expect a fucking tomorrow. I'm all in for that. Which might be stupid and reckless, but it feels so right and I want it *so* much—and I rarely treat myself to anything I want.

And maybe a fucking is *all* that I'm in for. Something unexpected and hot and wonderful.

Then done.

I ignore the pain that thought brings as I step back into my flannel shorts. My tree needs decorating. And maybe I won't have Logan forever. But I apparently have him wanting me for a little while—and that's one gift I won't haggle over. Until this ends, I'll take each day as it comes.

Even if the only day I get is tomorrow.

LOGAN

O NE MORE STOP," MY DAD SAYS, CROSSING AN address off our list and tossing the clipboard onto the dash of my truck. "Then you can go take care of whatever's been eating at you."

It's Emma. She's been eating at me.

Emma and her freezing apartment.

Driving around today with my dad, delivering meals and gifts to low income families, we've been to plenty of places where the thermostat is kept low, where parents and kids are bundled up inside their own homes. So I know what Emma's doing, and I'd love to take care of that electric bill for her. I'd love to take care of anything she needs.

But taking care of her *is* the problem. I've got a real bad feeling that throwing my money at her troubles will push her away. Just as she started pulling away on Friday, when I said I'd treat her to a drink. I want to be there for her in a way that she won't put on a goddamn balance sheet.

I just don't know what that is yet.

So frustration's been tearing at me since I left her last night. It's ripping at me now as I start up the truck, because her freezing apartment isn't my only worry.

I think I fucked up.

Last night I left her with the impression that the only reason I was coming back was for sex—thinking I'd keep it simple, so I could ease her into a deeper relationship over time.

But I don't think I can settle for just fucking, even for a short time. I want more *now*.

And I want to take care of her, give her everything I can. It killed me to drive away last night, leaving her in that cold apartment. Even knowing she was bundled up and safe—and that it probably wasn't her first night spent huddled under a blanket.

But it will be her last, damn it. "Who's next?"

"Millie Atwater."

He doesn't need to give me her address. Millie Atwater's been our last stop the past twelve years, ever since her granddaughter and her granddaughter's boyfriend got put away for selling meth, and Millie took in two young great-grandchildren.

Not so young anymore. Teenagers now, both of them. Probably at an age when receiving gifts and a holiday meal through a families-in-need program is more embarrassing than exciting, but when we arrived the weekend before Thanksgiving, I didn't see anything other than welcome on their faces. And as Millie's getting on in years, now they take care of their great-grandmother as much as she took care of them.

"You worried about that job in Florida this week?" my dad asks.

For a custom installation. Some bigwig ordered a bed too big to fit through any entrance, so I'll be flying across the country and assembling the parts we've already shipped to the site. Which I've done before, plenty of times—I figure if they're paying us six figures for a bed, then the least I can do is put it together at the location of their choice.

I won't like being away for three days while I'm starting up this relationship with Emma, but the installation itself isn't a problem. "No. That's all set," I tell him.

"You worried about Lucy being alone?"

Lucy, the stray dog that's adopted my house as her own. "No. Patrick will be stopping by to check in on her."

"Is it Emma?"

I shoot a surprised glance at my dad, trying to read his face. Beneath the Santa hat he's wearing, his expression's as neutral as it's ever been, which tells me he deliberately looks that way. My dad's not neutral about anything.

But there's no point in denying it. If he's got a problem with me chasing after his new office manager, it's better to hash it out now.

"Yeah, it's Emma," I tell him.

Slowly he nods, and I see the glimmer of worry I expected to see before. But I don't expect his reply.

"You be careful with her, son," he says solemnly.

My back goes up. "What the hell does that mean?"

My dad knows me. He knows I'm not going to fuck around with an employee, not unless I'm dead serious about her.

And I am.

"It just means that she hasn't always had it easy."

I know that. I'm surprised he does. "Are you talking about her foster homes—did she tell you something about them?"

"She didn't have to. I saw it for myself."

I frown at him. "When?"

"Six, maybe seven years back, when we were out delivering boxes. It was a house over on south Washington. One of the Christmas runs, it must have been, because you were right behind me with a box of wrapped gifts."

"*I* met her before?"

And don't remember? That can't be right. Seeing her for the first time a few weeks ago was like a kick in the balls and like coming home to a warm holiday meal, all at once. Six or seven years ago, she'd have been fifteen or sixteen, so she probably looked about the same as she does now. I can't imagine my reaction to her being much different when I was twenty.

"You didn't meet her. Probably didn't even see her. Because I was ahead of you when she opened the door. A little skinnier than she is now, and I'll never forget those big eyes, or the way she lit up when she saw my Santa hat. Or the way she *really* lit up when she saw the box I was carrying."

Which would have been a frozen turkey and all the dinner fixings, if I'd been carrying the wrapped gifts.

And I'm starting to remember this. "That was the time you called up Linda."

A friend of his who works in Child Services. It was one of the few times in my life I've seen him pissed. He'd been terrifyingly quiet as we headed back to the truck, and we sat there for a full ten minutes, while he watched that house as if debating whether to storm back in. Finally he used his cell to call his friend, and didn't tell me to drive away until after she reassured him that the girl would be taken care of that same day.

What had his conversation with Linda been about? Some bruises that he'd seen?

Dread settles in my gut like lead. "What happened?"

"She was wearing a long sleeved shirt, but the sleeves were rolled up—doing dishes, I think. And there were marks all over her wrists and just above. I didn't know what to make of them until her foster mother shows up at the door smelling like a whiskey factory. She grabs the girl by arm—hard enough you could tell it was hurting her—and the woman yanks her back into the house, hissing at me that they didn't need any charity. Then she slammed the door in my face."

Not the first door we've had slammed in our faces. Probably won't be the last. But it was the first time my dad ever called up Child Services after.

Rage has a burning lock on my throat, but I manage to ask, "Did Linda follow up with you?"

"I didn't give her a chance. I called her up the next day. She had one of their social workers visit that after-noon and had the girl in another house by that evening." His gaze slides over to meet mine. "It was the girl's sixth placement that year, Linda told me. Said some kids are difficult to place, they've got issues or special needs, but this was nothing the girl had done. Just shitty luck and a string of crappy homes that had slipped through the cracks. But when I followed up again a few weeks later, the girl seemed to have settled in all right to her new home. 'The girl,'" he suddenly says again, then chuckles. "Didn't know her name was Emma until she showed up for that interview."

"Did she recognize you?"

He shakes his head. "Back then, I don't think she really saw anything except the Santa hat and the box I was carrying. And don't you ever tell her."

"I won't." Emma might not care that my dad witnessed what had happened, or she might feel embarrassed and ashamed—or worry that it had something to do with being hired. She wouldn't have any reason to worry, but pride isn't always a rational thing. I wouldn't risk hurting her. "Does Marianne know?"

"No." And apparently my dad's thinking the same thing because he adds, "It was her references and interview that got her hired. Not pity."

I never questioned that. So I just nod, waiting for him to continue.

"Anyway," my dad says. "That girl has stayed with me all these years. Because I'll never forget how she looked at that box—like I was bringing her everything she ever hoped for. And I'll never forget the way she looked when that door was closing, and she realized she wasn't going to get it." His throat works for a second. "Sometimes she looks at you that way—like she looked at that box. And that's why I'm telling you to be careful with her. Don't give her something, then take it away. And before you start anything, you need to be sure."

"I'm sure," I tell him gruffly. "I'm more certain than I've ever been of anything."

A misty smile touches his eyes, his mouth. "Just like your mother. Always knowing when something's right."

Yeah. And when it's *not* right.

I fucked up last night. Instead of coming to Emma with everything I had to give, I only offered part of it.

That's not what'll happen tonight.

This time I don't leave a gift box. Just a note.

Put on your mask.
Unlock your door and wait.
Signed,
YOUR SECRET SANTA

I could do this without the mask—but it's sexy as hell on her. I think it excites Emma, too. When we fuck for the first time, though, she won't be wearing it. I'll be looking into her warm brown eyes as I sink my thick cock deep inside the lush heaven of her body.

But a blindfold is just right for an abduction.

When I open her door, Emma's up against the wall where she was standing the night before—and my reaction's about the same seeing her, except this time I know how she tastes. I know the heat of her mouth and the sweetness of her pussy. It's all I can do to stop myself from lifting her against that wall and plunging deep.

I hear the breath she draws as I step inside her living room. I see the lift of her small breasts beneath her pale blue top.

She was expecting me tonight. I think she's done her hair, though I can't really tell, because it always looks so soft and wavy, like I spent all night fucking her, my fingers buried in those thick golden strands. Makeup, too. Though her eyes are covered, her lips are a deep, glossy cherry that makes the color of the red satin mask look cheap in comparison.

Gone are the gloves and the thick sweater that she was swimming in yesterday. Instead she's wearing one of those little button-up sweaters that give thousands of horny teenagers wet dreams about their school librarian. She's paired it with that swingy little skirt I remember from her first day at work, though this time she isn't wearing tights. She's got striped socks on again. Red and white this time.

There's not a single doubt that I'll be going down on my knees again tonight.

But not yet.

I stride across the room toward the tree. She's decorated the branches and it looks damn pretty, but I'm not leaving the lights on to burn her place down. I yank the cord from the outlet and my gaze sweeps into the tiny kitchen. Nothing on the stove. Her keys are hanging from a peg by the front door.

That's all I need to know.

I head back to Emma, who's pressed up tight against the wall, and her toes are curling nervously against the threadbare carpet while I walk around her living room. Then as soon as I come near, she stops that nervous fidgeting and rises up on those toes, as if seeking a kiss.

Hell. I'm not disappointing her.

I bend my head and claim those cherry lips, loving the hitch of her breath when my tongue sweeps into the hot cavern of her mouth, loving her soft moan as she leans in against my chest and her tension immediately seems to melt. As if she's been waiting for this all day.

So have I. Which is why it's so damn hard to tear my mouth from hers, to stop this cold.

Need roughens my voice as I tell her, "You ready for me to take you, baby?"

A breath shudders through her parted lips, the glossy red smeared a little now and looking sexy as hell. "Yes."

All right, then. In a swift movement, I grip her waist and hoist her up onto my shoulder, her cute ass pointing up and her beautiful head hanging down.

A surprised scream is followed by a roll of her throaty laughter. "Logan!"

"Santa." To punctuate the reminder, I give her butt a little swat. "And like any good Santa, I'm hauling my gift sack around over my shoulder."

"This gift sack can walk into the bedroom, Santa."

If that was where we were going, I'd still carry her in. I stop by the couch long enough to grab the blanket she has folded neatly over one arm, and drape it over Emma's back. That ought to keep her warm until I get her into the truck and get the heaters going again.

Being covered up clues her in to the fact that I might not be taking her to the bed. "Logan?" she asks again, this time with a real question in her voice.

I snatch the keys off the hook and open her door. "Like I said," I tell her as I lock the handle and swing it closed, "I'm taking you."

"Where?"

"My place."

"Why?"

I'll tell her. But not while she's hanging upside down over my shoulder. "So I can show you my Christmas tree."

"Your Christmas tree?" Her giggles shake her against me. "Does your 'Christmas tree' have shiny balls hanging from it?"

Naughty girl. With a laugh, I swat her butt again, then can't stop myself from caressing those sweet curves through the blanket. She's got the sexiest ass.

"There are balls involved," I tell her. "But they're not too shiny."

"Is it a *big* tree?"

"The biggest you've ever seen, baby."

"That's probably true," is her dry response.

I don't want to think about any others she's seen. Jealousy's not something I'm accustomed to—and it's not as if I've been celibate all my life.

Because I didn't know Emma Williams was going to come crashing into it.

I open the truck and gently set her on the passenger seat. Her face is flushed, her mask still on—though it's slipped up above her eyebrows. Her soft brown eyes meet mine for a long moment, and her gaze searches my face, as if she's trying to figure out what I really intend.

Then deliberately, she pulls the mask down to cover

her eyes. A smile curves her lips.

That's an invitation to continue if I ever saw one. Quickly I buckle her in and head around the front of the truck.

"Do I smell pizza?" she says the moment I get into the driver's seat.

"Yup." Because eating at someone's house is different from going out to dinner or drinks. No bill arrives at the end of a visit, and she won't feel any obligation to repay me, except maybe to invite me into her place sometime for coffee. "You like pepperoni?"

"Who doesn't?"

Good question. "I figure you'll need your strength after you climb my Christmas tree," I tell her, and her husky laugh goes straight to my cock.

And I can't fucking help myself. With a groan, I reach across the seat and capture her face in my hands, drawing her in for a long taste of her mouth. When I finally let her go, she's breathing hard and her pussy's most likely soaking, which means I don't waste another second before putting the truck in gear and swinging toward home.

"How long until we're there?"

Her voice is strained, her fingers fisted in her lap. She's squirming in her seat like she was during the drive to the bank on Friday. Was she that hot and wet then? Hot and wet and I didn't touch her, didn't taste her?

I won't make the same mistake tonight.

"Ten minutes." Which might end up being the longest of my life. "You gonna make it?"

Her head falls back against the headrest and she gives a tortured laugh. "With or without shoving my fingers beneath my skirt?"

Already stiff and aching, my cock hardens to steel in a sudden, painful rush. "Do it, baby. Let me see you get those fingers all wet. Let me see you make yourself come."

Although then it'll become a real question whether we'll make it to my place without me pulling over and fucking her in my truck.

Biting her lip, she shakes her head. "It's not as good. I want your fingers."

"You'll get them." The promise is low and harsh. "As soon as we get there. My fingers, my tongue. I'll eat you all up, make sure your pussy's all soft and wet before I fuck you deep and hard."

"Oh god." A soft moan escapes her and her back arches, her hips pressing against the taut seatbelt. "Hurry," she pleads, and another frustrated moan is accompanied by a roll of her hips. "Or distract me. Tell me what you did today."

Thought about kissing her, licking her, fucking her. But that's not the distraction she's looking for. Or the one I need if I'm going to get us there in one piece.

"I drove around with my dad. Then spent a few hours at Murphy's watching the game with Shawn and

Tyrone." Because I went to Emma's place after finishing up at Millie Atwater's earlier, and she wasn't home. "You?"

"I went to the senior center on Oak."

I glance over. She's pulled her right foot up to the edge of the seat and has wrapped her arms around her knee, as if keeping a tight hold on herself. "You got family there?"

Although, shit—that can't be right. She doesn't know who her parents are.

But she doesn't seem to care that I just shoved my boot into my mouth again. Easily she says, "I was balancing checkbooks."

I grin. "Just grabbing old ladies' checkbooks and balancing them? You really do like those numbers to add up."

With a laugh, she shakes her head. "It's part of that citywide 'donate your professional time to people in need' program. Ever since I worked at the bank, I've been putting in about ten hours at the senior center every month." She rests her cheek on top of her bent knee, her face turned toward me as if looking at me through the mask. "Most of them are on fixed incomes. So sometimes it's just to make sure they don't overdraw or get slammed with fees. Other times because they're more likely to be taken advantage of, so it's to help them keep an eye on what money's being spent. Especially this time of year."

I know that program. My dad and I donate time every month, too. That's what we were doing today. In the winters, that means donating money for gifts and meals, then driving around and delivering them. The rest of the year, we're usually donating labor and materials. Weatherizing houses or repairing leaky roofs, mostly.

"So that was my day," she adds with a dismissive shrug, as if suddenly uncomfortable talking about herself. "How close are we now?"

Not close enough. The distraction's taken a bit of the edge off. But only a bit. And knowing that we're getting closer and that she's over there needing me as much as I need her just amps it right back up again.

That need's thick in the air between us the rest of the drive. The heavy tension smothers any pretense that we'll be able to distract ourselves from this. Everything's focused on getting her into my house, then getting into her.

Her breathing quickens as I slow to make the turn into my driveway. "Are we here?"

My answer's hardly more than an affirmative grunt. And any other time I'd have her take off that mask, show her my house, because it's part of what I'll be offering her. But I'll have to settle for showing her the inside and letting her see the rest tomorrow morning.

I don't wait for the garage to open. Braking hard in front of my porch, I tell her, "You stay there," before rounding the truck and yanking her door open. A second later I've scooped her up out of her seat and I'm hauling ass up the front steps, carrying her against my chest.

She's giggling again. "You forgot the pizza."

The pizza doesn't need to be fucked. "I'll get it after."

Though I've got to slow this down or I'll be inside her too fast. Our first time ought to be long and sweet, not a quick bang against my front door. So it's better to tease her and get her ready for my cock while that mask is still on. Because I want to be looking into her eyes when I make her mine—and as soon as the mask comes off, as soon as I see her gazing up at me with those big brown eyes, I don't know if I'll have any control.

Kicking my front door closed behind me, I head across the foyer and take the stairs two at a time. Emma's arms tighten around my shoulders, the hem of her skirt fluttering against my hand, her soft lips nibbling along the line of my jaw.

My cock's already about to explode. Christ, I've never needed anyone as much as I need her. But I've got to slow this down.

When I start up the second flight, a little laugh shakes through her. "This is a lot of stairs."

It's a lot of house. My bedroom is on the third floor, a big open loft overlooking the great room. I hit the lights as I reach the top of the stairs, because although she's wearing that mask, I want to see everything.

Starting with how she looks when I lay her on my bed, her golden hair pillowed beneath her head, her lush lips parted and her cheeks flushed. Groaning, I brace my hands beside her shoulders and allow myself a deep kiss before backing up to strip off my coat.

I yank off my boots and look up to see Emma sitting upright, her slender fingers unfastening the last button on her sweater, the sides falling open to reveal the silky white camisole that's clinging to the soft swell of her breasts, her pouting nipples clearly outlined through the thin fabric.

With a hungry growl, I catch her hands and push her flat against the bed again, my fingers trapping her wrists over her head. "Not so fast, baby. No unwrapping the presents until you've sat on Santa's lap and told him what you want."

Plaintively she moans and wriggles her sexy little body beneath me. "I want you inside me, hard and fast."

Ah, Christ. The way she's moving, that camisole's pulling even tighter across her breasts. Beneath the silk, her nipples look as hard as rivets. Those sweet buds must be aching.

Fuck, and I need a taste. Gruffly I ask, "You want me to suck on those pretty tits first?"

Her body goes utterly still except for the shuddering of her breath. "Yes," she whispers.

Holding her wrists in my left hand, I glide my right hand up the smooth length of her bare thigh. She starts to tremble as my palm travels beneath the hem of her skirt. "You want me to tease your clit while I do? You want me to fuck you with my fingers, get you hot and wet enough to take my big cock?"

Accompanied by a desperate moan, her hips lift off the bed as if to urge my slowly drifting hand even closer to its destination.

That's not an answer. Roughly I say, "Tell Santa that you want my fingers fucking your greedy little pussy."

"Yes." She's panting, the muscles of her thighs quivering. "*Yes.*"

My hand travels higher and I almost lose my fucking mind. She's already slippery wet and feverishly hot and there's not a single barrier to my touch. Hanging onto control by a thin thread, I grind out through clenched teeth, "Now tell Santa why you're not wearing any goddamn panties."

"Because—" She cries out as my fingers slick through the sultry lips of her pussy, her hips bucking, her back arching.

"Because?"

Helplessly she rocks her juicy cunt against my palm. "I thought you'd take me against the wall. At my house."

My mouth hovering above hers, I tease her snug entrance with my longest finger. "And you didn't want anything coming between us."

She's utterly still again. "Yes."

"Didn't want anything to slow me down."

"Yes."

My thumb slides up to circle her swollen clit, the

blunt tip of my middle finger pressing against her tight little opening. "And you wanted me inside you hard and fast."

"Yes." It's barely a breath.

And I'm going to give her what she wants.

My finger plunges deep at the same moment I capture those cherry red lips, craving the silken heat of her mouth. Her thighs snap closed around my wrist, as if trying to keep me in, but I'm not going anywhere. Her pussy is so unbelievably tight, clamping down on my finger in a scorching vise. I groan against her mouth, already imagining that velvet sheath gripping my thick cock, then lick past her lips, seeking the slick heaven of her kiss.

Instead I find her teeth clenched. Against me, her body's motionless, but it's not the stillness of anticipation. She's tense and shaking, her muscles locked.

As if she's hurting.

Heart thundering painfully in my chest, I lift my head. "Emma?"

She makes a little sound, a whimper through her clenched teeth. Above the manacle of my fingers, her hands are balled into fists, fingernails digging into the heels of her palms.

"Talk to me, baby."

"It's okay. I'm okay." Her ragged voice doesn't sound okay. "I just need another second to adjust."

Another second to adjust...to my *finger*? Oh sweet

Christ.

Emma's a virgin. And I just rammed into her with the tenderness of a jackhammer.

Fucking hell. My middle finger's still buried inside her but when I gently try to pull away, her thighs tighten around my wrist. I could overpower her, but I'd have to force her legs apart…and I'm not going to hurt her more than she already is.

Letting go of her wrists, I tug the mask up over her forehead. Her eyes are squeezed shut, tears glittering at the base of her dark lashes.

The sight fucking destroys me. My beautiful fighter. There's a storm of emotions ripping through me, sheer disbelief and primitive satisfaction and soul-sucking guilt—along with gut-wrenching relief that when I got to her apartment, I didn't just slam my cock into her and fuck her against the wall—but at the forefront of everything is the overwhelming need to take care of her now, to erase those tears.

Softly, I kiss the corner of her trembling mouth. "There's no rush, baby. We'll take as long as you need."

"Okay." A teardrop slides down her temple and soaks into her hair. "Sorry."

"No need for sorry."

"Well, *I'm* sorry." She laughs now, a choked little sound. "Because it was going really well."

"It still is going well." To reassure her that we're not finished here, I bend to kiss the side of her throat, where her pulse is racing just beneath her skin. "We'll just slow it way down. Until you adjust. Is it still hurting?"

"Not as much." Her thighs flex against my wrist, subtly pushing my hand against her, as if tentatively testing the feel of my finger moving within her tender flesh. She stops on a sharp breath, but her eyes are open now, the tears gone. That warm brown gaze meets mine and a wry, tremulous smile curves her lips. "I didn't think it would hurt. I've used my own fingers. And…tampons."

Her cheeks go scarlet at the last. Chuckling, I shake my head and hold up my free hand, because showing is more effective than telling. I'm pretty sure my smallest finger is bigger than any tampon. And when I press my palm against hers, the difference in our sizes couldn't be any plainer. She could wear my hand as a baseball mitt.

"Oh," she says softly.

"Oh," I echo teasingly before threading my fingers through hers and pushing her hand over her head again. "So a little change in plan. I'm not fucking you tonight."

Disappointment crumples her expression and boosts my ego about a thousand points. "We still can."

"We can still fool around," I tell her. "But I'm not fucking you until I can get two or three fingers into your pussy without hurting you. We'll take it slow, all right? Bit by bit. Just like a Christmas gift. Sometimes you tear off the wrapping paper, and sometimes you open it real carefully."

Her teeth clench in frustration, and she tilts her hips

up, forcing the penetration of my finger a little deeper. "It's not really hurting now."

And her pussy's slowly softening around me. But that doesn't change anything. "That's just one finger. My dick's a lot bigger. And if you're going to be screaming under me, I want it to be because it feels so damn good. Not because my cock is ripping you in half."

"Oh my god." She abruptly stops pushing against my hand. Her face scrunches into an expression of squirming discomfort. "When you put it like that…"

Laughing, I kiss the adorable wrinkles across the bridge of her nose. "I'll still make you feel good, sweetheart. We'll get your pussy used to taking something of this size. Tomorrow I'll give you a little more. And by Christmas I'll be fucking you, all right?"

For a long second, she appears torn between anticipation and disappointment. Finally she sighs. "All right."

Good. And now it's time to ease that disappointment.

The lush heat of her cunt still surrounds my finger. My thumb is nestled in the moist curls above her clit. But as incredible as she feels, I don't move that hand at all as I lean in and claim her cherry red lips. No light and sweet kiss this time. My tongue strokes hers, hot and slick, slowly fucking her mouth until she's moaning low in her throat and her pussy juices are flooding my palm.

When I lift my head her brown eyes are glazed and her lids heavy, as if in a passion-drugged haze. She hasn't eased up with her thighs yet, keeping my wrist trapped and my hand right where it is. The clasp of her virgin pussy is still tight as hell, but her inner walls are softer now, more elastic as her arousal deepens. I watch her expression for any sign of pain when my thumb slides over her swollen clitoris.

Back arching, her hips rock sharply, pushing my finger deeper. Her soft moan is cut off by a strangled cry of pleasure. Frantically rolls her hips as if seeking that same touch.

"Again," she pleads breathlessly. "Do that again."

Fuck, yes. Circling her clit, I gently pump my hand within the taut grip of her thighs. She's so damn wet, her nectar lubricating every thrust, and the sound of my finger fucking her tight channel is slick and sexy and driving me out of my head.

It's driving Emma out of hers, too. She's flushed and writhing, panting on one breath and moaning the next.

No pain left. So it's time for me to unwrap a little bit of my present.

Without slowing the thrust of my hand or the tease of my thumb over her clit, I bend my head and latch onto her left nipple, sucking the hardened flesh through the thin silk of her camisole. She cries out, her wrists tugging against my grip, and I let her go because I need that hand to get some of the clothes out of the way.

They aren't coming off. Not with my right hand caught between her thighs and Emma lying on her back.

Wrestling with her sweater isn't on my list of priorities right now, and pushing her camisole higher gives me what I want—more of Emma's beautiful body bared to my gaze.

And she's simply stunning. The white camisole rucked up by her collarbones doesn't look half as silky as her golden skin. Her small tits are soft round mouthfuls, her pouting nipples like rubies at their tips. Her stomach's soft with just a bit of inward curve at her sides that flares into the wider curve of her hips. The high waistline of her flirty skirt conceals her navel, but the hem is flipped up and I've got a full view of her long, long legs and those striped socks. Her knees are bent, her heels digging into the mattress as she rocks her hips to the rhythmic thrust of my finger, trying to take me even deeper.

My big hand's shielding her pussy, but I got an up-close view of that last night—the dark blond curls, the delicate pink flesh nestled between her glistening labia. I got a long, deep taste of all the sweet juices flowing from her virgin well.

But I get to taste the rest of her now.

With a hungry growl, I lower my head to her breast again. Her nipple's hard and hot against my tongue. The moment I suckle that taut bud into my mouth, her pussy clenches around my finger, her moan thick and deep in her throat. Her hands slide into my hair, and I fucking love how wild she is, pulling at me and then pushing as if she's so lost to pleasure she doesn't know what to do with herself, to do with me, and she's just grabbing whatever she can. Circling my tongue around her ruby nipple, I groan against her soft tit as her inner muscles ripple around me again. She's so damn sensitive. The way her cunt squeezes and pulls at my finger, when my big cock's deep inside her it'll be a miracle if I last more than a few seconds.

I won't last much longer *now*. Thrusting into her sultry pussy, tasting her golden skin, hearing her frantic moans, my cock's a throbbing volcanic rock and I'm about to blow a load into my fucking jeans.

But she's close, too. Her fingernails dig into my scalp and my name is a sobbing chant on her lips. There's no rhythm to her movements now, just chaotic need and desperate urgency. Every sound she makes drives me closer to the edge, and there's barely any control left as I move over her, straddling her thighs with my knees digging into the bed, my mouth finding hers again. I fuck my tongue past her lips the same way my finger's fucking into her, the way my cock needs to be fucking into her. Her swollen clit's so slippery with her juices that my thumb's gliding right over with almost no friction, faster and faster, then all at once she arches beneath me, screaming into my mouth as her virgin pussy clamps down, those tight inner muscles strangling my finger, her thighs squeezing my wrist.

And I can't stand it any longer. As soon as she comes

down, her thighs falling gently open, I rise up on my knees again. My right hand glistening with her cum, my left hand shaking with need, I tear open my jeans.

Her blond hair tangled around her head, Emma watches me drag my straining cock free of my briefs, her eyes glazed and her lush lips parted. My gaze locks on her flushed face as I fist my aching shaft. Pre-cum is already dripping from the bulging tip, and it only takes three rough strokes before I'm grunting like a fucking animal and cum spurts from my cock in thick streams, splattering across her belly and tits.

Holy fuck. Chest heaving, I collapse over her, barely catching my weight on my elbow. I bury my face in the sweat-slicked skin at her throat, my lungs bellowing like a steam engine.

I can feel the aftershocks passing through her body in erratic shudders. Her arms slip around my shoulders, her fingers threading into the hair on the back of my head, and as incredible as that orgasm felt, it doesn't come close to the feeling of being held by her after.

But I just made a sticky mess all over her chest. And this isn't taking care of her.

With a groan, I summon the strength to rise to my knees again, then can't get any farther because my brain shuts down at the sight of her lying there, her brown eyes glazed with satisfaction and her mouth bare of her cherry lipstick now, but still red and swollen from my kisses. The longer I stare the more she begins looking real shy, biting her lip and lowering her lashes, but she has no reason to worry.

"You're so fucking gorgeous, baby." That hair, those lips, those tits—and my seed painting her skin, splashed across her ruby nipples. But I know damn well how semen itches as it dries, so I tell her, "Don't move. I'll get something to clean you up. You lie right there so my cum doesn't get all over your clothes."

Not just my cum. Faint crimson streaks paint her inner thighs and my hand. Christ. No wonder it hurt her so bad. Not just tight and unaccustomed to taking anything inside her. After twenty-two years, whatever remained of her hymen must have been strong as steel and clinging to her pussy for dear life, and I ripped right through it.

Maybe it's better this way than with my cock, though. We'll take it slow, give her time to heal up.

A warm washcloth in hand, I return to the bed and find she hasn't moved much—except to tilt her head, looking back across the open floor of the loft, where a tall Douglas fir is decked out in lights and ornaments beneath the peaked roof.

She shoots me a sparkling grin that makes my heart inflate ten sizes larger within my chest. "You really did have a Christmas tree to show me."

Yeah, I did. I lean in for a kiss, then murmur against her smiling lips, "And is it big enough for you?"

Giggling, she wraps her arms around my neck.

"Apparently *too* big, considering that it's rip-me-in-half big."

"Then now is probably not the time to tell you that I've got two."

And even better than Emma Williams holding me on my bed after we come our brains out is Emma Williams holding me on my bed and laughing her beautiful head off.

When her laughter begins to taper off, I go in for another kiss. "Now let me clean you up, and then I'll show you my *really* big tree."

And pray that showing her everything else I've got to give her doesn't end up scaring her away.

LOGAN

Emma doesn't have to go downstairs before getting a look at my big tree. She can see it from the loft, a fifteen-foot Douglas fir that sits in front of the big windows facing the creek, but it's not until we're in the great room and I plug in the lights that the full height of it hits her. Her mouth drops open and she shakes her head.

"Why one so big?"

That's ripe for another joke, but I hold off this time and give her the truth. "The year I moved in, I had a smaller one in here—and it irritated the shit out me."

Her brows shoot up. "Irritated you?"

I gesture toward the high ceiling, the tall windows.

"The proportions were all off. So every time I looked at it was like scraping steel wool over my dick."

"Ohhhhh," she says slowly, her gaze slipping over my face as if seeing something new in me. "It's an artist thing."

I don't know about that. To my mind, I'm a builder, not an artist. But maybe it's the same thing in some ways. Cabinets and furniture are all about proportions, too.

And the irritation when those proportions are out of whack is probably something she understands. "Probably like when you can't find that error throwing a checkbook register off by a few pennies."

There's a flash of acknowledgment in her eyes, then her lips purse and she says dryly, "Yeah, but that doesn't feel like scraping steel wool over my dick."

I grin, and all at once her expression changes, lips parting softly and brown eyes widening as she stares at me.

That's a good expression, I think. A happy expression. But I'm not sure what to make of it. Gruffly I ask, "What?"

A hint of pink touches her cheeks, and her gaze flicks away like it used to when I thought she was scared of me. But this time her eyes come right back to mine again. "You haven't smiled at me before."

That can't be right. "The hell I haven't."

"It's true."

"You sure?"

She nods, then her blush deepens. "At least not that I've seen."

Because maybe every time I grinned at her, she was wearing that mask.

"I like it," she adds now, quietly.

"Well, you've given me a lot of reasons to smile." I catch her cheeks in my hands. "So you'll see it often."

"And your angry face."

"That's not my angry face," I say, but the sudden gleam in her eyes tells me she knows that. It's probably the face she saw as I was stroking my cock and splashing her tits with my cum. "But, yeah. You'll be seeing a lot of that, too."

She grins and I kiss that laughing smile before releasing her.

"Now look around the house if you like. I'm heading out for that pizza."

But she doesn't stray far from the tree in the short time I'm gone. She's standing by the window, looking out over the snow-filled backyard that slopes down toward the woods and the creek, then follows me into the kitchen.

I turn on the oven and slide the pizza inside to reheat. "You want a beer? Wine? Or if you want something harder, I can mix it up."

She slides onto one of the stools tucked up beneath the bar separating the kitchen and the great room. "I'll take a glass of wine."

"Any preferences?" Being a beer man, I don't drink it much myself, but I keep a few bottles on hand for visitors.

"Nothing too sweet." Her gaze alights on the tray at the end of the bar, which holds the collection of carvings I've been working on in my spare time. "Are those more ornaments—like the ones on your tree?"

"Yeah."

"You carved these?" She reaches for the tray, then stops. "Can I—?"

"Go ahead."

Her slender fingers pick out a tiny crib. "You made all of those carved ornaments on the tree, too?"

"I did. Keeps my hands busy while I'm doing other things." Like waiting for pizza to heat, or watching a game. "But those are for Marianne—for the Secret Santa thing."

A miniature nursery set that matches the full-sized one I'm giving her.

Emma cocks her brow and gives me a look. "So you're her Secret Santa, too?"

I laugh and shake my head. "Not the same. Whose name did you get?"

"It's supposed to be secret. So I'm not telling." Studiously she returns her attention to the other carvings in the tray, as if completely dismissing my presence.

Or trying not to give anything away. Because I saw

all the names remaining in the hat after she got hers, and there's a fifty-fifty chance that she picked out my name. Either mine or Shawn's. And the way she's deliberately not looking at me, I'm thinking it isn't Shawn.

But I'll be patient. After fetching her a glass, I screw the cork out of a bottle of chardonnay and pour.

As I'm setting the wine in front of her, she says, "I should probably warn you that I'm a lightweight."

Wordlessly, I take the glass back and tip in more.

She's giggling when I put the wine in front of her again. Her giggles quiet when she takes a sip, and her expression turns pensive. Her thoughtful gaze remains on me as I pop the cap from my beer, as I take a swig. All the while I return that look, wondering what's going on in her head.

I don't have to wonder for long.

With a sigh, she sets down her wine. "What is this, really?"

"What's what?"

"What are we doing here? This Secret Santa thing. And *this*." She gestures from me to herself. "You could have fucked me at my apartment."

I could have. But that's not all I'm after. And I figure the only way to tell her is bluntly.

"You want to know what this is?" I set my beer down and grip the edge of the counter, my gaze steady on hers as I say, "This time next year, I want you sitting there with my ring on your finger."

Her lips part on a sharp breath. Stunned, her gaze searches my face, and the naked yearning I've seen before in those warm brown eyes has returned.

Then disbelief replaces the longing. "Okay, what is it really?"

"That is 'really.'"

A laugh breaks from her, but it's an uncomfortable laugh, as if she can't figure out what the joke is but she's certain there must be one.

Shit. I didn't expect her to joyfully leap up and start planning our wedding. I *did* expect the disbelief, but time will prove the truth of what I'm saying.

That discomfort, though—it's as if I've prodded something tender and painful inside her, and hurting her was never my intention.

"It's no joke," I say softly.

The sad yearning filling her eyes again just rips me apart. As if she wants to believe that I'm serious…but simply can't.

So I'll just have to convince her.

With a heavy sigh, she shakes her head. "You don't even know me, Logan."

So her objection isn't *her* not knowing *me*? As if she could picture herself wanting me that much. She's just not picturing me wanting her. "I know enough to be certain you're the one for me."

"How?"

"I just know it. The same way I knew that I was

meant to build. The same way I know that room needs a big tree." With a tilt of my head, I indicate the tray of carvings. "Or the same way I can look at a hunk of wood and see what it'll be."

There's a brittle edge to her smile. "So you're going to whittle me down? Cut parts of me away until I'm what you want?"

"Shit, no. So that's a bad analogy. I'm talking about being able to imagine how it'll be between us." And my mouth's running faster than my head, trying to tell something that needs to be shown. I pick up my beer. "Bring your wine and come with me."

After a brief hesitation, she slides off her stool and cups her palm around her glass. Holding out my free hand, I tangle my fingers through hers and start across the great room.

"I designed this house," I tell her as we're passing the stairs, which marks the end of the open floor plan that encompasses the great room and the kitchen. Beyond the stairs is a more traditional layout with enclosed rooms. "It's got everything I want or could imagine wanting in a house. But half the rooms are empty. The bedrooms on the second floor, I figure eventually I'd have a wife, kids—a family to fill up those rooms. And then there's rooms like this."

I watch her face as I swing open the door. No need to look in—I designed the place, I know what's there.

"I installed the shelves myself," I say as her breath

catches and her fingers tighten on mine. "Because I wanted a big fucking library, with shelves on every wall. But the thing is, the only books I have are gifts that I've received, because everything I want to read, I download to my phone. So I've got this big empty room. But it never bothered me, because a part of me knew this room was never for me, anyway."

Her gaze flies to mine before she looks away, and there's that yearning again as she takes in all the empty shelves.

"But you can see this room being yours, can't you?" My voice deepens. "I think you can. You read a lot, so I think you're good at imagining what you can't see. You put on that mask and I bet you're still picturing everything that's happening."

Her cheeks flush and she darts another glance at me. This time I'm the one to look away, but it's so that she'll follow my gaze.

Raising our linked hands, I point to the bay window. "I think you can see yourself curled up there in the summer. And for the winters, I think you can picture a big comfy chair over there by the fireplace, because I sure as hell can imagine me coming in to find you reading on one—and thinking you're so damn sexy that I'm going to fuck you right there."

A shuddering little breath escapes her. Yeah, she's imagining that, too.

Her gaze slides around the library again, and she

takes a deep gulp of her wine before abruptly looking to me.

"Oh my god," she says. "You're *Beauty and the Beast-ing* me."

I don't understand any of that. "I'm what?"

"From the Disney movie. You're romancing me with a library."

I take a swallow of my beer and consider that. Finally I nod. "I suppose I am. And I like that you're the kind of girl who can be romanced by a library. But I'll tempt you with anything I have, if I need to."

Her gaze searches mine again. "But I don't understand what's tempting *you*."

Well, that's easy enough to explain.

"You mean, aside from you being a fighter who's still standing after all you've been through in your life? Aside from how you can be independent and say a balance sheet is less complicated than relationships, but still be so friendly and open at the same time? Aside from how sweet your mouth and your pussy taste? Aside from how you don't want to owe anybody anything, but you'll donate your time without any expectation of receiving something in return?" My fingers tightening on hers, I tug her closer. "Or maybe it's just because I'm about to take that pizza out of the oven and head to the couch, and I think you'll come with me. And I don't imagine either one of us will be doing anything much different from what we usually do on Sunday evenings, but somehow it'll be a hell of a lot better than it usually is, simply because we're here doing it together."

"That last part sounds really nice." Her eyes are soft and shining, her voice thick. "So what will we be doing on that couch?"

"Watching a movie, maybe." It doesn't matter, as long as she's with me. "Have you seen the one based on that Martian book you were reading yesterday?"

"Not yet."

"Then that's what we'll do." Because although I haven't erased her doubts, she's not running away—and when I bend my head, she rises to meet my kiss. Good enough for now.

Back in the kitchen, I'm not surprised to find my mutt standing in front of the oven. Emma's eyes widen and a pretty smile lights up her face.

"Who's this?"

"Lucy," I say, nudging the dog out of the way so I can open the oven door.

"Can I pet her?"

"Sure."

Setting her wine aside, Emma sinks onto her heels and starts scratching behind Lucy's ears. I don't stop her because this is another time when showing is better than telling.

Lucy looks up at Emma, who's telling her what a pretty girl she is, before walking away in the middle of the petting as if the human doesn't even exist.

"She's more like a cat than a dog," I say, sliding the pizza back into the cardboard box. "One day she showed up at my door, so I started feeding her. Now she's got a doggie door and a blanket on the far end of my couch, but I might as well be a nail in the wall for all the interest she shows in me. Whenever there's food available, she's right there, but otherwise she doesn't have any time for our human bullshit. Will you grab me another beer? Might as well bring that bottle of wine, too. You want a plate or are you all set with a napkin?"

"Napkin's good," she says and follows me to the big sectional sofa facing the flat screen. "Did you design all your own furniture, too?"

"This couch? Nah." I drop the pizza box onto the coffee table. "Some of the stuff in the house is out of the Crenshaw catalog, but this couch is from IKEA."

She chokes on her wine.

Grinning, I take the extra bottles out of her hand and set them next to the pizza box. "The way I see it, if I'm going to be spending time making furniture, I might as well make the company some money while I'm at it. That won't happen if I'm only building pieces to furnish my own house."

"Practical," she says, eyeing the couch as if trying to decide where she's supposed to sit.

"Yeah, it is." So are all the pockets for the remote and the cupholders that the IKEA shit comes with. "Why don't you take the chaise. I'll park my ass on the cushion next to it and put my feet up on the table here."

Gingerly she sits and scoots back against the cushy arm, legs curled up and those striped socks folded beneath her. Since she's not using the long end of the chaise, I move the pizza box there, where it'll be within easier reach for both of us.

And this is the fucking life. A sexy girl on my sofa, her wine in one hand and a pizza slice in the other. I've got my beer, a remote, and I couldn't ask for a damn thing more. I pull up the movie rentals onscreen.

As I'm flipping through the categories, Emma says, "I thought you watched football on Sundays?"

"Usually. But I'd rather do this with you." Though honesty forces me to add, "You won't be offended if I check the scores on my phone while we're watching, will you?"

"I won't be offended. But you should just put on football, instead."

I glance at her. She's got a bite of pizza between her teeth and is fighting with a long string of melted cheese that won't let go of her slice. "You like football?"

Mouth full, her initial answer is a shrug, then she finally wins the war with the cheese and swallows her bite before she tells me, "I like the exciting parts."

"The exciting parts?"

"Yep." She picks off a pepperoni and pops it into her mouth. "When you start yelling at the TV, that's my cue to start watching."

Chuckling, I reach past her for my second slice. "Sounds like you've done that before."

"I've lived with my share of families who had sports fans. And it was always the same—I'd be reading, and look up when someone started yelling, and I'd get to see the best parts of the game without having to slog through the boring parts."

"So you plan to read while I watch the game?"

"Unless you'd feel ignored."

"With you snuggled up against me? Hell no."

"All right. Although since your library shelves are practically empty, you'll have to let me use your phone." Her eyes take on a mischievous gleam. "You have books downloaded, right? I bet I can find something to read in there."

Hopefully. I hand over the device and ask, "I'm about to be judged, aren't I?"

She grins at me. "Oh yes."

And she really does start scrolling through all the titles as soon as she opens up the app. Holy shit. Never in my life would I have thought a woman looking through my digital library might be a nerve-wracking experience, but I never knew that woman would be Emma Williams. I try to see all the books through her eyes. I'm not a real highbrow reader. I've got some histories and biographies, but most of what I read are mysteries, thrillers, and horror off the bestseller lists. Anything with action and that doesn't spend too much time navel-gazing.

Now I'm spending more time watching her face than watching the game. She's sipping her wine while she continues scrolling through—as if looking at all the books I have is just as entertaining to her as reading them.

Suddenly I can't take the suspense anymore. Gruffly I ask her, "Have I lost all hope?"

"I'd say the opposite. In fact, you're in real danger of me stealing your phone," she says mildly, without looking up from the screen. "This is one of the mystery books that Nora Roberts wrote under another name, isn't it?"

I glance at the cover. "I think so. I don't pay much attention to the authors themselves. Just whether I like what they're writing."

"Did you like this one?"

"Yeah, it was all right. Don't start with that one, though—start with the first book. It's in there."

"Okay."

A few moments later she opens the first book and settles in, and my heart's suddenly ten times bigger than it was last Sunday when I was sitting here, wondering how and when I'd get Emma Williams to stop being afraid of me.

My dick feels ten times bigger, too. But I ignore it as best I can. Emma's likely still hurting from earlier, and although I plan to get my mouth on her later, my cock's going to have to wait a bit longer.

Until halftime rolls around, and Emma leans forward to set her wineglass on the table—then slips off the sofa and kneels on the floor between my legs. She looks up at me with heavy-lidded eyes, and the instant rush of blood to my cock has me gritting my teeth and struggling for control even before she's touched me.

"It's all right?" she asks softly, placing her hands on my knees.

"Fuck yes," I groan the response from low in my throat. Then I make myself tell her, "You don't have to."

"I know. But I want to." She starts running those hands up the tense muscles of my thighs and I'm in heaven. "But will you do something for me?"

"Any fucking thing in the world."

The ferocity of that response pulls a smile from her. "I just want you to take off your shirt. So I can look while I— Oh."

I'm already dragging it over my head and tossing it onto the table before leaning back against the cushion again. Her soft lips part, her gaze slipping over my torso. I'm never going to be one of those male model types, all waxed and lean. I'm built solidly, with thick muscles and a hairy chest.

The way Emma's looking at me, that's just fine with her. Her breathing gets heavier, her gaze dropping as her hands reach the V of my thighs. She hesitates, then skips right over the bulge of my erection, heading straight for my belt buckle.

And I realize what I should have realized the moment her knees hit the floor. "You ever done this before?"

"No." Her wry gaze flicks up to mine before returning my waist, where she's pulling my belt free. She opens the snap and starts easing the zipper down. "But I've seen some porn. Plus I've read a lot of books. And I…"

Her voice trails off. With the pressure of denim and the zipper easing up, my cock's already trying to bust free. I drag the elastic waist of my briefs down over the base of my shaft, and maybe she didn't get a good look before when I was stroking myself, but she sure does now. Thick and long, the fat head an angry red and already beaded with pre-cum.

"Oh," she whispers.

"You changing your mind?"

"No. It's just… I've imagined this. And, um. You're bigger."

And getting harder with her every word. But although it's killing me, I'm going to let her take her sweet time.

"What else did you imagine?"

Nervously she licks her lips, gaze darting to my face. "You looking like you do now. But I thought you were angry."

So I was mean and had her on her knees. "And what'd you do?"

Her eyes locked on mine, she leans forward until her hot breath is torturing the head of my cock. Her voice is a throaty whisper as she says, "Then you told me to make you come."

My dick's never been so fucking hard. On a low growl I tell her, "Make me come, then."

She moans as if that harsh demand is the sexiest thing she's ever heard. But the sexiest thing is her small hand wrapping around my thick shaft. It's her mouth opening up over the head of my cock. It's her pink tongue darting out to taste the drop of pre-cum at the tip.

Fuuuuck. My breath hisses through my teeth. I fist my hands in the cushions, stopping myself from burying my fingers in her hair and shoving my cock to the back of her throat and commanding her to suck.

It's her first time. It becomes a chant in my head, a mantra to keep control. *Her first time. Go easy.*

But Emma doesn't go easy on me. She bends over my cock, wraps both hands around my meaty shaft, and takes as much as she can into the sultry torment of her mouth. Without prompting, she starts sucking on me. Sucking and working her tongue and letting all that drool lubricate the twisting stroke of her hands, like she knows exactly what she's doing, but her inexperience is there in the careful way she never takes me deep enough to risk choking, as if she thinks gagging on my cock might ruin the effect instead of making it all even hotter. But that careful attention, that innocence is so fucking sexy. I can't look away, can't stop groaning her name. Her golden hair's a wavy curtain framing the erotic perfection of her face, those full lips wrapped around my dick—and her hungry gaze keeps flicking up to meet mine as if checking to see if she's doing this right, but it couldn't be any righter. She could be all teeth and jelly fingers and I'd still be ready to come just from that hungry look in her eyes telling me how much she wants this, how much she wants me to love it.

And I love it too damn much. My control's slipping with every slick caress of her tongue, every wet pull of her mouth, every tight pump of her hands.

"Harder now, baby." Through clenched teeth I make the rough demand. "You feel so goddamn good, sucking my dick like that. A little harder and you're gonna make me come."

As if just the thought of me coming deepens her own arousal, she moans around my cock. Immediately her rhythm becomes faster, harder.

"Fuck." Groaning, I fist my hands deeper into the cushions. Only a miracle is stopping me from thrusting into her mouth, from fucking her face. *Her first time.* But that thought isn't working as a leash on my control anymore. Because Emma Williams is sucking a cock for the very first time and it's mine.

The only cock she's ever wanted is *mine.*

"Gonna come, baby," I grit out. My big hands wrap around hers, tightening our grip on my shaft. "Pull back unless you want my cum filling up your mouth."

Oh fuck, she *does* want it. Because she doesn't pull

back. Instead she makes a deep hungry sound and sucks harder, and that's the fucking end of me. The orgasm bulldozes into me, my cock jerking in her grip and my cum exploding past her lips. Too deep, because now she chokes a little and draws back until just the bulging crown is in her mouth, but I couldn't stop this now if I wanted to, and her face, sweet Jesus. Her face—her eyes locked on mine and her skin flushed and her full lips still sucking right at the tip. Another pulse shoots down the length of my shaft as that look wrings every drop of cum from my dick.

Holy shit. My chest heaving too hard to get a word out, I cup her cheeks. It takes her a long second before she swallows my cum and she makes a funny face as she does it, and the next second I'm laughing breathlessly when she reaches for her wine and chases the taste by draining her glass.

"You'll get used to it," I tell her and she laughs, cheeks bright red and eyes gleaming. Then she laughs again when I add, "You must read some dirty, dirty books if that's where you learned to suck cock like that."

"Some." Smiling, she crawls up onto my lap, straddling my thighs as she kisses me with the flavor of chardonnay and cum on her lips. It's sexy as hell, and so is knowing that she's got no panties under her skirt, and her bare pussy is hovering right above my bare dick.

It's enough to get my cock stirring again and my mouth watering. "Are you wet?"

"Mmm-hmm," she hums against my lips, then says, "But halftime's over."

"Fuck the game."

She giggles and kisses me again. "And just think of how hot I'll be if I have to wait—sitting next to you, knowing that as soon as the game's done, you intend to eat my pussy. With every play, I'll be thinking about how much closer I am to having your mouth on me. Think of how wet I'll be *then*."

I'm not sure who she's trying to get hotter, me or her—but it's working.

"All right," I tell her, and she looks damn satisfied as she scoots over. After I tuck away my cock, I open my second beer and refill her wine, then sit back again.

This time when she starts reading, she turns sideways, leaning back against the cushioned arm of the sofa and draping her long legs over my lap. The hem of her skirt slides up, just a little. Not enough to see anything beneath. But these next two quarters are going to fucking kill me.

I slide my palm up one of those long striped socks before letting my hand rest on her lower thigh, my fingers stroking the inside of her knee.

This is the fucking life, I decide—a beer, a game, and a hot pussy waiting for me.

But I'm wrong. Because about five minutes later, I look over, and Emma's not reading anymore. Instead her eyes are closed and my phone is lying on her chest with her hand still loosely clasped around it. Beneath her sweater, her small breasts rise and fall on deep, even breaths.

And *this* is the life. The best life. One that's even better than I imagined. One where Emma is comfortable enough and trusts me enough that she'll fall asleep right next to me. Now I just have to persuade her that a life together would be better than she can imagine, too.

Starting with when she wakes up.

EMMA

THE GAME MUST BE OVER.

I didn't intend to nap, but I can't think of a better way to wake up than with Logan's tongue dragging over my clit. Oh my god. My pussy's already wet and aching, as if he's been trying to nudge me out of sleep for a while, and my body's way ahead of my brain.

Softly I moan, reaching for him. My fingers tangle in his hair as he lifts his head. He must have spread me out on the chaise, because I'm lying flat with my thighs open wide, and my feet aren't dangling off the cushions. Everything's dark—not due to the mask, because I'm faintly aware of Christmas lights shining somewhere off to the side—but as if he's already turned off the television and all the lamps.

Voice low and rough with amusement, he says, "Finally awake, then?"

Not all the way but getting there. "Mmm."

He seems to take that as a signal to redouble his efforts. His mouth lowers again, the firm grip of his hands pushing my thighs wider. Hungrily he latches onto my clit and even as I'm crying out with the agonizing pleasure of it, his fingers slip through my slick folds and press against my entrance.

"Let me know if it hurts, baby," he says gruffly, then begins easing a finger inside of me.

It doesn't hurt. The initial penetration stings a little, but then his tongue glides over my clit, and it just feels wondrous and full.

"It's good," I pant breathlessly. "So good."

A low groan is his response, his mouth never leaving my clit, his hand slowly thrusting. And I must have been close to an orgasm before I woke up, because I'm *so* close now, almost frantic with the need to come—then stiffening, stiffening, as a sharp stretching ache builds at the entrance of my sex. Because he's added another finger. Slowly he pushes it deeper, watching me, and it hurts but the pain's already fading, until I'm just left with that feeling of being stretched and overfilled.

"All right?"

"Yes," I whisper, though I'm not really too sure—until his mouth lowers again, and he slowly licks and tugs at my clit, and his fingers start thrusting gently, deeper and deeper. Then I'm truly all right, beyond all right, the sensations racing through me becoming more acute with every lick, every pump of his hand. And suddenly I'm right there again, right on the edge, but I'm higher, dizzy with the sheer pleasure of his touch. Then the world narrows with sudden solid clarity, narrows to the width of my skin and the stroke of his tongue, the incredible fullness of his fingers. I come with my back bowing, choking on my scream, my pussy squeezing that wonderful thickness inside me.

Groaning, Logan rides out my orgasm, then gently withdraws his fingers and softly licks the cream from my pussy lips before rising over me. His mouth finds mine in the dark, the tang of my arousal on his tongue and lips, and he smells so good—like soap and some woodsy fragrance.

Too soon, he breaks the kiss and murmurs against my lips, "Good morning."

"Good morning," I reply before I even realize what I've said. Then I do, and a couple of things hit me all at once.

It's Monday morning.

Logan is showered and fully dressed.

And I'm in his bed.

My gaze shoots to the window. Still dark out. But that doesn't mean anything. This time of year, the sun doesn't come up until *after* I'm supposed to be at work.

"Oh my god. What time is it?"

"Six thirty." With a grin, he stands and reaches for my hand to pull me up with him. "If you want to hop in the shower, I'll head down and start the coffee and some breakfast."

Six thirty. No need to panic, then. Except I feel panicky, anyway.

I try to hide it, smiling and babbling something like, "Shower, good, okay," before rushing to the bathroom. Inside, I stare at my flushed face in the mirror. My heart's racing and anxiety knots my gut. Because last night was perfect. *So* perfect. This morning was, too. But now reality's going to set in.

And I don't want it to.

But it does. It always does. That's when those amazing things he said last night—about us being together, about putting a ring on my finger—he won't be so certain about those things anymore. There will be something, *something* that changes his mind. And he won't want me any longer.

At least he wants me now. For a little while.

With two shower heads featuring multiple massage settings, beautiful cream tile and glass doors, his shower's as oversized and as incredible as the rest of his house is. I want to linger but I rush through, and emerge smelling as good as Logan did earlier. The anxiety in my gut has loosened some, but a heavy ache has taken up residence in my chest. Because I *can* see myself here, in this house, in this bedroom. I can see myself with Logan.

And when this is over, everything I imagine having with him is going to haunt me for the rest of my life.

I find a sweatshirt and sweatpants waiting for me, laid out on the bed. They're both far too big, but I'm able to pull the drawstring on the waist of the pants tight enough that they don't slide down over my hips. My own clothes I fold into a little pile and carry down the stairs with me.

The scent of coffee and bacon leads me to the kitchen. The rumble of my stomach sounds louder than my footsteps, and seems to announce my presence.

In a blue flannel shirt and black Carhartt carpenter pants, Logan looks up from the pan of scrambled eggs that he's scooping onto a pair of plates. Appreciation lights his icy blue eyes when he sees me in his sweats, but he doesn't say a word. He just lets his eyes tell me that he'd eat me up again, even when I'm drowning in shapeless clothes.

My cheeks heat. Feeling suddenly shy, I head for the coffee. "Did you already pour yourself one?"

"Yeah." He sets a mug and two plates on the bar. "You need cream and sugar?"

I shake my head. He takes the stool at the end of the bar—where he'll be sitting adjacent to me, instead of sitting side by side. We'll be looking at each other, I realize. And there will be no hiding from him.

I wonder if he knows I *want* to hide.

I set my mug next to my plate—then realize I might have been wrong about our seating arrangement. "This isn't mine, is it?"

It's piled high with more eggs and bacon than I can possibly eat. But a glance at the other plate tells me that it's just as full.

"Too much?" He takes the other stool. "I just made double of what I usually make."

Laughing, I demonstrate the same thing he demonstrated to me last night—holding up my hand against his. "That size difference is probably a good guideline for meal proportions, too."

"I guess I'm just not used to cooking for a woman," he says casually, as if he has no idea how telling me that lifts through my chest like some sweet song. "Eat what you can and we'll give Lucy the rest. And maybe she'll like us a bit better afterward."

I glance over to where the yellow dog is curled up on the floor in front of the refrigerator door, her eyes locked on Logan's big hands. "You think she might?"

"Nah. I've given her hundreds of these." He picks up a crispy piece of bacon from his plate and Lucy lifts her head. "And she wouldn't care if I got hit by a truck tomorrow, as long as the people who moved in here after my funeral still fed her."

He tosses the bacon Lucy's way. She leaps up and scarfs it out of the air, then lies down again—with her back to us, as if to let us know that she still doesn't care about our existence.

I grin and take a piece, too, but I'm not throwing it to the dog. Instead I start in on my own breakfast.

Logan digs in, too, and he's quiet until he's about halfway through. Then he says, "What are you doing on Christmas Day? Are you going to your friend Traci's place?"

Mouth full, I shake my head.

He frowns. "Are you staying at home by yourself?"

"Yes." It's what I've done every year since leaving my last foster home.

"Come with me to my dad's house." His pale blue gaze is steady on my face. "Spend it with us. It's just him and me."

Sharp yearning tightens my chest. But I shake my head. "Thank you, though."

"Why no?" He asks it softly.

I poke at my eggs. "It's just hard…being the outsider during Christmas."

"You speaking from experience?"

"Yes." And because I can see he's not going to just let this go without an explanation, I sigh and set down my fork. "I had some great foster families. And all of them had either their own kids, or relatives who showed up during the holidays. Whenever they did, they'd tell me, 'You must be so grateful to be a part of this great family.' And I *was* grateful, but…I never really felt a part."

"Of the family?"

"Yes." I don't think I can force down any more food through my aching throat, so I wrap my hands around my coffee mug, taking comfort in the warmth. "I was just there, looking in at what they had. But *I* never had it."

His jaw is tight. "Especially not when they said shit like that—telling you how you're lucky to be included."

I nod. "So Christmas was when I was never allowed to forget that any happiness I felt was due to someone else's generosity, and how I owe them for that."

His gaze is intense on mine, his voice like gravel. "It's not true generosity if they expect something in return—even if all they expect is gratitude. You don't owe anyone a damn thing, Emma."

"Well…some things I do." I owe a lot to those families. "I guess I just don't like it thrown in my face."

"Name one person who does," he says dryly, and the smile that reply pulls from me makes it easier to swallow when I take my next sip of coffee. "What about the families that weren't great? Did they do that, too?"

"Yes, but it wasn't exactly the same. I wouldn't have wanted to be a part of their families. And most of the time, they made it clear that anything I got would never have been given anyway, except as part of their obligation as a foster parent."

"Those gifts are the ones that came with a price?"

"Yes. Nothing was ever freely given. It was always held over our heads. One misstep, and either we wouldn't get it—or it would be taken away. Or they'd use it to remind us of what we owed them."

"If you came to my dad's, everything would be freely given. I have a feeling it would be at Traci's, too."

"I know it would be." And I do. Just like everything that Logan's given me here has been. "But I don't want to be the outsider."

"Well, that's a simple fix." A smile tilts the corners of his firm mouth but the solemn gravity of his gaze doesn't lighten. "We'll make you part of our family."

Sheer longing grips my heart. Oh my god, and he said it so *easily*. Eyes stinging, I try to cover my reaction by taking another sip of steaming coffee.

Gaze narrowing on my face, he leans in. "That's the solution, right? You won't be on the outside looking in if you become a part of a family—or if you make a new one. My dad and me, we'll be yours. And we'll keep you around Crenshaw's for a long, long time."

Though my throat's aching and thick, I manage a tiny smile. "That does sound really nice."

Eyes piercing, he regards me for endless moment. "But you don't really trust it, do you?"

I shrug.

"Why?" When I don't answer, he says gruffly, "You say I don't know you, baby. But I want to."

And there's no reason not to tell him. It's all ancient history. *Kind of* ancient history, since it still affects me now. But maybe while he needs the explanation, I need the reminder—because when Logan says he'll make me a part of his family, I want it so much.

But I've wanted it before.

I pull in a shuddering breath. "When I was little, there were a couple of times I thought I might become part of a family. Permanently a part of one."

"Adopted?"

"Yes. By the time I was older, I didn't expect it anymore. Younger kids are more likely to be adopted—and of course when I was little, I didn't know about the statistics, but the foster parents I was with would say certain things that made me think it was a possibility, and I'd hope. But there was always some deal breaker."

His eyebrows draw together in a dark frown. "What do you mean—a deal breaker? Their application was rejected?"

"No." That word sounds hoarse, so I take another sip before continuing. "It was always something about me. I didn't look enough like them, so no one would ever believe I was their real kid. Or I wasn't interested in the right hobbies or sports, and they wanted a kid who liked the things they did."

Those icy eyes suddenly burn with anger, and he's staring at me with his jaw clenched. "They *told* you this?"

"Not directly." I shrug. "But I don't think adults realize how much kids overhear. Or how much they pick up. There was one woman, I remember. I was five, and she used to take me to those beauty pageants for little girls. We were getting ready backstage, and she's brushing my hair while she's talking to one of the other moms—and the other woman asked her if she would make it permanent, because I was so pretty. And my foster mom said, 'My husband and I were thinking about it, but she doesn't really have any stage talent.'" And after all these years, I can still hear that response so clearly. After all these years, it still tastes so bitter. "Because I couldn't sing, or play an instrument, or dance. And she didn't think adding numbers in my head was a real talent. So that was the deal breaker. There was just always *something*."

Logan reaches across the bar and folds my hands in his. "So you're thinking I'm going to find something I don't like about you, and it'll be a deal breaker for me."

God. And he just zeroed right in on everything that's hurting my heart. Zeroed right in, and threw it out there in the open. Tears burning in my eyes, I try to pull away, but his fingers only tighten around mine.

"I won't," he says fiercely. "I won't, Emma."

I shake my head. The inside of my chest feels scraped raw. "You don't know me. And when you do—"

"I'll just want you more."

He sounds so sure. And it hurts so much, because I so desperately want to believe him.

But I don't know if I can dare to hope again.

His voice softens. "I'd put that ring on your finger now, Emma. I'd make it permanent right now. But I'm not asking that of you yet. I'm just asking you to share Christmas with us, so you can see how it might be. But you won't have to imagine anything. You'll see it's real—and so good—when it's happening. Just like last night was better than I imagined it would be. So think about coming, okay? There doesn't have to be any gifts involved. We'll just watch football and drink beer and then go for a walk in the snow along the creek, then sit down to dinner and eat more of my dad's Christmas roast than we should. Then I'll take you home and fuck you so hard."

A watery laugh bursts from me. Because of course it would come down to that between us.

His eyes gleam with amusement. "That last part has almost convinced you, hasn't it?"

All of it sounds wonderful. But the last part is just easiest to believe in. I know he wants me sexually. I want him, too. There's nothing to doubt there.

"Just think about coming," he says now, gently. "We'd love to have you with us."

Drawing in a deep breath, I gather my courage. "Okay. I'll think about it."

"Then think about this, too." His big hands cup my cheeks, keeping my gaze locked on his. "No matter what I might give you, you'll never owe me anything. That doesn't mean I won't ever ask anything from you, because I might ask a hell of a lot. When I get that ring on your finger, it means asking for your patience and your trust and your faith and your heart. But even if I ask for all that, you don't *owe* it. You should only do it because you want to give it. Because it makes you happy to give it. And everything I do for you, it'll be because I want to. Because it makes me happy. All right?"

His face is wavering through my tears. "All right," I whisper, and he kisses me, his mouth so warm, his hands so strong.

And my stupid heart begins to hope. But kissing him back makes me happy—and I want it more than anything.

So I do, for as long as I can.

It's not long enough.

Since I wasn't wearing any shoes when he abducted me, Logan has to carry me out to his truck—then into my apartment when we reach it.

As I'm unlocking the door, I tell him, "It'll just take me a couple of minutes to change clothes. Do you mind giving my car a jump before you take off?"

I lead us into the living room, which smells like cold pine—the best smell in the world, truly. But I don't think that I'll associate the scent with Christmas anymore. Instead I'll think of the man who's coming into the apartment right behind me.

"I don't mind giving you a jump, but since I'm flying out first thing tomorrow, I've got a better solution," he says.

"To that job in Florida?" My heart sinks a little. I'd forgotten about it—but he'll be gone for three days.

Right now, that seems like a lifetime. Three days is longer than how much time has passed from the moment he first kissed me to now.

Everything has changed so swiftly in that time…and I'm terrified that in three days, everything will change again.

"Yeah." As if he's just as reluctant to go as I am for him to be gone, Logan catches my hand and pulls me back for a sweet kiss before lifting his head. "Shawn's picking me up around four in the morning so we can head up to the airport. Why don't you stay with me tonight, then continuing staying at my place and using my truck until I get back on Thursday?"

Using the truck makes a little sense, considering the state of my car's battery. Staying at his house doesn't. "Why?"

"You need a reliable rig. I need someone to look after Lucy."

"Like house sitting?"

"Yeah. Like house sitting."

He says that as if he's just agreeing with me—not as if house sitting was how he was thinking of my stay there until I mentioned it.

Suspiciously I narrow my eyes at him. "You didn't make arrangements for Lucy already? I find that hard to believe."

"Of course I did. Patrick looks in on her, but he can't stay overnight. I'd rather have someone there." His voice deepens and he cups my face in his warm hands. "And I like the thought of you sleeping in my bed, Emma—or reading on my couch. And you can find out a lot about a man by being in his house. While you're there, you could look through anything. I don't care. Search my closets, my drawers. Poke around in my workshop. Dig through my computer. I'll give you all my passwords. I'll leave my tablet so you can read all my books. And I'll call you every night and whisper dirty things in your ear before you go to bed. All right?"

I don't know how I can say no to that, though I should. The more time I spend at his place, the more clearly I'll be able to imagine myself staying forever—and the harder it will be when this is over.

Not that it matters. It will be hard no matter when it ends. Today, tomorrow. Next month. It will always be harder.

So three days of harder is nothing.

"All right," I agree softly.

When he kisses me again, it still makes me as happy as it did before. I still want it more than anything. And it still doesn't last long enough.

I don't think it ever will.

EMMA

IT FEELS LIKE MUCH LONGER THAN THREE DAYS—and two nights.

Two nights spent warm and cozy in Logan's bed, reading his books, and talking with him over the phone—calls that end with his voice rough in my ear, telling me to come hard for him.

Two nights of coming for him, so hard.

Thursday seems to stretch out even more endlessly than the other two days did. I try to focus on work, hoping that the minutes will fly by more quickly. But the minutes begin dragging by even slower when Shawn calls into the office to let us know that a weather delay and traffic will put their arrival about an hour behind schedule.

Forty-five minutes later, I'm staring morosely at the clock on my computer when Marianne swings by, as cheery as ever. "Our Christmas party guests will be arriving soon, so go ahead and pack this up, hon—then run in to Bruce's office for a few minutes. Oh, and here's your Christmas bonus."

I stare at the envelope she drops on my desk. "A bonus?"

"Mmm-hmm." A concerned frown suddenly etches a line between her brows, and she leans in, her voice lowering. "You're going to see everyone's bonuses when they clear the account, so when you see the amount, I hope you don't feel as if you are appreciated less than anyone else. It's just that it's your first Christmas with Crenshaw's, so it won't be as much as some of the others."

"Oh, no—I just wasn't expecting a bonus at all." They hadn't been mentioned when Marianne and I ran the payroll this week.

"It's a little something that Bruce always writes up at the end of year. He considers it profit sharing, and he puts aside a percentage of his earnings to split up every Christmas—and the employees who've been here longest get the bigger share. So an employee who's put five years into the company receives five times as much as someone in their first year."

She says that last part with an apologetic tone again— as if still explaining why mine might be smaller. But I don't care how big it is. My throat's a burning lump as I say, "That must be a good incentive to stay."

Marianne gives me a look as if I just said the understatement of the year. "This is my tenth year—and that bonus is part of the reason it's so hard to leave."

"I can imagine." Thickly I say, "Thank you."

"You thank Bruce." She winks at me. "And it's past five o'clock somewhere in the world, so why don't you take him a little eggnog when you go in."

Nodding, I slide the envelope into my purse. Despite my curiosity, I won't tear it open and look. No matter how much it is, it's more money than I had before. Even if it's only twenty-five dollars, it means I can budget in a little host gift for Bruce when I go with Logan to his dad's house for Christmas.

It doesn't even occur to me until I'm knocking on his office door that I've officially made the decision to go.

Bruce calls for me to come in, then rises out of his chair with a broad smile when he sees the cup I'm holding. "Thank you, Emma. You didn't get one for yourself?"

Remembering how one glass of wine put me to sleep, I shake my head. "Probably better if I don't."

My boss grins, and it looks so much like his son's grin that my heart aches from missing him. "Well, if you decide to indulge, let me know if you need a ride home."

Hopefully I'll be getting a ride from his son. But I simply say, "Thank you. And thank you for the Christmas bonus."

He waves that off. "This company wouldn't be where it is without everyone putting their effort in. So I'm always happy to give something back. Did you pick up your Secret Santa gift off the party table yet?"

"Not yet."

His blue eyes are twinkling. "I think he got you something that you'll really enjoy."

Remembering the note and the mask Logan left at my door, I can't stop my blush. I know that's not what Bruce is referring to, but I can't help thinking that a Secret Santa *did* give me something I really enjoyed.

If Bruce notices my blush, he doesn't comment on it. Instead he gestures to the seating area by the window. Outside it's snowing again, fat flakes slowly drifting down. "Come chat with me for a minute, Emma."

This sounds more serious than I anticipated. Anxiety twists in my stomach as I sit.

He settles in and says, "Logan says you might be joining us at my place for Christmas."

My heart's pounding. "I think I will. If it's all right?"

"You'll always be welcome at my house, Emma. Not just Christmas. Anytime you like." And that's just like his son, too—offering it so easily and so sincerely, it makes my throat tighten and eyes sting. "Now, tell me how you're getting on here. Marianne says you're not having any problems and that we'll be in good hands on Monday when you start going it alone, but I want to hear it from you. Are you enjoying the work?"

"I am." I put all the truth of that in my voice.

"Logan tells me you like numbers but don't like the phones."

Every muscle in my body tenses. "Phones are all right, too."

On a sudden laugh, Bruce rocks forward in his chair. "Look at you. You just jumped to the worst possible conclusion, didn't you? Maybe worrying that you not liking phones will lose you this job."

I'd like to join in his laughter, but I can't. Because he's right. I'm terrified.

"Let me reassure you, then." He sits back again. "After that HGTV show, when we began expanding, I hired Marianne to help with the bookkeeping and the front office, while I took care of the back office here. Our catalog was taking off, Logan was making our custom shop into something special, and so she took the administrative pressure off me, seeing that payroll and bills were taken care of. While back here, I made sure everything was running smoothly in our shops. Because that takes up most of my time—coordinating shipments, managing inventory, all that."

He pauses as if waiting for a response. I'm not sure how this is supposed to reassure me yet, but I'm following along. Nodding, I tell him, "All right."

"Now, there's a reason I hired you specifically, Emma. That construction company you were with—you didn't just do their bookkeeping. When they started shedding their staff, you handled all their purchase orders, coordinated all of their material deliveries, the scheduling. Yeah?"

"Yes."

"And your boss there said that you were damn good at it. That you picked it all up without a hitch. He said that if they'd hired you two or three years earlier, maybe they wouldn't have had so many conflicts and delays that put them in the red and then put them under. So these past three weeks have been a walk in the park for you, haven't they?"

I'm not sure if I should say yes. "It's true that I have fewer responsibilities here."

His eyes are piercing mine. "Do you like that?"

I don't *dis*like it. But I could be more useful to this company than I am now. "I'd be happy to take on more, if that's what you're asking."

"It is." All at once he seems to sit easier, as if a huge weight just dropped from his shoulders. "I started this company with wood in my hands, Emma, but all I've had in my hands the past ten years is paper. And I miss being in the shop. I miss it like hell. So maybe over the next six months or so, I could show you this side of the business, move you into this office—and hire someone else to answer phones."

My chest is suddenly tight. "I'd like that," I tell me.

"Me, too." Expression satisfied, he looks around the

office. "You taking over all this would be the best Christmas present anyone could ever give me. Aside from that mug."

He gestures to the *World's #1 Dad* mug that never seems too far out of his reach.

I can't stop my grin. "Did Logan get you that?"

"It was my Secret Santa gift last year. He never admitted that it was from him, but…"

Who else would give him a *World's #1 Dad* mug? "Right."

"He's a thoughtful boy. Knows exactly what someone needs." Bruce raises his brows and gives me a significant look. "Even if they don't know it themselves."

He couldn't possibly know about the satin mask or how Logan pinned my hips to a wall and licked me to a screaming orgasm, but my face goes scarlet anyway. Because I definitely got what I needed.

A sharp knock at the door saves me, drawing Bruce's attention. Before he even replies to the knock, the door swings open and Logan strides through, his pale blue gaze fixed on me, his voice a low growl. "Marianne said you were in here. Christ, I've missed you."

My heart leaps into my throat, my gaze eating him up as he crosses the room with that long unhurried stride—and my ass is rooted to the spot. Bruce is sitting right here. Is Logan going to kiss me in front of him? Because he certainly looks as if he intends to.

Mildly my boss says, "Have I been missed?"

"Good to see you, too, Dad." Gripping the arms of my chair in his big hands, Logan leans down and swiftly touches his lips to mine. Voice low and intimate, he asks me, "How you doing, baby?"

There's apparently no point in hiding anything in front of his dad. Softly I reply, "Better now that you're back."

"Good to hear." His gaze burns into mine. "How's my dog?"

"Still indifferent to human life."

"And my truck?"

"Also indifferent to human life."

He grins and lightly kisses me again before turning to look at his father. "I think you've got guests in the front office."

Expression amused, Bruce looks to me. "Well, let me make certain we're through here first. I think we've settled everything. Haven't we, Emma?"

Filled with so much happiness that I wouldn't be surprised if someone said it was shining like a rainbow out of my eyes, I nod. "I think so."

"Then you and Logan can discuss what kind of desk you want him to make after you move in here." Eggnog in hand, Bruce rises to his feet. "I think if we rearrange this seating area and stick it over in that corner of the room, she'll have a nice view out the window. Maybe you should take a few minutes and make some measurements, son, before joining the party."

"I'll do that." Eyes slightly narrowed, Logan looks to me as his dad heads for the door. "You're moving in here?"

Quietly I reply, "I think I've been promoted. Your dad says he wants to work in the shop again."

That news seems to make Logan as happy as it made his dad, then the office door clicks shut, and in the next moment my face is in his hands and his mouth claiming my lips in a scorching kiss. My fingers tangle in his hair, and I softly moan when he lifts his head far too early.

"Shit." He pulls me to my feet and kisses me again before stopping, holding my face close, his ragged breaths mingling with mine. "I'll be walking around the party with my dick trying to bust out of my pants if I kiss you much more. So let's go out there, mingle, and leave as soon as we can."

"No arguments here," I tell him.

"If you had any, I'd just throw you over my shoulder and carry you off, anyway. Which reminds me"—he steps back and pulls two envelopes out of his back pocket, one apparently his bonus and the other a red holiday envelope—"I stopped by the conference room when I was looking for you. This had your name on it."

I take the red envelope. "My Secret Santa gift?"

"Yup."

"This isn't a pair of scented candles."

"You don't need those now that you've got a tree." He gives the envelope seal an encouraging tap. "So let's see what he ended up giving you."

I arch a brow at him. "You don't know?"

Grinning, he shakes his head. "Though I gave him a few ideas."

Good ideas, apparently. I carefully break the envelope seal and withdraw a gift card, and my smile is huge when I turn it around to show him. "From that bookstore downtown."

"Just right." He looks as pleased by his dad's choice as I am, then his gaze narrows on mine. "My gift wasn't on the table yet."

"Your Secret Santa is a slacker." With a laugh, I tuck away the card again, then grip his shirt collar and pull him down for another kiss. Against his lips I say huskily, "But don't worry. You won't end the day disappointed. Maybe I've got a little present for you tonight."

He grins against my mouth. "Oh yeah?"

"Mmm-hmm. A virgin pussy all wrapped up and waiting to go under your big Christmas tree."

Logan's big body tenses against mine. Catching my face in his big hands, he draws back, his pale blue gaze searching my eyes. "I don't want our first time to be like that, baby."

"Not…like what? With a virgin pussy? Because it's not going to get devirginized without you."

"I don't want it to be an exchange."

"An exchange?" I blink up at him in confusion, mentally rewinding our conversation. Slowly I realize where he's going with this, but I still can't quite believe it. "You…think I'm giving you my virginity in lieu of a Secret Santa gift?"

"I don't know," he says hoarsely. "But I know you're strapped for cash. I know you don't like to owe anyone. And that you like to keep things even."

Pain blooms through my chest. "I like *money* to be equal. Sex shouldn't even enter into it."

His jaw tightens, then on a heavy sigh he says, "You kissed me to keep things even when I brought the tree."

The hurt blossoms into anger. Pointedly I stab my finger into his chest. "No," I hiss at him, "*you* kissed *me*. I would have taken the tree as the gift it was. I was uncomfortable with the cost of it, sure. But *you're* the one who suggested that I should make up the difference—and I didn't think it was seriously a monetary repayment. I thought you kissed me because you *wanted* to kiss me."

Logan's face stills and I can see the realization sweep through his gaze. Because it all happened *exactly* as I just said. "I did do that."

Yeah, he did. I lift my chin. "So why do you think I kissed you back? Do you really think it was repayment?"

"No." Eyes closing, he drags his hands through his hair. "No, I don't."

"Good." My throat's raw, my eyes stinging. "Because if I was going repay people that way, I would have let someone at the electric company fuck me. Or I'd bang the guy at the auto shop. But I never thought of whoring myself out." His face whitens and my voice breaks as soon as the word *whoring* leaves my tongue. "It's great to know that you think I would."

"Emma, baby, no." Eyes tormented, his big hand catches mine.

"Don't touch me!" I yank my hand from his grip, stumbling back. "I don't want to touch you. Now that I know you think I'm trading myself for ten dollars instead of giving myself freely. God. If I'd said yes to your ring, would you think I was doing it for your house, your money?"

"No. Emma." His face bleak, he comes after me. "What I said about an exchange, I fucked it all up, because that's not what I meant. I swear to God, it's not."

Maybe he means that. I don't know. I just know that I'm so angry and hurt that I've got to get out of here before I start bawling. Blinded by tears, I haul open the door, hitting a wall of Christmas music and chatter. The party. Oh god. I have to walk through that, holding my head high. Somehow.

Gentle hands circle my waist. "Emma, please."

I hear the pain and apology in his voice, but I don't look back. If I do I'll just cry, and anger is the only thing that's going to get me through this.

So instead of tears, a harsh laugh rips from me, and I say, "You know what the funny thing is? I didn't even pick your name. So I'm going to take my cupcakes back from Shawn and let him pop my cherry instead, since apparently that's what I'm giving up as my Secret Santa gift."

Then I tear out of his embrace and slam the office door behind me.

LOGAN

MY DAD WARNED ME. CHRIST, HE WARNED me to be careful with her.

But I wasn't—and this time I'm the reason all the sweet hope and joy vanished from her eyes, replaced by hurt and despair. I don't wonder that a girl haunted him all these years. Emma's naked pain and her tears are going to haunt me for the rest of my life.

And if the rest of my life is what it takes, that's how long I'll spend making up for it.

But I don't rush after her. Hurrying is how I fucked up. In my rush to understand her, to know her, I took one thing she told me about herself and applied it across the board, making assumptions I never should have.

Assumptions that I'd have realized were incredibly fucking stupid, if I'd taken one second to think about them. But I didn't.

So I'm taking a second now. More than a second. Because when I go after her, I can't fuck this up again.

My heart's a heavy lump when I finally leave my dad's office. Immediately I run into Marianne, who's smiling and teary-eyed, the miniature nursery set in her hands.

"This is so wonderful, Logan." She pulls me down to kiss my cheek. "Thank you."

Throat tight, I only nod. My gaze is searching the front office for Emma.

"And here's yours, honey." Stopping by her desk— Emma's desk now—she opens one of the file cabinet drawers and withdraws a wrapped box. She presses the gift into my hands. "I know it's supposed to be secret, but I worried the context would be lost if you didn't know who it was from, and you'd be thinking double-yew-tee-eff when you opened it."

"Thank you," I say in a thick voice.

Her gaze narrows. "You all right, honey?"

"Just looking for Emma."

Her face softens. "Ah, well. She came through here in a rush a few minutes ago. So maybe she's in the restroom?"

She's not. She's not in the kitchen, the conference room, or the reception area, either. I swing back by my dad's office again, just to check, but she's not there.

What the hell?

She didn't drive off. Through the window in my dad's office I can see my truck. It's still out in the parking lot, covered in snow. She didn't get a ride. No one's left the party yet. She wouldn't walk home through the snow. She's angry and hurt, not foolish.

My gaze narrows on the shop across the lot. Maybe she's there. It would be easy enough for her to grab the keys and hike across the lot.

Still carrying Marianne's gift, I head outside. The Christmas music from inside the office is spilling out over the lot, so it takes me a moment to realize what else I'm hearing.

My truck's engine. A faint trail of exhaust rises from the tailpipe. So she's in there with the heater running, but hasn't bothered to clear the snow from the windows. She's not going anywhere. She's just hiding. And I've got a good idea why.

She doesn't want anyone to see her crying.

My heart aching, I stalk over to the truck and tap my fingers on the driver's side window. A moment later I hear the pop of the locks.

When I open the door, she's all the way across the seat on the passenger side, her face averted and wiping tears from her cheeks. Feeling as if a hacksaw is ripping my chest open, I haul up into the seat and pull the door closed, surrounding us in a cocoon of steel and glass and snow. I set the wrapped gift on the seat beside me. The overhead light goes off.

In the quiet darkness, my voice is a rough mess. "I'm so sorry, Emma. If I'd stopped to think for a second about what I was implying, I'd have known I was way off base."

"It doesn't matter." Her quavering voice and the tears still spilling down her cheeks immediately prove that's a lie. If it didn't matter, she wouldn't be crying. "Can you drive me home? I'm not going back to the party looking like this."

With a tearstained face that's my fucking fault. But I don't think she wants to hear any more apologies now. I don't think she wants to hear anything from me right now. So I silently grab the scraper and clear off the windows, then remain quiet on the drive to her apartment.

As soon as I stop, she grabs her purse and opens her door, hopping out. "Thanks for the ride."

She slams the door. As if she expects me to drive away.

Or as if she *wants* me to drive away.

That thought hurts like a motherfucker, but it doesn't matter. Whether she's expecting it or wanting it, I'm not leaving. I won't rush her, but I'm not backing off, either.

Emma's already at her apartment door when I catch up to her. Her mascara's in a raccoon mask around her eyes, but some of the angry fire has returned to her gaze.

My fighter. I knocked her down but she's up again.

Lips tight, she twists her key in the lock. "You really think you're coming in?"

"You said you had a virgin pussy all wrapped up for me."

"And you said you didn't want it," she snaps back and shoves her door open.

I'm behind her even as she turns to slam it in my face. Instead I have her up against the door a second later, my hand seizing her wrists and holding them over her head as she struggles against me.

Using my weight to trap her against the door, I lower my face to hers and growl, "I want it. I want *everything* you have to give. But I was so damn wrong about it not being an exchange. Every time you give yourself freely to me, Emma, you'll get something in return."

Renewed rage sparks in her eyes. "I don't want anything in return!"

"That's too bad, because you're going to get *me*," I say hoarsely, and her struggles abruptly cease. "You're going to get these rough hands that need to touch you. These eyes that will never tire of looking at you. These arms that will hold you steady or lift you up whenever you need their strength. This head that's crazy about every little thing you do." My voice deepens. "And you're going to get this heart that's already fallen in love with you."

Lips trembling, she looks up at me with wonder filling her big brown eyes. "Logan…"

Releasing her wrists, I gently catch her beautiful face in my hands. "And my big cock. You're going to get that, too."

Her sudden bright smile and husky laugh lift through me, easing the heavy ache in my chest. And I want to kiss her, but I'm not done yet.

"And my big mouth, baby," I add gruffly. "I'm so sorry."

"I know." Her eyes soften, and her hands come up to stroke my jaw, her touch the sweetest heaven. "I know you didn't mean it." Her breath shudders, and her fingers slip back to link together behind my neck. "But I think I've been waiting for you to find that deal breaker. Me being a whore seemed like it must be."

Ah, Christ. "Honest to God, even if you were, it wouldn't be a deal breaker for me." When she begins to laugh, as if that was supposed to be a joke, I shake my head and meet her gaze with mine. "Listen," I tell her solemnly. "Those supposed deal breakers that made you feel like you were lacking something—those were just excuses those assholes made so they wouldn't have to give anything to someone else. They just wanted to love little clones of themselves. They weren't willing to risk enough, to love someone else enough. But *I* will love you enough, Emma. You could be after my money and I'd love you so much that you wouldn't have any choice but to fall for me anyway."

A tremulous smile curves her lips. "That sounds about right. I don't think any woman has a chance against you."

"Too bad for them. I don't want any woman but you."

Another sigh shudders from her. She cradles my face in her hands. Her voice is soft as she confesses, "I'm in danger of falling so hard and so fast for you."

"Good." It's thick and rough. "Because I've already fallen hard. So I'll be right here waiting to catch you."

She whispers my name, her eyes shining with sudden tears, and her gaze earnestly searches mine. "I want you to know, that just because I'm not moving as fast as you, it doesn't mean I don't want you, or that I can't imagine a future with you. I want that *so* much. I just—"

"Have more reason to be wary."

"Not *more* reason. In the end, we're both risking the same thing. I'm just more accustomed to not getting what I want than you are, I think."

That's probably true. "So you're saying I'm a spoiled asshole."

I expect her to laugh, but instead she shakes her head and says softly, "No. I think you're an example of the universe actually rewarding someone who deserves to be rewarded. You give so much of yourself and so freely."

My heart swells. "Not any more than you do, baby. You're so damn perfect."

Her brows arch. "I have a temper."

Only a bit of one, and I like it when she fires it at me. "It works out. You have a temper, I don't. So we'll balance each other out."

She purses her lips. "I suspect that even if you did

have a temper, you'd say that would work out, too."

"I would. Because no matter what, I see it working. If I had a temper, I'd say we'd be in for some sparks flying between us." Tempted by those full lips, I lower my mouth to say against hers, "But we already generate plenty of sparks, yeah?"

"Yes," she breathes. "So can you please fuck me now?"

Hell yes, I can. Mouth capturing hers, I sweep her sexy little body up against my chest, carrying her into the bedroom. She's already trying to remove her clothes, twisting in my arms while trying not to break the kiss. But her house is still freezing and I'm not undressing her until she's covered.

Even if she's only covered with me.

Her room is simply decorated and neatly kept. There's nothing to trip over on my way to the bed. I toss her into the middle and come down over her, my mouth fucking hers, only raising my head to strip off her shirt and mine. Then I thread my fingers into her long golden hair and bring her back for another kiss.

But I need to taste more of her. Hungrily I capture her ruby nipple between my lips, her skin taut with cold, and she gasps as if burned by the heat of my mouth.

I rise up over her again, dragging one of the blankets with me all the way up to her shoulders before I disappear under it. I hear her laugh, then her sharp breath as my mouth reaches her stomach. Slowly I unbutton her jeans and drag them down her long legs, followed by her panties. The heady scent of her pussy fills the trapped air.

After three days, I'm starving for a taste.

Palming the underside of her thighs with my big hands, I spread her wide. Christ, her cunt's so fucking pretty. Pink and just dripping with juices.

A ravenous groan explodes from me on the first lick. Her flavor bursts over my tongue, salty and sweet, and I can't get enough. Lowering my head, I lose myself in the taste of her. Emma's hands fist in my hair and her erotic cries ring in my ears as I feast, suckling her clit, then dipping past her virgin entrance for more of her silky nectar. She's still so tight, snug around the thrust of my tongue.

Returning to her clit, I slide two fingers deep. She tenses before moaning, her pussy walls slowly accepting the thick intrusion.

My cock's even thicker. So although I'm dying to sink into her and the inside of my jeans is sticky with the pre-cum steadily dripping from the head of my dick, I take my time, lingering over her clit until the first ripples of her orgasm begin tightening her inner muscles. Then I add a third finger and do it again, until she's screaming and her hips are thrashing and we're both dripping with sweat. With shaking hands I shed my jeans and rip open a condom before settling between her thighs.

She's flushed, passion glazing her brown eyes, her lower lip swollen as if she's been biting it between her screams of pleasure. Leisurely I kiss her, my cock full of urgent need but my heart so content.

"Ready, baby?" I ask softly.

Her answer is another kiss, and her long legs circling my hips. Carefully I slide the head of my cock through the slick burning heat of her pussy, lodging against her entrance.

The delicate tissues there don't give way easily. I watch her face as I push harder, feeling the taut stretch around my cock's sensitive crown. Her warm eyes are locked on mine, and she bites her bottom lip again, a whimper sounding low in her throat.

Then her breathless, "Don't stop."

I won't. Threading my fingers through hers, I bear down. She gives a sharp cry, her fingers convulsively squeezing mine, and my teeth clench in sweet agony as the engorged head of my cock is suddenly enveloped in the tight, hot grip of her pussy. I push deeper, until my full length is buried inside her swollen channel, then go utterly still except for the soft kisses I press to her trembling lips.

"All right?" Tension and arousal grind each word to gravel.

Her eyes are gleaming with moisture as she nods, so I wait, slowly kissing her cheeks, her brow, sipping the tears from the corners of her eyes.

Tentatively she rocks her hips, the subtle movement sending a surge of pleasure through my cock.

I watch her face for any sign of pain. "Still all right?"

Breathlessly she nods, then bucks beneath me, driving my cock deeper into her slick pussy, and even as I'm gritting my teeth against the need to slam into her deep and hard, I hear her sharp gasp.

A little pain there. Softly I kiss her again, murmuring, "There's no hurry now, baby. We've got the rest of our lives to fuck hard and fast."

A shaky breath escapes her. "Okay."

Her quavering reply is a greater pleasure than the mind-blowing sensation of her cunt gripping my cock. Because that reply is an agreement that we'll be spending the rest of our lives together. A surge of possessive need pours through me in a heady rush, and I lower my head to claim her mouth again.

To claim *her*. Because I've tasted her sweetness. I've taken her innocence.

She's mine now.

Forever.

Bracing my elbows beside her shoulders, I begin moving inside her. Slowly, so slowly, withdrawing the full length of my rock hard erection before pressing back in, the taut inner walls of her virgin sheath reluctantly yielding to thickness of my cock with every deep stroke.

With a ragged moan, Emma breaks the kiss, her hands flattening against my back as if to use that solid plane for leverage. "Faster," she gasps, tilting her hips. "Oh my god. Faster now, Logan."

But I go slow. Even as she scratches at my shoulders, begging frantically for more, harder, please.

Slow. Even as she cries out my name with every endless thrust into the sultry grip of her pussy, her body writhing and her legs wrapping tighter around my hips to urge me deeper, faster.

Slow. Even as her cries become helpless panting sobs, ecstasy riding the edge of frustration that sharpens to erotic agony when I slip my fingers between us to find the swollen bud of her clit.

Slow. Until she bows beneath me, the inner muscles of her cunt clenching around my cock like a tight pumping fist, her choked scream the sweetest sound I've ever heard. In a powerful surge I bury myself deep, filling every inch of her sweet pussy and coming so hard that it feels as if I'm emptying my soul into her welcoming depths.

When her shudders ease, my mouth finds hers again, and I roll us over so that she's splayed bonelessly on top of me. For a long time we lay there wordlessly, until with a contented sigh, she lifts her head. With her bottom lip pinched between her teeth, she studies my face, her fingers lightly tracing the line of my jaw.

My gaze narrows on that trapped lip. "What?"

"I was just thinking about my Secret Santa." Her eyes gleam with amusement. "And how his Christmas tree was worth *way* more than ten dollars," she tells me, then shrieks with laughter when I immediately toss her onto her back again.

With a growl, I rise over her sexy body as it's still quivering with laughter. Swiftly I replace the condom before pushing her thighs wide and settling between them, my cock pressing against her entrance. "You've got your tree. So tell Santa what you want now, baby."

Giggling, she wraps her legs around me again. "A really big Yule log?"

So Santa gives one to her.

THIS TIME EMMA WAKES UP BEFORE ME. SHE'S ABSENT from the bed when I open my eyes, so I slide out from beneath the sweltering mound of blankets and haul on my jeans before blearily making my way into the bathroom. I'm in the middle of a piss when I realize my dick's not shriveling away from the kiss of freezing air. Emma turned up the heat.

I sure as hell hope she didn't do it for me.

Frowning, I finish up and make my way out of the bedroom. The scent of brewing coffee is overpowering the fragrance of her Christmas tree, but I don't find her in the kitchen. Instead she's sitting on the floor of her living room.

Crying.

My heart rips right out of my chest. And I must make a sound—probably like I'm fucking dying—because she turns to look at me, and I see I've made some assumptions again.

She *is* crying. But she's smiling, too.

"You okay, baby?" My voice is raw. Because she's smiling, but my heart is still recovering.

"Yes." Laughing, she wipes away her tears. Or tries to, because more just spill over. "Every column is in the black."

Frowning, I try to make sense of that and can't. "What?"

She waves her hand toward the laptop open on the floor in front of her—then she picks up a slip of paper. A check.

"The bonus," she says and starts choking up again. "It was five *thousand* dollars."

Oh yeah. It's been a damned good year for the company, which means a damned good year for all of us.

The best year so far. Though I haven't even looked at mine yet.

Reaching into my back pocket, I pull out the crumpled envelope I stuck there last night.

On a strangled gasp, Emma closes her eyes. "Oh my god, you left it in your *pocket*?"

"Yeah."

Where else should I put it? Hell, there's nowhere else to put it now, so after a peek at the amount, I shove it back in.

She moans a little. "A check like that in your back pocket. How many years have you been working there?"

"Ten, officially. But I've been getting bonuses since

Dad sold my first design."

She slits one eye open and peers at me through it. "So how long?"

"I'm on fourteen years."

Her eyes close again. "Holy shit."

Yeah, it's a nice little chunk of change. A sweet cherry on top of the design commissions I receive for the custom pieces and catalog sales.

Laughing with disbelief, she shakes her head. "Marianne said your dad puts in a percentage of profits and splits that between employees based on length of time. I figured it would be two to five percent. But this…" Her gaze goes distant for a long second, as if she's calculating in her head, then surprise widens her eyes. "He must give away half his profits."

"He does." I sink onto the floor beside her. "My mom helped him start up, way back when. She put up half the money. So he gives her fifty percent back to the employees—says he'd never be where he was without someone's generosity."

A smile curves her soft pink lips. "Neither would I."

Maybe a lot of us wouldn't be. I glance at her computer, frowning when I see the spreadsheet. "Now what's this? You didn't bring work home, did you?"

"No. It's my household budget."

I *knew* she'd have something like that. Grinning, I ask, "You track everything?"

"Everything. I even keep a food inventory." Sudden

excitement lights her eyes. "Let me take you to breakfast. I can take someone out to breakfast! So let me."

I love seeing her this happy. "All right," I tell her. "But that someone you take to breakfast better always be me."

Laughing, she leans forward to press a kiss to my lips, as if I've done her a favor by agreeing to be taken out. "And I can go get a battery today." Her expression dims a little. "Oh, except it's Christmas Eve. I guess an auto shop might not be able to fit me in."

"You can buy one," I tell her. "I'll put it in for you."

"But—"

"And you'll let me." I stop her before she can protest. "I'd do the same for Marianne or my dad, all right? It doesn't make any sense for you to pay a mechanic to install a battery when I'm right here with nothing better to do."

"All right." Her face brightens again. "But can we do it first thing after breakfast? We should also stop by the bank right away because they're probably closing early. Then I'll need to be alone the rest of the day."

Alone? I eye her suspiciously. "What are you planning?"

"I can't tell." She grins at me impishly and it's fucking adorable. "It's a secret."

"All right." I might do a few secret things myself— such as take another trip to the jewelry store.

I bought her a ring this week…but there's no need to rush this. I've been worrying that if I didn't grab onto her, she'd run away. So I charged in like a rutting bull moose, as if I've got one chance to claim a cow I've sniffed out.

But rushing isn't what Emma needs. As soon as I found out she was a virgin, I slowed everything way down. I should have done the same while building this relationship between us. Because I ended up taking better care of her pussy than I did with her heart, and I hurt her when I jumped to conclusions, started making assumptions.

And she's been living on the edge for so long, that now she's crying with happiness simply at the thought of having a few solid months ahead of her. Solid months that she earned on her own, not owed to anyone. She doesn't need someone charging in and throwing her off balance again. Better to be someone who is steady and solid at her side.

And she's here with me now. She knows my intentions and that doesn't scare her away. This thing with her, we can do bit by bit. We have the rest of our lives ahead of us.

So it's time to stop being a rutting bull moose and to start being a fucking *man*.

But that doesn't mean I won't be screwing her into oblivion as often as I can.

Gripping her hips, I lift her over onto my lap, facing me. "How you feeling? Sore?"

Her cheeks go pink. "Not *too* sore."

"So at least a little sore." Which means we wait for now. "And definitely not ready for a pounding."

Her lips plump out in a little pout. "Maybe not that."

"We'll hold off on that another day, then." Softly I kiss her before drawing back to ask, "Are you staying with me tonight? And going with me to my dad's tomorrow?"

"Yes and yes."

This time I kiss her long and slow, until she gently pulls away, but she doesn't go far. Instead she looks down at me with new tears in her eyes. But they aren't the tears of despair I remember—or the tears of joy from only minutes ago.

Instead her eyes are filled with hope.

EMMA

ON CHRISTMAS MORNING, I WAKE UP TO Logan's head between my legs again—but this time he's playing evil Santa, because he works me right up to the edge of an orgasm, then abruptly backs off the bed and pulls me to my feet.

Then I'm standing there with my pussy dripping and my body shaking with need as he drapes a red velvet robe around my shoulders. As soon as he's got the belt tied, he steps into a pair of flannel pajama pants, but he's not being any nicer to himself than he is to me. His huge erection pushes so hard against the front of the pajamas that the waistband is pulling away from the ridged muscles of his abdomen.

Grinning, he drops a kiss to my lips. "Time to open our presents."

I know exactly where my Christmas present is. I reach for his cock, but he laughs and grabs my hand, pulling me toward the loft's tree. Last night, there were only two presents beneath it—the one I brought for him, and another that he said was from his Secret Santa and that he hadn't opened yet. Now there are three more small boxes, one with my name scrawled across the gold wrapping paper in familiar black marker, and the other two marked with his name, written by the same hand.

I laugh. "Looks like you've been a good boy this year."

"Hell yeah, I have."

He kneels in front of the tree and pulls me down to the floor with him, and I can't recall ever having so much fun on Christmas morning. Even the needy ache of my body just heightens the overall anticipation as he places the box marked with my name on my lap. Then he reaches for the gift I brought, and his biceps flex as he drags the heavy box out from beneath the branches.

Feeling as if the entire world is bright and shiny, I meet his icy blue eyes. He looks just as eager to open his as I am to open mine. "So do we open carefully or rip it all off?"

His answer is to tear the wrapping paper around his box to shreds.

Laughing, I do the same to the pretty gold paper, then my heart stops when I reveal the gift underneath, the red box stamped with the jeweler's signature.

"Oh my god," I whisper and carefully open the box. A large diamond pendant is nestled upon a bed of black velvet. Glittering beneath the colorful lights of the Christmas tree, symmetrical rays of diamond chips set between six larger gems form a stunning snowflake dangling on a platinum chain.

I raise my stunned gaze to Logan's, who has stopped opening his gift to watch my reaction.

"No haggling," he says softly.

"I wasn't going to." My throat is thick. "Will you put it on me?"

His eyes darken as I turn slightly away, lifting my hair from the back of my neck and watching him over my shoulder. His hands are so big, scarred and callused after years of building, yet his fingers so sensitive. He deftly opens a clasp that I would have fumbled over forever.

He moves closer behind me, until I can feel the heat of his body. As the pendant settles into the hollow of my throat, I whisper huskily, "Thank you."

His response is a warm kiss against my nape. My eyes are burning when I turn back, my throat a solid lump.

"All right?" he asks gruffly.

When I nod, he bends his head and kisses me softly before drawing back.

"Now I'm going to see what's in that box. Because it's

so damn heavy, I'm guessing you filled it with coal."

I laugh, shaking my head, my hand going to the unfamiliar weight of the pendant lying against my throat. My heart seems to clench tighter as he rips away the final strip of packing tape holding the box closed.

A grin widens his mouth when he looks in at the assortment of books inside. "So I get to judge you now?"

"Yes." A nervous giggle shakes through me. "It's twenty of my favorites—well, twenty of my top fifty, maybe, because you own a lot of my favorites already. So I didn't buy any repeats."

"Are there any of those dirty ones in here?"

My cheeks heat. "Quite a few."

"Hell yeah. I'm going to read those first." Then his voice deepens when he glances at me. "You're already filling up the shelves in your library, baby."

My heart gives a heavy thump. "And you look really angry now."

His icy gaze hardens. "By now you know what this face means."

"Yeah, I do." And my pussy's aching again, my skin tight with anticipation.

On a low growl he says, "Then you open those other two gifts, baby. And I'll give your sweet pussy the hard fucking it's been waiting for."

Breathing slow and heavy, I look to the remaining gifts. There are three left: his present from his Secret Santa and the two others marked with his name.

Reaching under the tree, he tosses the gold-wrapped gifts to me. "They're for me, baby. But you might as well open them, since you'll be the one wearing them."

Clutching them in my lap, I say breathlessly, "Your Secret Santa gift first."

Because I've got a feeling that as soon as we open these, we won't be getting to that one for a while.

Logan seems to agree. Almost impatiently he tears the wrapping from the gift, then abruptly freezes, staring at what he just revealed. The strangled noise he makes almost makes my heart stop, then I realize— It's a laugh. He's choking on a laugh. Because he's laughing so deep and so hard that he's not even making a sound, but his eyes are watering, and his head's bowed as his shoulders shake uncontrollably.

And I can't even figure out what the gift is. There's no packaging—just a short black corrugated tube with smooth cylinders attached to each end. It looks to me like some weird alien sex toy…which might account for his reaction.

"What is it?"

Dragging in a deep breath, he regains some control. He wipes his eyes, then takes another deep breath before he tells me in a strained voice, "It's a bull moose call."

I frown. And that's from his Secret Santa? "What's it used for?"

Another shudder of laughter shakes through him. "When you blow it, you sound like a bull moose. It's usually used for hunting."

Oh. "So you hunt moose?"

"No." Grinning, he puts the moose call aside and his gaze drops to the gifts on my lap. "Now your turn. The square one, first."

There's a square, and a rectangle. Setting aside the second, I carefully begin to pick at the tape, gently peeling back the folds of wrapping paper at the end.

Logan growls. "Rip it open."

He's not the only evil Santa. Deliberately teasing, I gingerly begin to pick at the tape closing the opposite end.

Abruptly he reaches for me, strong fingers catching my chin. Expression hard, eyes glittering, he says in a soft voice, "As soon as those are open and you're wearing them, I'm going to put you on your knees and get my thick cock into you as deep and as hard as I can."

Oh god. I rip the package open, my hands shaking with the force of the need raging through me.

A pair of silk stockings in red and white stripes. They're longer than my knee-high socks, with a lacy band around the top.

"Now put those on." Logan watches me, his big hand stroking the bulge of his cock through his flannel pants. "Let me see those stripes go all the way up those long, sexy legs."

Not all the way up. Just to mid-thigh, where the elasticized lace holds them in place. They're soft and feel deliciously luxurious against my skin, so despite my desperate need I take my time, pointing my toes and rolling each one slowly over my knee and up the length of my thigh.

Logan's teeth are gritted, a muscle flexing in his jaw by the time I've finished. "Now the other gift."

I don't hesitate before opening this one: a sleep mask, made of the softest velvet in a deep, cherry red.

A red velvet that matches the robe I'm wearing. He'd given me another gift without my even realizing it.

My breath shuddering through parted lips, I slip the mask over my head. The last thing I see is Logan, watching me with ravenous hunger burning in his icy gaze, his big hand stroking the thick length of his cock.

"Stand up now, baby."

His soft growl is already closer. Muscles trembling, I rise to my feet. Immediately there's a tug at my waist—Logan loosening the belt of my robe. The heavy material gapes open at the front and prickles of excitement race over my skin. Then callused palms glide over my shoulders, pushing at the sleeves, and with a whisper of crumpling velvet the robe falls to the floor.

Leaving me clad only in my stockings, the diamond pendant, and my mask. I stand shivering, knowing Logan's looking at me wearing nothing but the gifts he just gave to me.

"You're so fucking beautiful, Emma." His harsh voice comes from directly in front of me. "I could just look at you forever. But you want more than that, don't you?"

So much more. "Yes," I whisper.

"I'll give it to you, baby."

Without warning, strong arms sweep me up against a broad chest. I gasp, then his mouth finds mine as he carries me—to the bed, where he gently sets me down, my head supported by a soft pillow.

But his hands on my hips aren't gentle. They're firm and unyielding as he rolls me over onto my stomach.

"Up on your knees, Emma," comes his rough command. "Elbows on the bed, legs spread."

With my bottom high in the air and my sex exposed to his gaze. Face flaming behind the mask, I get my knees under me, my pussy feeling swollen and wet and so needy.

Because I'm already ready, I realize. Because he worked me up so far, then left me hanging, stewing in my need as we opened the gifts.

Evil Santa. Planning this all along.

And that's so damn hot.

The rip of a condom wrapper is followed by the dip of the mattress beneath his weight. I bite my lip as long fingers slick through the folds of my pussy.

A rough groan sounds behind me. "So hot and wet. You going to take everything I have to give, baby?"

"Yes," I reply, then begin shaking in anticipation as the blunt head of his cock lodges firmly at my entrance.

"Push back, Emma." His voice is hoarse with need.

"If you want what I have to give you, then you need to take it first."

Oh god. Rising up on my hands, I press back, seeking that incredible sensation of being filled. But there's only pressure, so much pressure.

"I'm big, baby." Each word sounds tortured. "You've got to push harder."

To take the thick head of his cock. I can picture that flared crown, remember the feel and taste of it beneath my tongue. And now the stretch of my delicate flesh around it as I push back harder. Suddenly he breaches my entrance, that broad head lodged just inside me, the ecstasy of taking him overwhelming every other feeling.

With a soft cry, I collapse onto my elbows again as hard hands grip my hips.

"Ah, Emma." Raw and deep, his voice is pure gravel, pure emotion. "Look at the way you give yourself to me. I'm so crazy fucking in love with you."

And even as that pleasure washes through me, with one slick thrust, he buries his cock deep. So deep I can barely breathe, then he fucks hard into me again and I scream against my pillow, my hands fisting as I'm bombarded with sensations, my breasts jolting with every sharp thrust, my nipples on fire, my pussy full, so full, the slap of our skin so wet and the rhythm so fast.

Cock pounding into me, Logan's fingers tangle in my hair and he pulls me back harder, fucks deeper. "You like this, baby?"

"Yes." It's a breathless, sobbing cry. "It's so good."

His groaning laugh is followed by, "*Too* good, baby. I'm not going to last. So we need to make you feel even better."

Releasing my hair, his hand slips between my legs. The stroke of his fingers across my over-sensitized clit is like an electric shock, searing every nerve inside me, the sharp pleasure of his thrusting cock suddenly too much, too much, but he's fucking me deep and hard and fast, my pussy clenching around him, his fingers delivering another slick jolt to my clit and then I'm coming, screaming as my inner muscles clamp down on his thick shaft, clutching him tight even as he shoves hard into me a final time. He abruptly stills, and the heavy pulse of his erection deep inside me makes me shudder in ecstasy again.

I collapse forward and Logan comes with me, his weight heavy but I love it, love the sweaty press of his hair-roughened chest against my back, the fullness of his softening cock still inside me.

Then he mutters, "The fucking condom," and I moan when he gently withdraws. He disappears into the bathroom and returns a moment later, sliding into bed and pulling me against his side.

Utterly wrung out, I manage to mumble, "This is the best Christmas ever."

His huff of laughter sounds like wry agreement, but a moment later he says, "I bet next year is even better."

I won't bet against that. I rise up on my elbow, looking down at him, and my heart is so full and happy that I don't know what else this could be. "Are you ready to catch me?"

Abruptly he sits up, framing my face in his hands. "Are you falling?"

Overwhelmed by the emotion, tears burn my eyes. "So hard."

"I'm right here, baby." His voice is hoarse, his icy gaze searching mine. "I always will be."

I can see that, too. So clearly. *Always.*

So I give him everything I can.

"I love you, Logan Crenshaw." My heart in my throat, I wreath my arms around his shoulders, holding him close. "I am so crazy fucking in love with you."

And his beautiful grin in response, his fierce kiss— they're the sweetest gifts I could ever imagine.

LOGAN

ONE YEAR LATER

I FIND EMMA IN THE LIBRARY, STRETCHED OUT ON her belly on the chaise longue in front of the fireplace. A short stack of books is sitting on the floor next to the chaise—the books she received at my dad's house today.

There are plenty more books scattered around the room, waiting to be shelved. She finally gave up her apartment and moved into my house three months ago, and the last time I saw her spreadsheet, the rent line was empty and a book budget had taken its place. So she's filling those shelves with books faster than she can read them.

And it's easy to see what happened here. She was just putting the books away, she said. But she probably opened one and got caught up, losing track of time— and if she's truly engrossed, she becomes completely oblivious to anything happening around her.

It's just another thing I've discovered about her in the past year. Just another thing that I love about her.

I knew Emma Williams was right for me the second I met her. But I had no idea how much I'd love her when I finally got to know her.

I didn't know I'd ever love anyone this much.

And she's so deep in her book, she doesn't realize I'm there until my fingers are sliding up the backs of her long, long legs. She's wearing a swingy little skirt again, different from the one she was wearing last year when I met her, but just as capable of driving me out of my fucking mind.

"Shhhhh," I tell her when she tries to roll onto her side. "Keep reading. And stay quiet."

"Why?" she whispers.

"Because you don't want Logan walking in and seeing Santa pushing this skirt up over your ass."

A little giggle shakes through her. "You're my Secret Santa?"

"Yes."

"Are you going to give me something, Santa?"

My voice deepens to a growl. "I'm going to take something, baby. But don't make any sound. Because

ALL HE WANTS FOR CHRISTMAS

Kati Wilde

ALL HE WANTS FOR CHRISTMAS

Detective Cole Matthews has worked toward one goal: being damn good at his job. But after taking a bullet in the line of duty almost destroys everything he's worked for, he's not in the mood to play nice or to look after some pampered rich girl at her daddy's request. There's only one woman he wants by his side…the sweet angel who saved his life.

But this Christmas, heaven might be a little closer than one grumpy detective could ever believe…

KATI WILDE

ALL HE WANTS FOR CHRISTMAS

SECRET SANTA &
ALL HE WANTS FOR CHRISTMAS

Also by Kati Wilde

The Hellfire Riders MC Romance
(Discreet Cover Editions)
Saxon
Blowback
Gunner
Bull & Duke
Stone
(Original Covers & Ebooks)
The Hellfire Riders: Saxon & Jenny
The Hellfire Riders: Jack & Lily
Breaking It All
Giving It All
Craving It All
Faking It All
Losing It All

Contemporary Holiday Romances
(Discreet Cover Editions)
Secret Santa & All He Wants For Christmas
The Wedding Night Before Christmas
(Original Covers & Ebooks)
Secret Santa
All He Wants For Christmas
The Wedding Night

The Dead Lands
(Discreet Cover Editions)

THE MIDWINTER BRIDE

(MORE DISCREET COVERS COMING SOON)

(Original Covers & Ebooks)

THE MIDWINTER MAIL-ORDER BRIDE

THE MIDNIGHT BRIDE

PRETTY BRIDE

THE MIDSUMMER BRIDE

(COMING SOON)

Wolfkin & Berserkers

BEAUTY IN SPRING

HIGH MOON

TEACHER'S PET WOLF

SHERIFF'S BAD BEAR

(COMING SOON)

Contemporary Romance

GOING NOWHERE FAST[1]

THE KING'S HORRIBLE BRIDE

Fantasy Romance

EVIL TWIN[2]

---

[1] Includes cameos by the Hellfire Riders

[2] Set in the same world as the Dead Lands

ALL HE WANTS FOR
CHRISTMAS

COLE

WALKING INTO THE STATION'S KITCHEN A step ahead of me, my partner cocks his head. "Do you hear this shit?"

I hear a whole bunch of shit. His voice, first of all. Then there's the jingle of keys hanging from Lieutenant McCarey's belt and the clink of his spoon as he stirs his coffee. Somewhere behind me is faint ring of a phone from one of the desks in the patrol room.

Loudest of all is the grinding of my teeth. My thigh's screaming like every single stitch tore open on the short walk up the stairs from the locker room. But there's no blood seeping through my black pants, so the stitches didn't actually rip. It just feels like they did.

"They're piping in 'Jingle Bells,'" Huertas continues as I suck up the pain and try not to hobble my way to the water cooler. "We've still got clowns in holding who are sleeping off their Halloween benders—literal frickin' clowns—and they've got Christmas music playing?"

Frickin' isn't what he usually says, but the lieutenant's here so he's dialing back the *fuck*s. Except McCarey's not paying any more attention to Huertas's bellyaching than I am. He's focused on me, instead.

"Most guys who catch a couple of bullets take it easy for a while," he says. "You sure you want to be coming in already?"

Thanks to the bastard who intended to shoot up the county building, I already sat on my ass at home for two fucking weeks. Just last Friday, a grand jury ruled that I was justified firing my weapon, but I've still got a psych exam and physical exam to pass before I'm cleared for full duty. So it'll be another few months before I'm allowed to do more than sit on my ass at the station, but at least I'll be working. "Desk duty *is* taking it easy."

He eyes my hair, still wet from my shower. "And what do you call hitting the weight room an hour before shift?"

"I call it the bare minimum, sir." I've worked too damn hard getting to this point to sleep in now. The lieutenant knows that eventually I'll be gunning for his job, but he's not too worried. I only earned my detective's shield two years back, so by the time I've made lieutenant, he'll

have his captain's bars or be sitting in the deputy chief's chair.

And I don't expect to get that far. I don't care if I get that far, either. I piss people off too easy and as soon as you rise past lieutenant, it's all politics. Better to let the higher-ups play nice. I'm happy down in the trenches.

"Just upper body, LT," Huertas tosses in. "I've got my eyes on him. No leg work until it's cleared by the doc. And you know Cole never uses his head, anyway, so no worries about his recovery there."

The lieutenant's gaze flicks to the scabbed-over furrow above my ear, where one of Lowery's bullets gave me a closer shave than dictated by police regulation. "Just don't hesitate to take more time if you're not feeling up to it yet. Even desk duty can hit you harder than you expect, and you're more likely to set yourself back if you push too hard too fast."

Desk duty is already a setback. But I just nod and say, "If I start feeling like I can't hack it, I'll put in for more leave."

McCarey's bullshit detector isn't broken, so he doesn't believe a word of that, but we've both said what we needed to say. Except apparently he's got one more thing to tell me. "Chief's expecting you in his office at start of shift."

Shit. Nothing good ever comes from a visit to the chief of police's office. He's a damn fine cop with a long history in this department, but a big part of his job is

making sure relations between the public, the DA's office, and the police run nice and smooth. So being called in usually means there's a bump in the road—and nobody wants to be the one who gets steamrolled.

"Probably going to pin a big gold medal on your chest," is Huertas's smirking conclusion as I head out, teeth gritted at every step.

It won't be a medal. Eventually, I'll probably end up getting a commendation for taking Lowery down before he got off more than a short burst of gunfire, but I already received a handshake from both the mayor and Chief Jackson while I was still in the hospital. More likely Lowery's lawyer is yanking someone's chain or trying to discredit me before we even make it to trial, and I'm going to end up on administrative leave again.

Except as soon as I enter the chief's big corner office, I realize I've gotten it wrong. Because Chief Jackson isn't even at his desk; instead he's parked over on the east side of the room, where a short leather couch and two club chairs are set up around a coffee table.

No need to introduce the man sitting with him. Caucasian, dark blue eyes, and graying black hair that frames distinguished features. Six-two and a solid two hundred pounds. A suit that likely costs a month's salary—of *my* salary. John Bennet is a big name in this small city, descending from one of the founding families or some crap like that. Guys like him are why I'll never play politics. He's currently sitting on one of the asses

the mayor has to kiss every once in a while, especially come fundraising time. To his credit, Bennet puts his money where his mouth is—but word from City Hall is that he likes to throw his weight around along with his money.

I don't have to deal with that shit. Usually. Looks like I am now.

"Detective Matthews." Stars gleaming on the shoulders of his uniform, Jackson stands to perform the introduction. Bennet rises more slowly, cold blue eyes measuring me as he goes. "You know John Bennet?"

"Only by sight." Because I *can* play nice, I stick out my hand. "Pleasure."

"After what you did for the city, I'd say the pleasure's mine, detective." His grip is dry and firm and his voice contains the echo of the hallowed halls of some Ivy League school. He's sure as hell not used to being shorter than anyone else in the room, though—and doesn't like it much, either. He puffs out his chest a bit and rocks up onto the balls of his feet. Probably he's thinking about taking out his dick to measure against mine.

Better he doesn't. He'd lose that contest, too. And I've got nothing to prove. All his posturing is just funny. Soon enough, though, it'll be irritating.

Seriously, who has time for this shit?

"You're looking well," Bennet adds, his blue eyes skimming over me, lingering on the stripe alongside my head before roaming down to my leg, as if trying to see

where the bullet ripped through the muscle in my upper thigh. I'm standing steady as a rock, giving him nothing. "I hear you've been cleared for light duty?"

"That's right. This shift will be the first one I've worked since the incident." I glance at the chief. "Nothing better than being on the job, sir."

Jackson's no fool. He knows I'm more worried about administrative leave than whatever the hell Bennet's here for. "We'll get you back out there as soon as we can, detective."

Bennet heads to the leather couch again. The chief sinks into one of the club chairs. It's awkward as hell standing now, but I only plan on sitting once today—into the rolling chair in front of my desk—and staying there once I'm down. The stitches in my leg won't allow for much else.

"A big fellow like you, I imagine a desk's not your style?" Bennet asks.

I shrug. "There are always calls to make and reports to file. So I get plenty of time at a desk even when I'm on full duty."

Doing that part of the job is just that—part of the job. I don't mind it. What chafes is not being able to do anything else.

"I'll testify to that." The chief sits back. "I spent most of my time as a detective spinning the dial on my phone, that's for damn sure. It's easier to track people down these days, what with everyone carrying their

smartphones. The paperwork, though…" He laughs. "Hell, I'm still trying to catch up on that."

"Yes, sir," I say, and leave it there. I was called in for a reason. I'm hoping someone gets around to that reason before too damn long.

The chief does. Probably because he's not one to waste time on small talk, either. "Luckily, detective, Bennet here has a request that might liven up your routine. You know his daughter is an assistant to the county medical examiner?"

It'd be hard not to know. The ME's office is in the county building that shares a courtyard with this station, and just about every dead body in the city moves through that morgue. And I'd heard that Bennet's little princess had gotten a job there, though I haven't met her myself. I don't give a fuck about some spoiled rich girl whose daddy pulled enough strings to get her a job filing papers or making coffee or whatever. I don't know what she does over there. But I know a lot of the guys around here suddenly found any reason to head over to the county building to pick up autopsy reports instead of waiting for them to land in their inboxes.

Bennet offers a smile. "It's more of a favor to ask than a request, Detective Matthews. Given your recent injuries, however, I will understand if you deem it too strenuous."

Does he think that'll prod me into accepting whatever he's angling for? My ego isn't so delicate that I'll

agree to something without first finding out what the hell it is I'm agreeing to. "I suppose my doctor will have to make that decision, then."

That smile tightens. "Not *physically* strenuous. It might lengthen the hours in your day, though. You see, Mia is somewhat…headstrong. And she's entering into a rather independent phase."

He pauses as if to give me a chance to respond. But I've got nothing to say. If she's rebelling that might explain the morgue. Maybe she's going through a goth period, like so many teenagers do. But I still don't see what the hell this has to do with me.

The chief says, "She's moving into your apartment building, detective."

"Yeah?" That surprises me. I still don't give a flying fuck, but it surprises me. By my standards, I live in a real nice place. Rent's on the upper end of what I can afford, but I don't have any family or a girlfriend or many expenses except a beer with Huertas or a pizza now and then. But by Bennet standards, it's a dump. "Not exactly the kind of place you'd expect her to live?"

Bennet seems grateful that I was the one to say it and saved him the trouble of explaining to the guy who lives in a shithole that his place *is* a shithole. Hard to ask for a favor when you're insulting someone. "Not exactly," he agrees. "My wife and I would prefer her to remain at home, of course, but Mia seems determined to move out, and the harder we argue against it the more stubborn

she's becoming. So"—he spreads his hands, a ruby glinting on his pinky ring—"I was hoping you might agree to keep an eye on her. Not actively *watching* her...but just to make certain she stays out of trouble."

He's got to be fucking kidding. I look to the chief. He's regarding me impassively, but I already know how he wants me to answer. He knew what Bennet would ask and he still called me in.

I return my gaze to Bennet and have to unclench my jaw before answering. "Just keeping an eye out?"

He nods. "And letting me know if there's anything I should be concerned about. If she's getting visitors, people hanging around her who shouldn't be. It's well known that she's my only heir. But even without the Bennet name, a girl with a trust fund the size of Mia's always draws the wrong kind of attention from conmen looking for an easy payday."

So he doesn't want his little girl getting fucked by the wrong men. That's pretty goddamn creepy. So is a cop watching a girl and reporting to her daddy.

This fucker doesn't seem to care, though. "You sure *my* attention's not the wrong type?"

He laughs and gestures to the chief. "I already spoke with Mike here about your character. He assures me you aren't a ladies' man."

That's true. I'm too much of an asshole. Any woman smart enough to be interesting is also smart enough to run away after about an hour in my company. I'm not

likely to be attracted to some rebellious teenager, anyway. And no woman's pussy is worth the kind of trouble that banging Bennet's daughter could bring down on me.

Maybe one woman would be worth it. Except I don't even know if I dreamed her. When you're bleeding out on the steps of the county courthouse, it's hard to trust a vision of an angel hovering above you, gazing down with pale blue eyes and telling you in a throaty voice to *hold on, detective, just hold on*, and *we have to get some pressure on his leg!*

But to Bennet, I only say, "I'm focused on the job right now. Not women."

That seems to satisfy whatever is going on in that slick head. Rising to his feet, he holds out his hand again. Sealing the deal. "I appreciate you doing this favor for me, detective. And if I can ever do anything for you in return…"

He leaves that open. But I don't ever intend to fill it. Going to a guy like Bennet expecting him to return a favor just puts you in debt to him.

So I shake his hand and say, "Seeing to your daughter's safety is all part of the job."

Bennet smiles at that, then looks to the chief. "Say hello to Brenda for me, Mike."

"I'll do that," Chief Jackson says. "Give my best to Patricia."

With a perfunctory nod, Bennet leaves. And I don't say a word, not a fucking word, because I'm an asshole

but one thing I'll never do is mouth off to the chief of police.

He sighs and heads to his desk. "If you're wondering whether you're under orders to keep an eye on Mia Bennet, that answer is no."

Thank fuck. "We just let Bennet think it?"

"Works for me." Jackson drops into his chair, eyes me critically. "You have any issue playing that game, detective?"

"No, sir."

"Good. Truth is, I've known Mia almost her entire life—and she's not going through a phase. This is how she's always been. She's just getting better at pushing back."

"Against him?" His little girl must have some steel in her, then.

"And against her mother, which is really saying something." He shakes his head. "Mia's a good girl. Smart, too. Any trouble she gets into, she's more than capable of getting herself out. Have you met her yet?"

"Don't think so. Unless it was in passing, and I didn't notice."

That seems to amuse him. "You'd notice her. Mia is… memorable."

"I'll take your word for it, sir." There's only one woman who's ever stuck in my head longer than a few days. I don't know who she is—or even if she's real. But as soon as I'm at a hundred percent again, nothing will stop me

from finding her.

But nothing I've ever wanted has simply dropped into my lap. I've had to fight for it all, had to earn everything I have. So if I want her, whoever she is?

That means it's time to get back to work.

COLE

Just fifteen more yards. Fifteen fucking yards. Five to my apartment building. Five to the elevator. Five to my apartment door.

It feels like fifteen miles, but even that's not right. Before Lowery's bullet ripped through my leg, fifteen miles would have been nothing but time. My head wouldn't have been swimming and my thigh feeling as if a dull, serrated blade was sawing through my bone with every step.

And I left my crutches at my place this morning. So damn stupid. But I was getting around all right. Sure, walking hurt like a son of a bitch, but I could deal with that pain. Now I'll be lucky to make it home without

bawling like a baby.

Thank fuck I threw out all the powerful meds the docs prescribed for me. Today I might be tempted to use them. I haven't been popping anything stronger than ibuprofen because I'm too familiar with the shit that happens after someone starts relying on opioids. All the calls that come in, from murders and sex crimes to theft, a good percentage of them trace back to some addiction or another. And no one's immune. Not housewives or doctors or teachers—or cops. They get into it trying to ease the pain, then can't get out. So I won't risk getting into it. Even if it leaves me flat on my face.

I punch in my code at the door and nearly black out swinging it open. Despite the bullet that grazed off my skull, my head doesn't give me much trouble. Just aches now and then. So this dizziness is more likely related to the way my heart's pounding and my skin's drenched in sweat. Because my body doesn't know what to do with the pain.

And because I'm pushing too hard. Just like the lieutenant warned me about. But I've *always* pushed too hard. I've worked for one damn thing my entire life. I'm not letting a piece of shit like Lowery steal it away.

A vision of pale blue eyes flashes through my memory. Everything inside me wants to push for that, too. To find her. To get a taste of her. Just a little taste of her heaven. But right now, I'm in hell—and that's no place for an angel.

❄ 22 ❄

I don't know if I'll ever be back at one hundred percent. Shit, a woman like that, even my one hundred percent isn't good enough. So I'll get back to where I need to be, back to where I'm worth something again, before I even try.

And I've always pushed hard for the job—but for the first time in my life, I want more than that. I want to be able to stand in front of her. Carry her to a bed. Kiss her from velvet softness of her lips to the sweetness between her thighs, making her come over and over again. She deserves a man who can give her that.

Not a man who can barely walk through a door without fainting.

Gritting my teeth, I start across the lobby. Like the rest of the building, it's nothing fancy. Just an open space with a waiting area on the left, a bank of mailboxes on the right, and a hallway leading to the stairs. Today I don't bother with the mail. When I moved into this place, it was the building's proximity to the station that made it worth the high rent. Right now, though, every penny I've paid is worth it for the elevator.

Almost there. Thank fuck.

My chest's heaving like I sprinted a marathon when I enter the hallway. The relief of *almost there* vanishes in an instant. A huge leather couch is shoved halfway into the elevator. Trying to wrestle it in from this end is a blond white male, six-one and with 'fucking frat boy' written all over him. Almost literally, given the Greek

letters that arc across the front of his university hoodie.

"No, you've got to lift up that end. Shit, you're going to—" Wincing, he breaks off as a heavy thunk sounds. Laughter mixes with concern as he says, "Is your hand okay?"

I don't hear anything from inside the elevator, but the response is clear when frat boy begins laughing harder. "At least your middle finger's not broken."

For fuck's sake. I raise my voice over the goddamn gigglefest. "Will this take much longer?"

Frat boy's head whips around. "Oh shit. Sorry, man. Uh…" His gaze zips from the couch to the inside of the elevator before zooming back to me. "The way this is going, the stairs might be the best option."

"The stairs *aren't* a fucking option. So maybe just back that shit out of there so I can—"

The head that pokes past the elevator doors stops me cold. My angel. Who's looking just as shocked to see *me*.

And who's looking just as beautiful as before. Even more so. That hazy vision on the courthouse steps was dominated by her pale blue eyes, filled with the husky warmth of her voice. I knew she had dark hair, but it's thick and black and sleeked back into a ponytail in a way that leaves her stunning features exposed and vulnerable to my starving gaze. Like a desperate man I fill myself up on the sight of her. I remember red velvet lips, but she must have been wearing lipstick that day, because now they're pink and full and parted softly as she stares

at me in wordless surprise and with widened eyes.

Those eyes have haunted my dreams. But not just while I'm sleeping. Every damn waking moment.

Without thinking, I step closer to her—and my knee almost gives out. Pain rips up my leg. *Fuck.* I almost shout the curse, but instead grind my teeth and brace my hand against the wall to stop myself from face-planting right in front of her.

I hear her soft exclamation as she scrambles over the couch. But it's all a dim roar in my head, because a few realizations are hitting me hard and fast.

Bennet talked about his daughter like she was a rebellious teenager going through a phase. Instead she's twenty-five, give or take a year or two. Long past the age when any father should be asking a cop to report back on who's visiting her apartment.

And she's taken. By a fucker who already has his shit together, is probably already at a hundred percent. You're a cop long enough, you can size up people pretty damn fast. Frat boy is from decent money, went to a good college—not some asshole who had to claw his way up out of the gutter just to look at her. His fraternity sweatshirt has some years on it, too, which means he's probably already out of school and working, a lawyer or stockbroker or some white collar shit that pulls in a ton of cash and can give Mia Bennet the life she's used to. The kind she deserves.

I shouldn't be so twisted up by the knowledge that

my angel already has a man. I should have known. A woman like her, of course someone snatched her up.

"Detective Matthews." Her voice is warm and with a rusty edge, just like I remember it. She's so damn close, looking up at me with concern furrowing her brow. She's five-nine or so, taller than I thought she would be, but just as curvy as I dreamed in her dark leggings and thin zip-up hoodie. Her hand hovers just inches from my chest, as if she's thinking she might need to hold me up but is worried that touching me will hurt me worse. "Are you all right?"

"No." The hoarse answer is too fucking honest. "But I will be. Give me a minute."

It'll take longer than a minute before I'm all right. Maybe a lifetime.

But a minute is all my leg needs.

"Okay." Watching me closely, as if not really believing that a minute is all it'll take and she expects me to keel over any second, Mia Bennet crosses her arms beneath her breasts and waits.

Her gaze continually roams my face, settling on my mouth for an instant like the lightest kiss. And despite the agony ripping up my leg, my dick decides to get in on the action. That's when I learn that when your upper thigh is stitched up, a hard cock is just another thing that adds to the pain, like it's yanking on muscles and nerves that shouldn't be yanked. My breath hisses from between my clenched teeth.

Mia frowns. "Detective Matthews—"

"I'm all right." It's a harsh rasp. "Just another second."

"Okay." She tilts her head, that long ponytail swinging against the back of her shoulder. "So you live here?"

More like I'm dying here. "I would if I could get to my place."

A shadow crosses her face. "Sorry. We'll get out of your way—"

"Hold on," the frat boy interrupts. "Did you say 'Matthews'? This is the guy who stopped that fucker from shooting up the building where you work?"

"Yes," she says softly, her eyes still locked on mine.

"Oh, man." He comes at me with hand extended. "Jason Lewis. And thank you. Mia's the best thing in my life, so you saved mine, too."

Now I'm wishing him dead. Ignoring his hand, I answer flatly, "Sure."

My resentment bounces right off him. Grinning, he says, "You've got to let me take you for a drink sometime—"

I stop him with a hostile stare. "I'll settle for you getting that elevator clear."

"Oh shit. Yeah." Still in good cheer, he grabs hold of the sofa arm and begins hauling it back out into the hallway.

Mia's still right in front of me, close enough to touch, her gaze running all over my face. But the light in her eyes is darker now, worry pleating her brows. "So you

are healing up?"

"I am. Thanks to you, if I'm remembering right."

A hint of pink touches her cheeks. "I didn't do much. The EMTs were there right after me, so…" She trails off with a shrug. "I heard the grand jury cleared you for the OIS?"

For firing my gun, shooting Lowery. "I was back on duty today."

Her face brightens with a smile and my heart just seizes in my chest. Christ. *Christ.* Simply seeing her is heaven. Seeing her happy? I'd give anything to see it again. Give anything to be the one who always puts that smile on her beautiful face. I've never wanted anyone so fucking bad. And she'll be so close, every day. But someone else will be holding her. Kissing her.

This is pure hell. "You're moving in for a while, then?" At her nod, I add, "I hear your daddy isn't too happy about that."

A surprised laugh bursts from her, followed by a disbelieving shake of her head. "Did he go to Chief Jackson? Probably after my boss told him she wouldn't try to convince me to change my mind."

"Maybe you should. You don't really belong in a place like this."

Her expression freezes. A shadow darkens her eyes as she stares at me for an endless moment. Then she glances over her shoulder and steps back. "Looks like Jason's got the elevator clear. I'm glad you're feeling

better, detective."

I'm not feeling better. I've never felt like so much shit, not even in the seconds after the bullet tore up my leg. I'm aware of her gaze following every limping step I take past her.

Then another realization hits me. The apartment across from mine has been standing empty for a month. Holding the elevator door open, I ask gruffly, "What number you in?"

Her face brightens again, as if she's happy I bothered to ask. "Three-oh-six."

Fuck. I let go of the elevator door, letting it slide closed.

Not just in the same building. Right across the hall. And not just knowing someone is holding her, fucking her. Maybe hearing it. Maybe seeing him kiss her goodbye in the morning and disappearing through that door together at night.

Suddenly the most painful thing I'm feeling isn't my leg, or even my goddamn dick. It's centered right in my chest, instead.

MIA

"Hate to break it to you, sis," Jason tells me. "But it looks like your hero is an asshole."

"Yeah." Clearly the detective wasn't thrilled when I gave him my apartment number. When the elevator's indicator stops on three, the reason why is obvious, too. Cole Matthews doesn't think I belong here. And I'm not only in the same building, but apparently on the same floor. "But some people are jerks when they're hurting. And he was just shot two weeks ago."

Jason jabs the down arrow, calling for the elevator again. "And some people are jerks when they *aren't* hurting. Guess which one he probably is?"

I know what he is. Cole Matthews *is* an asshole. But

word is, he's a gruff and blunt asshole, not a mean and vicious one. That distinction makes all the difference in the world to me.

Not that I ever talked to him before the day Lowery showed up at the courthouse with a semi-automatic rifle. But I knew who Cole Matthews was. He's hard to miss. Not only is Cole tall as hell, he's built like Superman. And if that weren't enough, he's… Well, he's not *handsome*, really. Not like Jason is, or my father is. Instead his features are overly bold, with dark slashing brows and a brooding stare over a strong nose, and absolutely magnetic—as if forged from iron that pulls your attention in his direction the moment you enter his sphere of influence.

So, yeah. I noticed him.

I don't think he ever noticed me. I can't recall our eyes ever meeting before that awful day. Working in Joan Childers's office puts me in contact with a lot of law enforcement, though, and the city and county administrative community downtown is small. So I hear my share of gossip, and some of it involves Detective Matthews. Nothing disturbing. No harassment or groping. Usually it's a lab assistant griping about him badgering them for quick results on tests, or some abrupt remark he made to the forensic technicians at a crime scene. Both Dr. Childers and Chief Jackson like the detective, though—and I can think of few people whose opinions I respect more than theirs. Hell, neither of them like my

parents much, so I'd say they're pretty good judges of character.

"He did look in bad shape," Jason concedes as the empty elevator dings open.

He had. Pale beneath his tan, face gleaming with sweat. But better than the last time I saw him. Blood was streaming down the side of his head and pooling on the concrete steps, and I was desperately trying to stop the bleeding in his thigh. He got lucky. Both of Lowery's bullets could have been fatal so easily. Just a few millimeters and it would have penetrated his skull instead of grazing off of it. Just a few millimeters and lead could have shattered his femur or ripped open his femoral artery.

I was lucky that day, too. Just a few seconds, and another of Lowery's bullets would have hit me.

It's strange how life can seem to change so slowly... then all at once, change in a flash. Strange how choices that seemed so difficult are suddenly so easy and obvious. For years I've been pushing back against what my parents want me to be. Then in one pull of a trigger, I simply don't care what they want. I'm done pushing back, because what they want is not even a factor in my life anymore.

Not that they'll make it easy. They never make anything easy.

"So this time," Jason says, "I'm going to get in there and lift that end up while you push this end in. All right?"

"Yep." We can be smarter than my furniture. Though maybe next time I'll just pay for movers to bring it in. When I bought the sofa, I thought, *Oooh, this is what it's like to be independent! I'll haul my new couch into my own home!*

First living-by-myself lesson learned: Hire professionals to carry the heavy stuff.

Jason clambers over the sofa and tosses back, "So did you find out if he has a girlfriend?"

My cheeks catch fire. Because I don't need to find out—I already know he doesn't.

I don't respond but my red face must give me away. Jason starts laughing so hard he can't heft his end of the sofa.

"Maybe you can bake him some cupcakes or something."

This time I flip him off, because he knows I've never baked anything. Unless you count helping a friend slice up cookie dough when I was over at her house. My mother never allowed me to go anywhere near our own kitchen, claiming that my presence there would only create more work for the staff—first when they felt obligated to help me, then when they had to clean up my mess. Besides, a Bennet simply didn't belong in the kitchen. A Bennet belongs on a seat in a boardroom or at the head of our charity foundation.

But now that I'm living by myself, I *should* be able to bake. And making cupcakes actually sounds kind of fun.

Not that I'll be making them for Cole Matthews. I can't deny that the thought of him eventually getting a girlfriend or a wife twists up something hot and painful inside of me. And I can't deny that I think he's gorgeous, and that everything I've learned about him tells me he's a dedicated, hardworking, loyal man. The detective sounds like everything a woman could want.

But for a long, long time, I've been told that I'm not someone a good man would want. And it's all shit, I *know* it's shit. That doesn't mean I'm ready to hang my heart out as a target. I need to build up a little more armor before I let anyone start taking shots at it.

Then maybe tiny pellets like *You don't really belong in a place like this* wouldn't pierce so deeply. Because I don't think he meant anything hurtful by it. He was just bluntly saying what a lot of people probably believe. Still, I'm so used to being wounded, all I heard was: *You don't belong.*

But I do. I belong in Apartment 306. Because I've got my lease, signed and paid for.

And I'm not going to let *anyone* ever make me feel worthless again. Not my parents, not random assholes—and certainly not overly blunt, grumpy detectives. Not even the ones who are big, sexy heroes. This is my life, dammit.

So I'm finally going to start living it.

MIA

IT TURNS OUT, I *LOVE* LEARNING TO LIVE BY MYSELF. I love turning this apartment into a home of my very own. And I love YouTube, because it doesn't matter what I want to know—someone has uploaded a step-by-step tutorial about how to do it.

And it's all so fun. Even chores as simple as washing my new dishes or sweeping my wooden floors. Maybe one day the thrill will wear off, but two weeks after moving in, I'm still enjoying all of it. Especially laundry, and that moment when I pull the clothes from the dryer and they're so warm and smell so good. And after taking on so many projects at home, God knows I dirty a lot of clothes. The apartments each have hookups but I haven't

bought my washer and dryer yet—and I don't know if I will. When I use the small laundry room in the basement, the whole process feels like an adventure. First sorting the clothes. Then traipsing down the stairs. Then feeding the machines detergent and quarters.

As far I can tell, only a few people in the building use the coin-operated machines, so the laundry room is always quiet. I use both available washers, colors in one and whites in the other. Then I race upstairs again, praying the door across the hall won't open while I'm running around in my little shorts and thin sleep shirt… and also praying it will.

It doesn't.

So I just have to fill the time until my laundry's dry and until I go to bed. I prop my tablet on the kitchen counter and fire up an episode of *The Great British Bake Off* while I mix up some muffins—which turned out to be surprisingly easy now that I have all of the ingredients and equipment. My results won't look anything like the bakes on the show, but a girl can dream and the contestants are all so *nice*. I slide the first batch into the oven before running down to throw my clothes into the dryers. About a second after I make it back to my apartment, I hear Cole leave his. I stand there with my hands braced against the door, forcing myself not to spy on him through the peephole, wondering if he'll ever knock.

He doesn't. Instead the faint ding of the elevator

arriving on our floor tells me that he's going out.

On a date? It's Sunday night and probably too late for that. Maybe just picking up something from the corner store.

Suddenly torn by worry, I gnaw my bottom lip. It's snowing outside. The sidewalks are pretty slick. And he's getting around more easily now, especially in the mornings. By the afternoons, though, he usually seems to break out the crutches—and crutches plus snow and ice might be a problem. So maybe if I don't hear him come back before I go to bed, I'll make a trip to the corner store, too.

Then he'll probably think I'm stalking him. I see him almost every day. We leave for work about the same time, come home around the same time. We don't say much when our paths cross in the hallway. Usually he just answers my greeting with a stiff nod and a brooding glare.

And just like before the shooting—and before I moved into this apartment building—I occasionally see him while I'm at work. The difference now is that he sees me, too. Every time I notice him, he's already noticed me. His dark gaze never leaves me. Then I pretend to be unaware and get out from under that unrelenting stare as fast as I can. It's cowardly, I know. But I don't know how to handle the crazy way my heart starts pounding when he's near. And I can't bear those stiff greetings, as if he'd rather not talk to me at all. It's gotten so bad

that I'll use the stairs so I'm not stuck in the elevator with him, my heart going a mile a minute and my body on fire, while he watches me. Doesn't talk to me. Just watches me.

Like he did on Friday morning. Since Cole's on light duty, most of the missing persons cases are being funneled in his direction. So when a call came in regarding a missing elderly man only a day after an elderly man was found slumped over dead on a park bench, with no identification and no signs of physical trauma, it's no surprise the detective came down to the autopsy suite to see if the unidentified man was his missing person.

Also no surprise, it *was* his missing person. Preliminary identification turned out to be a simple matter, thanks to a distinctive military tattoo.

The surprise came when Cole stayed through the rest of the autopsy—saying he would wait until Dr. Childers discovered a probable cause of death. My boss is both meticulous and methodical, so the autopsy takes anywhere from a full hour to an entire morning. And it's gruesome. I don't mind that, but most people do. Even cops. So they typically don't hover; they'll wait for Childers to call with her preliminary findings. And given the deceased's history of heart disease, this case was pretty clearly going to be filed under 'natural causes.' Nothing unusual, no foul play. Just a man who went for a walk but who probably had a cardiac event before he made it back home.

Cole had to know it, too. Yet still he remained. And every time I looked up, he was watching me. I would like to think it's because I looked *sooooo* sexy that day… but as an autopsy technician, I'm dressed head-to-toe in shapeless blue scrubs, a surgical mask, and a hair net. Only my eyes are visible, but even they are shielded by clear safety glasses.

So yeah. Cole probably didn't stay because I looked so damn hot. And he didn't talk much. Just followed me with his brooding stare while I took photos and samples and opened the skull.

I might have thought the quiet was usual for him, since he doesn't ever talk much around me. But partway through the procedure, Childers teased him for his atypical silence and asked if he was trying to scare her new technician—me—before assuring him that I'd already seen worse than anything he could deliver.

I'm not sure that's true. I suspect that if Cole tried, he could do terrible, terrible things to my heart. He just wouldn't leave any visible marks.

Three minutes before my second batch of muffins are supposed to come out, my timer goes off to warn me about the end of the dryer's cycle. I wait to pull the muffins from the oven before racing downstairs.

And Cole's not at the corner store. Instead he's in the laundry room, wearing nothing but a pair of light gray sweatpants, casually leaning back against one of the washing machines, his phone in hand. The noises

coming from the device sound like he's watching a football game, and a half-empty beer bottle sits within his reach on the nearby table—as if he's been killing time down here instead of running back and forth like I have been.

I stop dead, suddenly far too aware of my thin shirt and my little shorts.

And his bare chest and stomach. His torso appears carved from granite. Holy shit, the pectorals on the man. And the abdominals. And the Adonis belt. And there's a happy trail of dark hair running straight down. And a soft bulge beneath his waistband.

I tear my gaze upward again and meet his eyes, which are narrowed on my face.

Scowling, he asks, "Is your shit I'm waiting on?"

My cheeks flame. Even I know that when there aren't any available machines, leaving your clothes in the dryer is not proper communal laundry etiquette.

"Sorry." Grabbing my basket from the table where I left it, I edge past him. Bending over in front of the machine, I begin pulling out clothes as fast as I can. They're still hot, my face is hot, everything in this laundry room is burning me alive. "You need both?"

"Just one."

"Okay. This one's empty." I slide my basket over. My heart's pounding like I just dug a six-foot-deep hole instead of emptied a dryer. Desperately I search for something to say. "How was your weekend?"

"Long." He starts throwing handfuls of wet laundry into the first machine. "Yours?"

I try not to stare at the flex of his biceps but it's hard. His arms are beautifully cut, muscles and tendons like organic steel, all working in gorgeous harmony. "Productive."

He grunts and slams the dryer shut. "Is 'productive' why I smelled paint in the hall?"

I nod and drag the last of my clothes into the basket. "I'm sampling different colors on my walls before I commit to anything."

"You're painting your place yourself?" His voice sounds doubtful—but if he doubts that I'd do it myself or whether I *can* do it myself, I'm not certain.

"I was going to hire someone, but…" I shrug. "Home Depot has a ton of online tutorials and do-it-yourself workshops at the store. So I can learn to do it. And I'm not in a rush, so if I screw it up I can do it over."

"Or hire someone to clean up your mess."

I probably won't. But we'll see. I heft my basket onto my hip. Usually I'd take it all upstairs to fold and put away, but…he's talking to me.

And his chest is bare and tanned and sprinkled with dark hair.

I set my basket onto the folding table. He starts his dryer and walks over to my side—not limping. But when he leans back against the edge of the table, he keeps his weight off his left leg.

Then he just looks down at me.

Every inch of my skin feels flushed and prickly under that dark stare. My nipples are hard little bullets poking against the thin fabric of my shirt, but it's not cold in this basement. Not cold at all.

Cole reaches for his beer. "When I heard you were working for Childers, I figured you were filing papers or some shit. Not opening up DBs."

Dead bodies. "Oh, I file a lot of papers, too. The day I'm not writing up a report is probably the day I'll be on that slab."

That brings a faint smile to his lips. "You and me both. So how'd you end up in the morgue?"

Probably the most frequent question I hear, aside from "How can you stand it?" I suppose a detective who investigates how those people end up in the morgue knows how I stand it. He has to stand it, too, in his own way.

As for the rest...I suppose there are a lot of reasons. But most are reasons that expose too much of me and are difficult to share. So I give him the easier one.

"I like puzzles," I tell him. "And figuring things out."

Childers does most of the figuring out; I just help. But after a few years, I'll probably go to medical school and study forensic pathology, and eventually do the same thing she is. I'm not in a rush, though. I've got time to get there.

"You like puzzles, so you decide to take people apart

and sew them back together?" He shakes his head. "You could just pick up a Sunday crossword, instead."

"I already did that today. In pen. So if I didn't work in a morgue, what would I do with the rest of the week?"

He grins in response and my heart skips a beat. It's the first time I've made him really smile. I can barely tear my gaze away as he lifts his beer, takes a swig.

"So what about you?" I reach for a pair of jeans, careful not to touch the hot metal rivets. I learned that lesson last week. "Why'd you become a detective?"

If Cole also has reasons that are difficult to express, he's not sharing them either. "Because I hate puzzles. I like the world better when the mysteries are solved."

I laugh. "Fair enough. Though if you like things solved, you're in the wrong business."

His eyes narrow again. "I'd argue that our solve rate is pretty damn good. It's just in the courts where it doesn't look as impressive."

"Because most of the time you can figure out what happened?" But proving it is another matter. "Yet finding evidence that holds up against a legal defense is a little more difficult."

He nods and takes another drink, then holds out the bottle to me, silently offering.

I hate beer. And it's a little warm. But taking that bottle, placing my lips where his have been, and tipping back a small sip feels like the sexiest thing I've ever done.

"Thank you," I whisper huskily and hand the beer

back. Despite the drink, my tongue feels thick and my throat dry, but the rest of me is so, so wet. Deep inside me, everything's melting, tightening. And that bulge beneath his waistband isn't soft anymore.

I'm playing with so much fire here. I know I am. I'm not ready for this kind of thing. But I think it's going to happen anyway. I just pray my heart has enough armor to survive the inevitable end.

He's watching me again, with a dark, smoldering gaze that burns every inch of my skin. "You're one hell of a puzzle to me, Mia."

A pang strikes my chest. Softly I ask, "Does that mean you hate me?"

"No." And his voice sounds deeper, rougher when he says, "I just wonder what the hell you're doing here, instead of living in your daddy's big mansion overlooking the city."

"What I'm doing here, aside from folding laundry?"

"Yeah."

Asking why I'm renting an apartment in a building I could easily buy, then. Or maybe asking why I'm here beside him. The first question's easier to answer. "Have you met my father?"

"Unfortunately."

That blunt response makes me smile. "Would *you* want to live with him?"

His bark of laughter is answer enough.

I shrug. "Puzzle solved, then."

"I don't think so." But Cole doesn't add what he *does* think. Instead I'm aware of his gaze settling on my breasts. On their hardened tips.

Which just makes them feel tighter, hotter. Aching for something more substantial than a look.

This time when he takes a swig, the heated intensity of his expression suggests that he's imagining something else on his tongue. Heart thundering, I reach into the basket for the next item. Soft cashmere slides beneath my fingertips…and my sweater is now the size of a doll's sweater.

Struck by dismay, I lay it out on the table. Cole chokes on his beer.

"Oh no. It's my favorite winter sweater," I mourn, trying to stretch the tiny white sleeves back to their original length. They aren't going. "But I looked at the label. It said you could wash it on the delicate cycle."

His broad shoulders shaking with his laughter, Cole asks, "What'd it say about drying?"

"I don't know." I look inside the side seam for the tag—which is the same size as it was before, but seems huge now in that tiny garment. "Oh. 'Lay flat to dry.' Whoops."

"A hell of a whoops." His amusement settles into a wry grin. "You sure you want to give up all those maids and that mansion now?"

Why does he bring that up again? Suddenly irritated, I tell him, "You know you're kind of an asshole, right?"

"You only say that because you don't know me very well." His gaze slips down my body and lingers on my bare legs. "When you get to know me better, you'll see there's no 'kind of' about it. I'm a complete asshole."

Despite myself, I have to laugh. At least he admits it, I guess. And it's nothing I didn't already know. "You can have it," I tell him generously and hold out the tiny sweater. "You can use it as a mitten. Just tie the neck closed and stick your thumb into a sleeve. It'll be super soft and warm."

"For one hand?" He raises a brow. "Usually I just use lotion."

My cheeks heat. I only meant to turn my silly mistake into a joke but he's turned it another direction. But I won't back down. "Well, it *is* really soft. And if you get it all messy, it's washable."

His voice roughens. "On the gentle cycle."

A little breathlessly, I nod. "Then while it's wet, lay it out flat."

His gaze locked on my face, he sets his beer aside. "Are you flirting with me, Mia?"

Oh god. Am I doing a terrible job of it? So bad that he isn't sure whether I am or not?

But no backing down.

"Yes," I whisper.

Something in his eyes hardens. "Not getting enough attention upstairs, then?"

Considering that he ignores me… "Not really."

"Fuck." A bitter laugh breaks from him. "Well, if you're so desperate for more, I don't mind giving you *my* attention."

Desperate? I can't even say he's wrong, though. I feel desperate right now. For a kiss, a touch—anything he's willing to give. Still, he's a jerk for throwing it in my face.

"You *are* an asshole," I tell him.

"I really am, angel." Before I can react, he spins me around. I come to a stop with the small of my back against the edge of the folding table, his palms flattened on the surface at either side of my hips, my body caged by the iron strength in his arms. With his gaze fixed on my lips, his head lowers until his mouth hovers just above mine. "But I'll damn my own soul to Hell for the chance to touch you."

Bracing my hands against his chest—his gloriously hard, warm, bare chest—I pant against his lips. "It won't cost your soul. I swear."

"Kiss me, then," he rasps, and his long fingers tangle in my hair. "But if you start this, Mia, it's all on you."

What will be on me? His soul? Why is he making this all sound like a horrible decision, as if someone other than me might be hurt by it? As if *he* might be hurt by it?

Is it that bad, what I'm doing? Suddenly uncertain, I hesitate.

Abruptly Cole's face softens. "Forget everything I just said," he tells me gruffly. "If you need me to, I'll take

all the blame."

What blame? But suddenly it doesn't matter, because his mouth brushes mine. He kisses me as if I'm soft and delicate, gently coaxing my lips apart. A shiver races over my skin when his tongue slides deeper, yet this is nothing like I expected. Everything I know about Cole Matthews is sharp and direct. But his kiss is restrained, as if he's covered his every rough edge beneath a blanket of warm velvet.

Still it's hotter than anything I've known before. A soft moan rises from my throat. My thighs clench as if trying to ease the melting ache between them. Maybe he won't lose control, but I'm already on the verge of it.

God, I want him to lose control. I want to drive him crazy with lust. I want him to feel like I do.

I drag my fingernails down his chest. Hardened muscles become chiseled stone in the wake of my touch. When my hands reach his ridged abdomen, he abruptly crowds closer, pressing his body full-length against mine. And he's big. Everywhere. Surrounding me. Against me. His thick erection pushes against my stomach but I want that rigid length between my legs, where I can rub against him. Whimpering with desire, I link my arms around his neck, trying to lift myself to the height I need.

A rough growl reverberates through his chest. In a sudden movement, he tears his mouth from mine and hefts me up onto the table, then steps between my

parted thighs.

His dark gaze bores into mine. Unlike his restrained kiss, his voice is harsh and unyielding. "This is what you want, angel? You and me, messing around in this dirty basement, where anyone might walk in and see?"

"Yes," I breathe. "I'd want this anywhere."

"Fuck," he groans the curse like my answer hurts him. Hands braced beside my thighs, he rocks back and takes a long look at me, from my bare legs to my kiss-swollen lips, as if deciding where to go next. After an endless moment, his gaze drops to my chest. I'm leaning back slightly, my palms flat against the table's surface, my spine arched and my hardened nipples on display beneath the thin cotton of my shirt. "You going to let me get my mouth on those pretty tits, angel?"

A shudder of desire rips through me. His eyes darken as I tremble against him.

"If you want to," I whisper.

"More than my next breath." His voice roughens. "And your pussy? You going to let me lick that, too?"

Oh my god. Just hearing him say it makes me dizzy with need. My heart thunders, my pulse filling my ears and making my response seem thick and slow, as if I'm speaking underwater. "If you'd like to."

Grimly he shakes his head. "Wrong answer, angel. What matters is if *you* would like it."

How could I know if I'd like it? But I think I would. Just imagining his mouth between my legs makes

everything inside me feel so taut and hot. The reality has to be as good.

"I would." And I'll beg him if I have to.

I might have to. Because he still doesn't move. From his great height, he studies me, tension holding him in a steely grip, his every muscle standing in sharp relief beneath his skin. As if all this restraint is taking effort. As if he wants me almost as much as I want him, but he's not ready to give in.

Apparently for good reason. With a tortured groan, he tells me, "If I touch you now, angel, there's a real chance I won't stop. If I don't stop, we risk getting busted for indecent exposure. Maybe you can survive that—but if I lose my head, I lose my job. So does touching you sound like a good idea?"

Yes. But I shake my head.

A gleam in his eyes tells me he's thinking the same. *Yes.* But no. "That doesn't mean you can't touch yourself."

My breath stops. "Me?"

"I won't let anyone see." His head dips closer, his gravelly voice abrading my skin with every teasing word. "You can touch yourself the way I want to. Slide your hand right into your little shorts, see if your pussy's hot and wet."

I don't know if it's a suggestion or a command, but I immediately comply—feeling sexy and naughty and in love with the way his expression goes hard and hungry when he realizes what I'm doing. His gaze zeroes in on

my hand as I dip my fingertips past the waistband of my shorts.

"Right in there, angel. Fuck, yes. Get those fingers all over your pussy." He groans again when my hand disappears beneath the soft fabric. "Tell me how wet you are."

"*So* wet. Drenched." Simply drowning in desire, and the caress of my fingers over my clit feels so good, but I can't tear my gaze from his face. He's watching the concealed movement of my hand as if everything he wants and needs is right there. "And so hot."

His hands grasp the edge of the table in a white-knuckled grip. Holding himself back. "Are your fingers all slippery?"

"Yes." My answer is hardly more than a soft moan.

"Give me a taste of it," he growls the order. When I pause, uncertain how to do that, his burning gaze lifts from between my legs to meet mine. "I'm going to lick those pussy juices right off your fingers."

Oh god. Trembling with excitement, my heart racing, I pull my hand free of my sleep shorts. My glistening fingers quiver a little as I begin to raise them, but I don't go fast enough, because Cole abruptly grips my wrist and brings my hand to his mouth.

His ravenous gaze holding mine, he slowly drags his tongue up the length of my middle finger, and that long, hot lick seems to touch every part of me, inside and out. My entire body clenches when he sucks lightly on the tip of my finger, then melts into a dizzying swirl

of need. I'm shaking all over, my breath coming in soft pants, my senses a riot of sensation and overwhelmed by sheer erotic thrill. Because *Cole Matthews* is licking my fingers in the basement of our apartment building as if the taste of my arousal is the sweetest treat anyone could give him.

I laugh breathlessly. "This is the dirtiest thing I've ever done."

"*This* is?" His tongue flicks into the juncture between my first and second fingers, so unexpectedly suggestive that it steals my breath, and I can only nod in response. "Jesus fucking Christ. If that brainless frat boy doesn't do anything dirtier than this, no wonder you're looking for more."

I'm so aroused, I apparently can't even think anymore, because I didn't understand any of that. "What frat boy?"

His jaw clenches, and he releases my hand. Bracing his palms beside my legs, he lowers his head until his face is right up in mine. Through gritted teeth, he says, "That fucker Jason Lewis. Your pretty little boyfriend. Remember?"

I stare up at him, too astonished to even laugh. Beyond the absurdity of someone as gorgeous as Cole Matthews calling anyone else 'pretty' like it was an insult…well, there's all the rest of the absurdity. He thinks Jason is my boyfriend? "You must be the last person in this city to know that while my mother was pregnant with me, my father was cheating on her with

his secretary—and he knocked her up, too. All this time, I thought that *I* was the last to know. But I'm apparently only second-to-last. Yay."

A frown darkens his face. "What does that mean?"

"It means the brainless frat boy is my brother." And the laughter is starting to break through. *Brainless frat boy*. Jason will get a kick out of that.

Cole's body is utterly still. Hoarsely he echoes, "Your *brother*?"

"Half-brother, technically. But not half in all the ways that matter."

I'm not sure Cole really hears me. He seems thunderstruck, disbelieving. His gaze wildly searches my face.

Then it all changes. His expression settles into taut lines—a look that grabs me by the throat, hot and feral and possessive.

"Fuck the risk," he rasps, then clasps his palm around the back of my neck and drags me in for a devastating kiss.

No restraint this time. His fingers tighten in my hair, angling my head back for a deep stroke of his tongue. Need clamps down hard within my center and explodes through my veins. *This*. This is what I wanted. Just like this. He devours my mouth with hungry licks, his palm cupping my breast, his thumb teasing my nipple. Every flick across the hardened tip sparks erotic wildfires deep inside me, scorching every nerve on a direct line to my clit.

His steely forearm drops around my waist and he hauls me closer. His huge erection lodges against my pussy—and this is it, this is going to happen. We've got almost nothing between us, just a pair of sweats and a pair of shorts. A few tugs of fabric and a thrust and he'll be fucking me, because neither one of us is slowing down. This is not how I imagined my first time. It's even better than I imagined, because he's so hungry for me, and I'm desperate for him, not just giving into curiosity or settling for someone who doesn't drive me this crazy. His big hand pushes down the back of my shorts, palming my ass and holding me firmly against that thick length as he rocks between my legs, forcing my sensitive flesh to feel every solid inch that will soon be deep inside me—

And he goes absolutely rigid. His body. His mouth. His hands.

"Cole?" I whisper against his lips.

His breath slowly hisses through his teeth. And I realize he's pushed up against me, and my legs are tightly wrapped around him—and either one of those things could have pulled on muscles that shouldn't be pulled. Not considering where he was shot.

Hardly daring to breath, I ask, "Your leg?"

A short nod is the answer. Then a gritted, "Fuck."

"It's okay," I say and carefully begin to unwind my legs. "Stop me if I make it worse."

"You're making it worse," he immediately grates out.

I freeze.

A tremor wracks his big frame, followed by a soft grunt. A laugh, I realize. The best laugh he can manage right now. "Bad enough we have to stop," he says a moment later, his voice strained. "Not having your thighs squeezing me tight is worse."

It is. I hate letting him go.

I hate hurting him even more. Slowly I scoot back farther onto the table. His eyes are closed, his mouth in a flat line edged with white. "Was it me pressing against you? Or the way you were moving?"

"Moving."

His clipped reply tells me the pain isn't easing yet. Softly I bite my lip, waiting, afraid that anything I do will jar his leg and increase his agony. "Should I run upstairs to get your crutches?"

"No. It'll just be a minute." He gives another short grunt of a laugh. "Though maybe a lot longer before I can follow through on what we started."

Before we can have sex. A hot little thrill races through me again at the thought of it—and the wondrous delight of knowing that he eventually wants to try again—but I do my best not to seem like an overeager dork with a crush when I say breezily, "That's okay. I'd rather not have you crying and screaming while I'm trying to get off."

He laughs again, harder this time, then his muscles go rigid again and he groans. "Shit. And me, I'm glad

I'm not poaching on another man's territory, after all."

Which must have been the reason for all that talk about damning his soul and blaming. Because he'd despised the thought of touching someone else's woman. Yet he'd wanted me enough to touch me anyway.

For an instant, that feels amazing. Like a blast of warmth through my heart, which is so used to the cold. My mother's frigid disdain. My father's icy control. In all my life, Jason's really been the only person to want me for who I am.

And Cole wanted me so much that he'd betrayed his principles just to have me.

But it only feels amazing for an instant. Because in the next moment, I realize who Cole believed *I* was. A woman who would cheat on her boyfriend. Who would flirt with a guy and fuck him in a laundry room, even though she was seeing someone else. And if he believed that of me…well, that's not the kind of woman you'd want anything *more* from than a fuck in a laundry room.

Cole might have wanted me. But if I was who he'd believed, whatever he felt couldn't be the kind of want that would last beyond a furtive screw or two.

And he knows better now, but the ache of that realization is blooming in my heart like a corpse flower. Maybe it won't bloom long, but right now it's huge and fetid, turning all the sweet warmth into a rotten poison. He believed I was a cheater. Someone so selfish, I would hurt a guy as sweet as Jason without a second thought.

He wanted me. But whoever he wanted—that selfish, cheating girl—isn't who I am.

And I *knew* my heart didn't have enough armor yet. Which must be why it hurts so much now. I was so stupid to start this. So desperate for someone to see *me*, to want *me*. And if that someone was Cole Matthews, who'd fascinated me from the moment I first saw him? To suddenly have him kiss me was like a wish come true.

Maybe I should have been careful about what I wished for.

Throat aching, I avert my face, unable to bear seeing his pain, unable to bear how helpless I am to stop it— unable to bear how beautiful he is to me. I haven't dared move much, so he's still incredibly close, his hands braced on the edge of the table, my knees drawn up between us.

For a long time it seems the only sound is the tumble of the dryer. But it couldn't have been more than a minute or two before his quiet, "You all right?" draws my gaze to his face again. His eyes are dark and intense on mine, with a frown shadowing his expression—as if he can sense the hurt that's still blooming inside me.

And I might not be a selfish cheater, but I'm apparently a liar. "Yes," I tell him. "You?"

"Yeah. But wishing I'd killed Lowery."

The man who shot him. Despite the pain in my heart, I have to smile at that blunt reply. But I don't have it in me to give any other response. I simply don't know what to say.

"Shit." Hard fingers catch my chin, force my gaze to his. His eyes search mine. "You're not moving, but I can feel you backing away from me. What's going on in your head?"

A whole mess of things that I can't control and don't want to share. I don't know how to do this relationship stuff, even if that relationship only consisted of a few hot kisses. And I don't know how to get out of this without hurting more and exposing how stupidly vulnerable I am.

Voice thick, I finally say, "I think that maybe I better go now."

And wait until this storm of uncertainty passes. Until I can think clearly again.

His brows push together in a dark frown. Bitterness laces his harsh tone. "You're disappointed, then? Maybe wishing you're with someone in good enough shape to give you what you need."

The pain that pierces my chest leaves me speechless. I had been afraid of more hurt. But I didn't know it was actually coming. Because maybe now Cole doesn't see a cheater when he looks at me, but he must see someone shallow and petty to suggest something like that, even though I've never given him reason to believe it. Which makes *him* a judgmental dickhead who'll immediately assume the worst of someone—and makes me an idiot for thinking he might be different.

But I'm not sticking around to let him hurt me some

more. Jerking my chin out of his grip, I hop down from the table and began tossing my clothes into my basket. "This was a mistake," I tell him, and only the tightness ballooning in my chest keeps the tears burning in my throat at bay.

"A mistake?" he echoes hoarsely. His hot gaze follows me as I push past him. "Seems to me you were having a fucking good time. So you're just walking away from what we could have had here?"

No. I'm not walking away; I'm running away. Before I cry right in front of him.

But pride stops me before I take a single step. My breath hitches, yet still I manage to force out the words. "I'm not who you think I am. And if I'm disappointed, it's only because you're even more of an asshole than you said you were."

Then I run.

COLE

MIA'S RUNNING AWAY FROM ME, BUT I CAN'T chase after her. If I try there won't be some amazing romantic scene where I sweep her up into my arms. Instead I'd end up flat on my ass. So I watch her go, my heart like a hot lump of lead burning in my chest.

A mistake, she called this. Me touching her, kissing her. *A mistake.*

That's something I get told often while I'm on the job. Every time we bring someone into the interview room.

You've made a mistake, detective. I didn't steal anything. If you think I killed anyone, you're mistaken.

You're making a big mistake, accusing me of this.

They're wrong. They're all wrong. It's never a mistake talking to someone during an investigation. Because even if they're not guilty, we can rule them out, or get information we didn't have before.

But I'm not thinking of them now. Instead I'm thinking of someone else telling me I was making a mistake—but back then, I was the one walking out the door. It was the last thing my dad ever said to me. *You're making a big mistake, you little bastard. You think you're going to make something of yourself? Those fuckers out there are never going to let you, just like they never gave me a chance. They'll always look at you like a piece of shit. Then you'll come crawling back home, begging for help from your old man.*

Since then, not a second has passed that I haven't proven him wrong. I've never gone back home. I made something of myself. And the sweetest part of it is, my old man taught me a hell of a lot about the job without even meaning to. He taught me how a man will use aggression and belligerence to conceal his inadequacy and fear. He taught me how many excuses a man will make when he's done wrong, how he'll paint himself as a victim. He taught me that a man will imagine everyone else is thinking and acting just like him, no matter how weak or corrupt it is. He never imagines anyone is truly better than he is, just better at pretending they are.

Hell, I use that in the interview room all the time.

Just let the bastards run their mouths, ask them what they believe happened, and often what they accuse others of thinking and doing—turns out that's exactly what the bastard thought and did.

This time I'm the bastard. Mia was already pulling away from me before she said this was a mistake, but maybe that's because I called her brother a brainless fucker. Or maybe it's what she said about her dad cheating on her mom, and there I was, assuming she was cheating, too. Maybe all that was sinking in.

Her saying that this was a mistake, though—that came right after I asked her if she was disappointed I couldn't fuck her. When the truth is, that was all me, feeling like a tiny, inadequate piece of shit because I couldn't give my woman what she needed. I just projected that crap all over her.

Some days there's more of my old man in me than I want to admit. But I've spent most my life finding those parts and scratching them out. Right now, he'd be cursing Mia, calling her a whore and a tease.

Me, I'll do what I should have from the start—thinking instead of raging, listening instead of talking. And she said something loud and clear. *I'm not who you think I am.*

So I'll find out who Mia Bennet is. That shouldn't be too damn hard. I'm a detective, for fuck's sake. Reading people is my job. But I've got to stop assuming shit— and stop letting my dick lead the way. And, considering

my leg's so fucked that my dick isn't going to be doing any leading for a while, that shouldn't be too damn hard, either. The hardest thing might be getting her to talk to me again.

But I'll find a way. I've had a taste of her and it was the sweetest damn thing I've ever known. Maybe another taste is more than I deserve. Or maybe that's just my old man in me again, saying I don't have a chance in hell of being with someone like her.

She's too damn good for me, that's a fact. But she's too damn good for any man. So if she's going to be with anyone, might as well be me. I just have to work harder to get there. That's all right, though. That's what I've been doing all my life.

My leg still feels like a shark made a snack out of it, so I settle back to wait. She left that tiny white sweater on the table. And Christ, it's soft as hell. I'd joked about wearing it like a mitten and stroking my cock, but feeling it now, maybe it's not such a joke.

Especially since I remember seeing her wear it last week. She'd just come out of her apartment, that dark hair pulled back in the ponytail she's always sporting for work, her lips like red velvet, and this white cashmere clinging to her full breasts. Just so fucking beautiful—and now I know how soft it felt against her skin. So, yeah. I'll be wrapping this little sweater around my dick before the night's out.

Along with something else. Because I kill the time

until the dryer stops by watching a game on my phone that I'm only half-paying attention to, because I'm still thinking of her legs in those little shorts, her nipples through that thin shirt. And there's a sock in my dryer, the one she unloaded as fast as she could. A sock…and a pair of panties.

A little thong. Black lace that's cupped her pussy. That's soaked up her juices.

Like a fucking stalker I sniff them, though there's nothing left of her scent on the fabric. Still, I know what she smells like, tastes like. The heady flavor that I licked from her fingers still lingers on my tongue.

And that was the dirtiest thing she'd ever done.

I stare at the panties as that realization sweeps through me. When she'd said it, I was so fucking torn up thinking about her boyfriend never touching her like she ought to be touched. But now it hits me again. *That* was the dirtiest thing she'd ever done? Then she's either not done much…or it's been done badly.

Christ. Maybe that's another reason she pulled away. I came on to her like a freight train. Almost fucked her against a table. And I know what kind of man I am. I'm big and demanding and vulgar. There was no doubt she was right there with me, wildly turned on and looking forward to the ride. But, hell. As soon as we slowed down a little, maybe she started having second thoughts.

And maybe that means I shouldn't slow down again. But more likely, pushing too hard will just set me further

back with her than I already am.

So I've got to slow it down. Even if it kills me.

But at least now I've got a good reason to knock on her door.

Which is where I'm standing a few minutes later. There's a long wait between my knock and the door swinging open, and the reason why strikes me the second I see her. She's put on a big sweatshirt and a long pair of pajama pants. My chest tightens. I don't know whether those oversized clothes are supposed to say "hands off" or to serve as some sort of protection, but either way they're a clear sign that she doesn't want to pick up where we left off.

Her pale blue eyes regard me warily. "Detective."

So we're back to that, even though she panted my name against my lips. All right.

That wary light fades when I hold up the sock. "This yours?"

"Yes." As if relieved to discover the sock was what brought me to her door, some of the rigidity leaves her posture when she reaches for it. "Thank you."

Since I'm keeping her panties, she shouldn't be thanking me. But I don't mention those at all and risk embarrassing her. Instead I draw in a deep breath. There's the paint I smelled earlier—and something warmer, spicier, familiar. "You making pumpkin pies?"

"Pumpkin muffins." Her tone is guarded, and her gaze lands on my bare chest before skittering away. "I

plan to give them out to our neighbors, since mostly everyone's been really nice about me moving so much stuff in and having my deliveries in the way all the time."

Not all that much stuff, as far as I can see. In the living room, there's just that big leather couch and a huge stack of boxes. "You better at baking than you are at laundry?"

Her lips twitch a little. "I think so. I haven't done it much. But it's just science, and I'm pretty good at that."

Tasty science. Generously I offer, "I'll test one, if you want me to."

"Yeah, well. I said my neighbors were *mostly* nice. So you don't get any of my muffins."

I grin. Maybe she's wary, but she's sassy, too. And I'm crazy about her. "You going to invite me in?"

"No."

"That's all right." I brace my shoulder against the door frame and look over her head. "I can be nosy from here. Is that all stuff from IKEA?"

She glances over her shoulder at the boxes marked with the store's brand. "Yes."

"You going to assemble it yourself?"

She seems to stiffen a little before shrugging, and I realize what she thinks I'm going to say. Why doesn't a rich girl just pay for better furniture…or to have it assembled for her?

And that *is* what I was thinking. But maybe she already told me the answer.

"Because you like puzzles," I say.

The look she gives me is more surprised than guarded. And maybe I hit that nail on the head, or maybe it's more than that. Because she's baking, and she mentioned going to Home Depot, taking classes…she just likes *doing* things. Putting shit together. Figuring out how it works. Not just dead bodies. Everything.

That's sexy as fuck.

"Some of that stuff will take two people to put together and move around," I tell her. "You need help, knock at my door."

Again that wary surprise flickers in her eyes. "Thanks."

Yeah, I bet she won't. She's got a brother to help her. Still, I mean it when I say, "The painting, too. Those the colors you're thinking of?"

On the far wall, long stripes of rust, brown, and a deep golden yellow are painted in thick swatches. Mia turns to regard them from across the room. "I don't know. I wonder if I'm too influenced by the season. Maybe next month I'll be picking out red and green."

Now that she mentions it, those colors do scream *Thanksgiving*—which is only four days away. "Maybe that's not so bad. You like the holidays?"

"Historically, no." A wry little smile tugs at her lips when she turns to face me again. "But I'm hoping the future ones will be better."

"Now that you've moved out of your parents' place?"

She nods.

"I know how that goes," I tell her. "If you think I'm an asshole, you should meet my dad."

Not that I'd ever wish that on anyone. But her smile widens briefly before a shadow falls across her expression again. Maybe thinking about *why* she called me an asshole. And why I deserved to be called one.

So it's time for an apology. "Listen, Mia…" I probably should have practiced this ahead of time. What the hell do I say? That I was in a jealous snit? That I'm terrified I'll never be at one hundred percent and be able to give her what she needs? "I made some shitty assumptions, and I shouldn't have."

Though her shoulders stiffen up again and her focus goes a little distant, she doesn't toss the apology back in my face. Instead she quietly says, "Thank you."

So far so good, then. "I'd like to make it up to you."

"Make it up to me?" Her brow furrows and her light blue gaze returns to mine. "You just did. You don't owe me anything."

"Then I'd like to give you something." Something other than a tongue down her throat in a laundry room. "Let me take you out tomorrow night. A drink, dinner. Whatever you like."

"No." Her eyes are suddenly huge, the emotion shining from their depths dark and bruised, but her mouth is firm with resolve. "You said it yourself: You're an asshole."

True. "But I'm an asshole who wants you. At my side.

In my bed. Everywhere."

Her breath stops. Her gaze searches mine, as if she's desperate to see whether I mean it. As if she *wants* to believe it. Then her eyes close and, as if want and belief don't matter at all, she breathes, "I can't."

"No?" My voice roughens. "Because I remember how it was between us. Like a fucking wildfire. You remember?"

"No."

"Liar. You want a reminder? I'll give you one right here."

She doesn't need one. When her eyes fly open again, the memory is burning right there. But she's shaking her head.

And I know I'm pushing hard, but I can't fucking stop. "You don't think we'd be good together? Because we will, angel. In bed and out of it."

It's as if my words strip her expression bare, revealing naked desire—and wavering indecision. I push again, gently.

"You want this as much as I do," I tell her softly.

"Maybe I do." Her chin lifts. All at once her eyes are glistening with tears, but the pale blue behind them has hardened into ice. Her voice is thick and ragged. "But I've spent my life wanting. I'm tired of the people who I most want to see *me* only seeing that I'm not what they expect me to be, and then being disappointed in who I am. And I made a promise to myself not to waste time

on people who make me feel like shit—like you did. You apologized, and thank you. But I'm not taking the risk of it happening again."

Push too hard, something will break. I pushed too hard and it's like seeing someone rip open right in front of me. Everything hidden is suddenly exposed. *I'm not who you think I am.* And she's someone who's been wounded over and over. Now she's terrified it will happen again.

Terrified of me. My angel is scared of *me*. Chest a solid ache, I promise her hoarsely, "I won't hurt you, Mia."

Eyes glittering, she steps back. "Because I'm not going to *let* you."

And she slams the door in my face.

COLE

I REMEMBER BACK IN GRADE SCHOOL, WHEN HOLI-days seemed like they ought to be the most magical fucking thing that ever were, that this time of year the teachers used to go around the class and make everyone say what we were thankful for. So Thanksgiving was the holiday I hated the most. Christmas, you could put your head down and claim you didn't celebrate it and the other kids might give you shit but no one else would challenge that claim, and you got enough time off over winter break that no one really gave a fuck anyway. But Thanksgiving, you attended school right up until the day before. Then they'd ask for that thankful shit.

And what the hell was I going to say? I'm thankful

my father passed out before he started in with his fists? I'm thankful he moved his ass off the couch long enough that I could scrounge up enough change beneath the cushions to buy a fucking loaf of bread? I'm thankful my mom took off when I was little and left me behind with him?

On some days, I was kind of thankful for that. Thankful at least one of us got out.

Now I'm all the way out and understand why holidays seem a lot more magical. It's just all a matter of who you spend them with—and these days I've got a whole list of shit I'm truly thankful for.

My leg's a constant dull ache that flares up into teeth-gritting, screaming agony when I go too long and too far, or twist wrong. But in a few months, I'll be back to regular duty. A setback but not derailed. I'm thankful for that.

I've got a family that isn't blood but runs blue and true. I've known that since I joined the force, but it's never been more apparent than these past weeks, ever since I was shot. And I'm thankful as hell for my partner. You trust a man at your back, that's one thing. But Gabe Huertas has become a brother, and that's something a hell of a lot more.

And Mia… I'm thankful she hasn't moved out, considering how I fucked up.

I pushed too damn hard. I knew I was doing it and did it anyway. And it's one thing to push when you're up

against something strong. She *is* strong, no doubt. But she's like one of those packages of chips that won't tear open no matter how hard you pull, until you finally find that tiny notch that lets you rip it wide open. I found that notch and tore her right up. So she's strong, but she's fragile, too. I hadn't realized how fragile she was.

And all this week I've heard her come and go—avoiding me, I'm pretty fucking sure—but everything inside me is coming and going with her. Today, she left around noon. Heading to her parents' mansion. Because despite her saying that she hopes her holidays will be better now that she's moved out, she's attending their Thanksgiving dinner. At least that's what I picked up while listening to her and Childers chatting during the autopsy last Friday. Also got the feeling she didn't want to go, but that she felt obligated to.

Me, I've been invited over to Huertas's, so I get my ass in gear around five. I've been resting most of the day, doing nothing more strenuous than swearing at the refs in a football game, so I'm good without crutches for a few hours. I head out of my place with a bottle of wine for Gabe's wife and a six pack of beer for us.

I'm locking my door when the elevator dings and opens. Carrying a canvas grocery bag, Mia comes striding out and my heart stutters in my chest. For dinner at a mansion, no surprise she dressed up. She looks like a million bucks in a long belted coat that nips in at her waist and shows off her curves, and tall boots with heels

that add four inches to her height. I'd barely have to bend my head to kiss her. Her hair is in a thick, messy braid over her shoulder. And I fucked everything up, but my brain and my dick don't care. The only thing I can think of is taking that coat off. Wrapping that thick braid around my fist.

Her gaze catches mine and her step falters. The stuttering lightness in my chest transforms into something heavy and tight, because she smiles but her eyes have a glittery, hard shine. Like she's angry but also real fucking hurt and one of those things has her on the verge of crying.

I head straight down the hall toward her. She slammed the door in my face but I'm sure as hell not letting her get past me without making sure she doesn't need help.

Gruffly I ask, "You all right, angel?"

The hurt shines through the anger, as if my question tips the scale further in that direction. Or maybe she just didn't expect anyone to care. Suddenly her eyes are swimming. "Yes." Her voice thick, she comes to a halt in front of me. "Just feeling really stupid, thinking anything would ever change with them."

"With your folks?"

She nods and I see her rally, see the deep shuddering breath she draws in, the squaring of her shoulders. Her gaze flicks to the wine bottle and the beer. "You're headed out?"

"To Huertas's place."

"Your partner's?"

"Yeah."

"Do you want to take a pie?"

"A what?"

She lifts up the canvas bag. The sides are pulled tight, as if it's got something heavy inside—and about as big around as a pie. "I baked one but my mother didn't want to offer it to her guests. It's not 'traditional' enough."

"What the hell kind of pie isn't traditional enough?"

"Coconut lime." She shrugs. "It seemed like it might be refreshing after a heavy dinner."

"Fuck yes, it does." I tuck the bottle of wine under my arm and take the bag from her. It's heavier than I expect a pie to be but maybe it came out of the oven like a brick. Doesn't matter. I'll eat it. She should, too. "Come with me."

Her brow furrows, as if what I said didn't make any sense. "What?"

"To Huertas's place. They've got room at their table and his wife's always telling me to bring someone. Sofia's great, too. His whole family is. You'll like them."

Something like yearning passes over Mia's face before she shakes her head. "I'm not very good company today."

"Neither am I. I'm a fucking asshole, remember. But they still put up with me."

A soft smile graces her lips, then vanishes on a sigh.

"I really can't. I know better than to let my parents get to me…but I'm hanging on by a thread here. And I don't want to be that girl who falls apart all over you and your friends. Jason will be over in a little while, anyway."

I don't know what her parents said to her but I'm not leaving her like this. "Then I'll stay with you until he gets here. That way you're not alone."

A little laugh escapes her, but it's not a laugh of amusement—more like she can't think of anything worse than falling apart all over me. "No. Thank you. But I'll be okay."

"Mia," I say hoarsely. "Let me help you."

She shakes her head, backing away. "Please give my regards to Detective Huertas and his wife. And a happy Thanksgiving to you, Cole."

Fuck. But aside from running her down and tackling her, there's no stopping her from leaving. To her retreating back, I say, "To you, too, angel."

She's getting away now. But here's something else to be thankful for: I've got a pie plate to return. And a reason to knock on her door.

Because there's no damn way I'll sleep again without knowing she's okay.

MIA

I'M A FULL GLASS INTO A BOTTLE OF RED WHEN Jason arrives. His dinner at his mom's house went a lot better than mine did. No surprise there, maybe. Anything goes better than Thanksgiving dinner with my family. For most of my life, I didn't know Jason was the reason for the tension between my mother and father—or maybe he was a symptom of that tension. I don't know when they started hating each other. And by the time I learned that my father had a son the same age as me, I was a senior in high school.

But everyone else apparently knew from the beginning that my father had gotten his secretary pregnant—an affair in a long line of affairs. And all the while, my

mother took out her humiliation and bitterness on me. Jason's never did on him. So he can go to Thanksgiving dinner and come away from it, and his only regret is that inviting me to join them would be too damn awkward. His mom sounds lovely but I wouldn't ever ask her to add me to their family gathering.

So Jason and I get together afterward. It's been six years now. Usually we meet up at his place, but this time we did at mine.

By the time I've finished with my second glass of wine, I've bent his sympathetic ear with every shitty thing my mother and father did and said. Halfway through my third glass, he's passed out on my couch in a food coma.

But it's okay, because I'm done. I'm truly done with them. And I don't feel sad or upset, except that I spent so much of my life trying to be what they wanted. No more. And if today is a day for feeling thankful, I'll be thankful for that.

And more thankful that I found Jason when I did. Thankful for Lowery's bullets, too, in a twisted way. When I realized how close I'd come to dying, it had been almost stupidly simple to let go of everything that had hurt me for so long.

I'm thankful for Cole Matthews, too. In a very real sense, he saved my life that day—and not just by shooting Lowery. Maybe that's why I can't let go of him as easily as everything else. He's the reason I'm alive, so

a part of me belongs to him. Maybe a part of me will *always* belong to him.

Even if it does, it's only a part of me. But the rest of me seems determined to hang on to him, too.

I shouldn't blame myself for that. I shouldn't call myself an idiot. If I want to feel like shit and hear someone tell me how stupid I am, I could just go back to my parents' house. And really, who *wouldn't* be a little crazy about Cole Matthews? Especially after being kissed by him?

No one. That's who.

Except maybe my condescending iceberg of a mother.

More than a little tipsy, I lift my glass in a silent toast to her immensely cold heart, then carry the bottle of wine toward my bedroom, intending to find a heart-warming holiday movie to fall asleep to. I'm halfway across the living room when a knock sounds at my door. Wearing a flannel pajama shirt that hangs halfway to my knees and fuzzy red socks, I make a wavering detour and—because I'm drunk but not stupid—take a look through the peephole to see who it is.

And there he is. The one I can't let go. His hair's slightly disheveled. And he's been pushing his leg too hard again. The dumb jerk won't use his crutches as much as he should. His lips are tight, the edges of his mouth pale with strain. He shouldn't be on his feet at all, let alone coming to see me.

But he's not a robber, so I haul open the door.

Immediately his dark gaze runs all over me, from head to toe. Funny how much he does that now. I remember just a few minutes before Lowery started shooting, that I spotted Cole walking down the courthouse steps. Of course he didn't see me. But I thought then, *Look at me. Please. For once, just see me.*

Only a few minutes later, he did see me—when he was bleeding on the ground. He looked up into my eyes with such wonder and awe that even amidst all the terror, my heart felt like it would burst. But that bullet to his head must have knocked something loose in his brain at the time, because he hasn't looked at me like that again.

He's not looking at me like that now. Instead his gaze is searching and intense, his voice gruff. "You okay?"

Because the last time he saw me, I was a mess. But I'm better now. "Mmm-hmm," I tell him, showing him my bottle of wine. "Look. All good."

That doesn't seem to reassure him. He frowns. "You drank all that yourself?"

"I did. But don't worry," I add, suddenly realizing why he's frowning. "I don't make it a habit. I've seen *waaaaaay* too many livers."

"I bet." He glances past me. "Your brother's here, too? You've got someone with you?"

"My brainless frat boy boyfriend." I grin at Cole when he winces. "Jason thought that was hilarious. Before he passed out. Not from this"—I lift the bottle again—"but from all the stuffing and mashed potatoes.

Everyone blames the turkey but tryptophan only gets to your head so easily because your body's busy digesting all the carbs. Though the wine probably helps a little, too. Did you eat a lot?"

"Yeah, I did. Too much."

"Did you have to loosen your belt? But you have really hard abdominal muscles. I bet you didn't have to. While I was in training, I assisted during an autopsy on a guy who'd just finished Easter dinner. And he had a dozen eggs in his stomach. That wasn't what killed him—he was stabbed in the neck—but a dozen eggs! Did you eat *that* much?"

"Not quite." Laughter lights his dark eyes as he braces his shoulder against the door—taking the weight off his leg, I realize—and he holds out a small plastic container. "I brought this back for you."

I stare blankly at the little food storage tub. "What is it? Are those leftovers?" Excitement zips through me. "I've never had Thanksgiving leftovers before."

He shakes his head. "It's a piece of your pie. Didn't seem fair that you didn't get any. So I saved you some. Heroically, I'll add. I had to fight off Huertas *and* his kids when they went back for seconds—and his little girls are vicious. I barely survived."

Touched, I take the container. "So they liked the pie?"

"It was fucking amazing. To tell the truth, I almost ate this piece instead of giving it to you. But Sofia wanted to wash your dish before returning it, so Huertas will bring

it to work with him in the morning. And since I didn't bring your pie plate back, I had to bring something."

I don't care about the dish. "You should come in, then," I tell him, stepping back and opening the door wider. "We'll share this piece of pie and the rest of this wine, and you'll sit and rest your leg like you should."

He doesn't move right away. Instead he stares at me, then groans and drags a hand though his hair. "I shouldn't. You're drunk."

I frown at him. "What does that mean? Should I be afraid of you? Are you going to have sex with me while I'm impaired? That's gross. And not heroic at all."

His expression darkens. "Fuck no. But sex isn't the only way a guy like me can take advantage of someone who's drunk."

"A guy like you?"

"I want to get into your head even more than I want to get into your panties, angel."

Is that all? Joke's on him, then, because there's nothing *in* my head right now. Just mushy mush. "Jason's here and can protect my secrets," I remind him, then grab his hand when he still hesitates. "C'mon, Detective Matthews."

I pull him into my apartment—somehow I've only got hold of his forefinger, but that's apparently enough. He mutters something like, "I'm going to Hell," but kicks the door closed behind him and lets me lead him into the kitchen…though he probably knows where it is.

"Does your apartment look just like this?" I ask. "Same layout?"

"Pretty much."

I guess I don't have a reason to keep hold of his finger then. Sadly I let go, then head across the kitchen for plates and forks. "Since Jason's taking up the sofa, we'll have to stick to these barstools. I haven't put the dining set together yet."

"Works for me. I don't even have a dining set."

No dining set? I blink and look back at him. "Do you want one for Christmas?"

"No." With a laugh, he settles onto one of the stools at the breakfast bar. "Shit. Is this what happens when you drink too much? You become generous?"

"I'm always generous." I set the dessert plate in front of him. "It's a good thing, though. One day I'll run the Bennet Foundation and give away *lots* of money for the betterment of the city. Whenever my father asks why I'm wasting time in the medical examiner's office, I tell him that the best way to learn how we can improve every citizen's life is to be intimately familiar with what's killing them. Which is true, but not the only reason. And he thinks it's a stupid reason, anyway, but I don't. Do you want red wine or white or something else?"

"Water's good."

It takes an absurd amount of concentration to fill his glass with ice and water from the filtered pitcher in the refrigerator, and when I turn back to him, he's looking

over his shoulder at Jason. My brother's sprawled face-down on the sofa beneath a blanket.

Cole glances at me again as I sit on the stool beside his. "What'd you mean when you said you were the second-to-last person to know you had a brother?"

"Just that." Reaching for the plastic container, I pop open the lid. "I found out during a school dance, my senior year of high school. No surprise, my father sent me to St. Mary's, so we had to invite boys from other schools. One of the girls invited Jason."

"Why 'no surprise'? You aren't Catholic. And wait a second." He stops me as I begin to lift the pie from the container. "Why don't we just share it straight from the tub? Then you won't have dishes to clean."

"I like washing dishes," I tell him and set the pale green slice onto his plate. Some of the decorative whipped cream has softened and lost its shape, but otherwise it all held together well. "And my father is a pompous, controlling dick-weasel. So he thought if I was at a private girls' school, he could more easily direct my education and my social life."

"But he couldn't?"

"Not the education part. My social life…he was pretty good at controlling that. I didn't have many friends." Knife in hand, I frown over the slice, trying to figure out what's wrong with the shape of it, but my brain's not cooperating. "If I cut this in half, one side is all crust and the other half is just a point. That doesn't seem even."

With gentle fingers, Cole takes the knife and neatly cuts lengthwise down the center of the slice. "I don't believe the other girls didn't like you, angel."

"Some did," I admit. "But it was hard to trust any of them. Do you know that my freshman year, my father asked some of my friends to watch me? And tell him what I was doing and who I was talking to? And they *did*?"

His face darkens. "It sure as fuck doesn't surprise me."

"Yeah." My throat tightens as the memory of that betrayal hits me again, but I shake it off. That's all done with. "So I had friends, but after that, I always felt…a little distant from them. And of course that made some of the girls believe I was just a snob. *They* didn't like me much. And one of those girls was the one who brought Jason. Because even they had heard the rumors about the son my father had with his secretary. And this girl thought I'd be embarrassed when he showed up, or I'd be put in my place, or something."

"And what were you?"

"I didn't even know who he was. Just some guy that this girl brought over to talk to me. It was weird, because I didn't know her well. I thought maybe she was showing off her hot new boyfriend. I saw that *he* was embarrassed, but I was clueless. Then someone finally explained it, and my reaction…wasn't pretty." With my fork, I toy with the whipped cream, too mortified to look Cole in the eyes. "I suppose this is the part that I

should be careful about telling you. If you want to get into my head."

"Then don't tell me."

"I won't. Because I was *horrible*. I instantly hated him. So much. I thought his existence was the reason my father was never satisfied with anything I did, and why my mother was always disappointed in me, too. Because we weren't enough—*I* wasn't enough—to make my father happy. Not when he apparently had a perfect golden boy with another woman. So I said he wasn't my brother, that if my father really cared about him, he'd have given Jason the Bennet name. Then I was glad that hurt him." Sick shame churns in my stomach at the memory. "Then I ran out of there, bawling my head off— which of course got around to my mother, and then *she* was mad at me for embarrassing the Bennet name by being such a crybaby in public. And for acknowledging Jason at all. Sometimes I think she doesn't care that my father cheats on her. She just doesn't like being humili- ated by everyone knowing about it."

Cole's quiet for a moment. Then he says, "Seems to me Jason eventually forgave you."

Dull heat climbs up my face. "When I pulled my head out of my ass. And it turns out, Jason resented me, too, except he'd known about my existence for a lot longer. But he thought I was the princess who got all of our father's time and attention. Only after we met again—okay, what really happened was I tracked him

down and accused him of stealing my father—and we realized that our dear dad was just a selfish dickhead all around. And that I missed out on eighteen years of having a brother."

"But you're making up for it."

"Trying to," I agree. "I'm trying to make up for a lot of things I never did. Like making pies for Thanksgiving. Of course, I think that will go a lot better if I don't include my parents in the future." Listening to myself whine, I sigh. "But maybe I shouldn't complain about crappy holidays. It's not like I was hungry or didn't receive any gifts. My parents were just…who they are."

Cole's shaking his head. "You're right," he says quietly. "You'll do better without them. This is something I can tell you for sure, Mia. When I was a kid, we didn't have shit. We were poor as fuck. And—"

"See?" My face is burning. "I'll shut up."

"Don't you dare. Because if you let me finish, I'll tell you that I had friends who were in the same boat. Didn't have shit to their name. But they loved every damn holiday and Christmas, even if all they got was a pair of socks, because their families made something special of it. Just being together in that time was special to them. Me and my old man, though… Some years he had a girlfriend, some years he had a job, and some years that made it worse and some years that made it better. But I'll tell you the best Christmas I ever had was the first one away from home, sitting alone at a Denny's, eating

their turkey dinner. Because I was away from all that shit. You get away from that shit, too. And it'll get better. *This* Christmas, it'll be better. Because you'll make it better. And I'll help you."

His fierce expression wavers in front of me as tears fill my eyes. My heart's aching as I slide off my stool, and a hot lump of emotion is balled up in my throat. With me standing and him sitting, my height is about even with his, but I'm not close enough to see him properly, not with my vision all blurry. His hands curve around my waist when I push closer, all but straddling his right thigh, my arms linking around his neck.

With my face right up to his, I whisper, "Is this hurting your leg?"

"No, angel." He groans his answer, so he might be lying. Or maybe because I'm also making him hard in all the places he's not already hard. His chest can't get any harder. I'm pressed up tight against him, my breasts flattened against those steely pecs, and he's warm and solid and so wonderful.

"I like your face," I tell him.

I also like what telling him does to that face. He laughs a little, lines forming at the sides of his dark eyes, that smile making his mouth so wide and kissable. "I like your face, too."

Unable to resist, I unlace my fingers from behind his neck and trace those smiling lips with the fingertips of my right hand. "And I like your mouth. Even when you

look at me all frowningly for a long time."

Softly he says, "When did I do that?"

"Last Friday. When Dr. Childers and I were working on Eldon Jameson. You were staring at me and looked so unhappy with me. Were you?"

A heavy sigh slips past my fingers. "Not with you. But I don't like the idea of you down there, knowing the kind of shit you must see. It's not all old men and natural causes. Sometimes it's Hell." Gently he skims the backs of his knuckles down my cheek. "And an angel doesn't belong in Hell."

That's sweet. But he's got it all wrong. "I'm not an angel."

"Considering you were hovering over me when I thought I was dying, you better let me decide that."

"Then I'm an angel," I concede, since I can't argue with that impeccable logic. "But maybe think of it like this, instead: Heaven's already full of all the angels it needs. So Hell could use some more. Especially since I'll be one of the last people who ever takes care of the dead. I'll treat them with dignity and respect. And what we do *is* hard sometimes, but I'll do right by them and their loved ones. Like you try to do. Are you going to stop investigating just because it's hard sometimes?"

He doesn't answer that. He doesn't need to.

Suddenly exhausted, I lay my cheek against his shoulder. "Anyway, I can do that thing where you…separate yourself. Detach. Maybe I learned it from my mother.

The difference is that I come back. Re-attach. And go out into the world like that. With all my feelings intact."

"And that's when you're afraid of getting hurt?"

"Or of hurting someone else. But I'm not afraid in the autopsy suite. Maybe the best thing about dead people is that they can't hurt you…and you can't hurt them. You can hurt *for* them, and for the people they left behind. But on a one-to-one basis? No. You should take me to bed."

"Mia…" My name trails off on a hoarse groan. His hands tighten on my hips. "Don't think I'm rejecting you, because I *do* want you, but—"

"I'm so drunk, I don't think I can make it there without someone beside me, keeping me steady."

"Ah." His deep chuckle sounds against my ear. "You didn't eat any of your pie yet, though."

"Because I don't like pie."

"You don't like pie." He echoes it flatly, like the words are gibberish he's trying hard to understand.

"I don't really like any sweets. I only like baking them. And giving them away." I snuggle my face against his warm neck. He smells so good, with some kind of spicy cologne lingering against his skin. "But if I'd said that you could have the whole piece, I couldn't have lured you into my apartment. You would have just taken the pie over to your place. So I said we'd share. But I'll give my half to Jason."

Amusement deepens his voice. "You're a wily drunk."

"Mmm-hmmm." The whole world shifts and reels dizzily around me. I cling tighter to his shoulders. My voice rises in alarm as I realize what just happened and why I'm suddenly floating. "You don't have to carry me. Your leg—"

"Can do this." His tone allows no argument. "And the day I can't is the day I don't deserve to touch you at all."

"You're wrong," I tell him. "So wrong, you stubborn jerk."

But he's not listening. And Cole might be a stubborn jerk, but he manages to carry me down the hall without dropping me or limping too badly. My room's dark, only lit by a lamp on the nightstand. By the time he reaches my bed and sets me gently down, his taut features show the strain of his effort. So the last thing he needs to do is walk down the hall again.

I catch his hand. "Lie with me until I fall asleep."

His gaze narrows, as if he's wondering whether I'm being wily again.

"I'll be out within five minutes. And the rest will be good for your leg," I tell him before he can argue.

"Only five minutes, then." A storm moves across his expression, leaving behind a dark cloud. "Because last time I was here, Mia, you slammed your door in my face. I don't know why you invited me in here now and what changed, but I'm sure as hell not going to risk you hating my guts when you wake up, wondering if I took

advantage of you being drunk…more than I already have."

Self-recrimination edges the last with harsh bitterness. I roll over into the center of the bed, feel his long, hard body as he slides up behind me. "You didn't get anything out of my head that I wouldn't want you to know."

"A few days ago, you didn't want me to know anything."

I yawn and punch my pillow into place against my shoulder. "A few days ago, I didn't really trust you wouldn't hurt me."

"Now you do?"

"Mmm-hmmm."

"Why?"

"Because you offered to stay with me to make sure I'm okay." And I didn't know men were so talkative in bed. "Now, *shhhhhh*."

Frustration joins the laugh shaking his big body against me. "All right, angel." His silence lasts only a few seconds, but in that time I fall almost completely under. Until I hear him say, "What kind of mattress is this? This is the most comfortable shit I've ever been on."

"Like a cuddle from a cloud," I murmur. "Do you want one for Christmas?"

His laugh shakes against me again. His strong arms pull me in tighter against his chest, and I feel the brush of his lips against my temple. "No, angel. That's not what I want for Christmas."

"Tell me what you do want, then."

"Don't buy me anything."

"I don't know if I'll buy it. But I'm giving something to all my neighbors. Your gift is harder to figure out, though. You saved my life, so it should be something special."

"You've got that backwards, angel." His voice roughens. "You saved me, remember?"

"Not backwards. And *shhhhhh*."

He finally shhhs.

COLE

ETTING GO OF MIA'S WARM, SLUMBERING FORM and rising up out of the mattress that's like a gentle floating pull into sleep is about the hardest thing I've ever done. I want to stay, want to wake up beside her, with Mia still in my arms.

But this shit isn't right. Maybe she really has changed her mind about giving me a chance. Until she says it sober, though, I sure as hell shouldn't be touching her.

She was right about the short rest doing me good. My leg's not screaming at me so badly as I make my way back toward the kitchen. I'm not a bit surprised to see Mia's brother sitting on the barstool she vacated, finishing the pie she'd left out. He's been awake this whole

damn time—and he made sure I knew it, too. Looked me straight in the eyes while Mia was getting my water. I'm not sure if he heard every word she said, but more than likely. And I'm pretty fucking sure if I'd lingered in her bedroom much longer, he'd have come to haul me out.

I can't even be pissed about that. She's got someone looking out for her. And it's real clear that isn't something she's had all her life.

"She's asleep," I tell him. "And is going to wake up with a hell of a hangover. You gonna be here?"

With his fork, he points to the couch. "All night."

It's still relatively early. Not even eleven o'clock. Plenty of time for her to sleep. "Is she working in the morning or does she have the day off?"

"Working." Jason lifts his chin, gesturing to the other stool. "You want to have a seat?"

For a chat? "No."

My refusal doesn't faze him. As easygoing as ever, he replies, "Stand, then. Do you want to know what she didn't tell you?"

"Depends on why you're telling me."

"Because you said you'd help her make this upcoming holiday better. You meant that?"

"Of course I fucking meant it. I wouldn't have said it otherwise."

Nodding, he scrapes up the last bite of pie. "This really is good. And Mia's mother told her that she didn't

know what was more tasteless: a pie that looked as if it came from a roadside diner, or her own daughter. It was the first thing Patricia said when Mia got to the Bennet mansion today."

For a second, I can't see past the rage blinding me. Then I take the fucking seat.

And her brother's face isn't showing much, but a seething moment of silence passes before he continues. "Mia will just say her mother is cold, but it's a particular kind of cold that's done a number on her. Because Patricia doesn't just slip the knife in; she twists it. Their dinners aren't like most people's, you know? Not even on regular days. But on Thanksgiving they've got a fancy chef, invite the city's best. So Patricia makes Mia go and apologize to the chef for insulting him, because by bringing a pie she's insinuating that what he's made for their guests isn't good enough. Patricia's saying all this right in front of him, by the way. Because Mia's pretty sturdy on her own, standing up for herself—but drag someone else in, suggest they've been hurt by what she's done, and it just fucks her over. But of course Patricia knows that, so she'll use Mia to hurt someone else, because it hurts Mia even more. And the way Mia tells it, the chef is just completely fucking embarrassed and doesn't know what the hell to do, except to say no harm is done and the pie looks good, then Patricia turns that around and tells Mia that he just feels sorry for how pathetic she is. You want a beer?"

I think I need one. "Yeah," I say hoarsely.

Jason heads to the fridge. "Not that our dear old dad is any better. Because he's hoping to make a deal with a developer to build up that strip along the waterfront, so he makes sure that Mia sits right next to this fucker and tells her to be really nice to him. And Mia, she'll be nice to everyone—until they get flirty and handsy. Because who the fuck knows what our dad's suggesting to this guy before the dinner to make him think she'll welcome it. It's not the first time, either. And two guesses who gets blamed when she ends up telling the guy off, or slapping his hands away, or the deal falls through."

Using her as fucking bait. I *knew* there was some creepy shit behind Bennet's favor. Watching her, making sure she doesn't get a boyfriend or publicly date the wrong man, maybe souring the lure.

"You got any names?" My tone lets him know exactly what I'd do with them.

"Aside from our dad?" Jason shakes his head. Instead of coming back around to the barstool, he stands on the opposite side of the counter, slides my beer over before twisting open his own. "Mia says she's always handled it. And maybe she has. Apparently this guy apologized to her. And she says that she'll never go to their dinners again, so it doesn't matter."

It matters. "Her mom does this shit, too?"

"Oh, no. Patricia is always trying to set her up, but with men our age, and all from good families. Trying to

get her married off, I guess. And I honest-to-God don't know if she's doing it so that she can finally wash her hands of a daughter she never wanted in the first place, or to spite her husband and spoil his little honey trap, or to protect Mia from that shit—because she and Mia look a lot alike, and it's hard to believe Bennet started that crap with his daughter and not his wife."

"Yeah, it is." And might explain a hell of a lot about Mia's mother. Still wouldn't excuse the way she treats her.

Her brother leans forward, bracing his forearms on the counter. "So that was Mia's Thanksgiving. And you ask why I'm telling you, it's because she *knows* they're full of shit. Like, if she believed bringing that pie really was an insult, she wouldn't have given it to you. And she knows what they've done to her."

"Cut her open every single day of her life." No wonder she feels safer around dead people. *They can't hurt you.*

"Pretty much. She told you that she and I have been making up for lost time since we were eighteen. And that's true…but the first two years after Mia found out about me, she spent most of the time terrified that I was going to decide she was a worthless piece of shit, just like her parents told her she was. It was a while before she trusted that I wouldn't." His mouth twists and his eyes remain steady on mine. "She's been healing ever since, and she's trusting you a hell of a lot more quickly than she did me. But she's still easy to hurt. So

if you can't handle this shit, and can't handle what'll be coming at you when her parents find out she's looking in your direction, let her know right away."

"I can handle it." I'll stand strong through anything she needs me to. "And in the meantime, I'll find a way to blow their goddamn house down."

"Oh, well." He suddenly grins. "No worries about that. Mia has a plan of her own, for after she takes control of the Bennet family's assets and the foundation. So it'll just be a few more years."

"And that sounds too fucking long."

Her brother shrugs. "She'll be the first to tell you: She's not in a rush."

COLE

Chief Jackson's assistant finds me a few minutes on his schedule just after noon. Going directly to him isn't something I'd usually do. If I have a problem, I take it to my lieutenant. But since this started with the chief, and was never an official part of my job, I take it straight there, instead.

He knows I don't jump up the chain of command, either. So he takes one look at me from behind his desk and says, "Is this about Mia?"

"Yes, sir."

Concern furrows his brow. "Is she in trouble?"

"Getting out of it, I think, now that she's away from her parents. But there might be a shit storm coming our

direction."

He leans back in his chair, eyes narrowing. "What kind of shit storm?"

"In the form of John Bennet. Because I'm going to marry Mia, sir."

Chief's got one hell of a poker face. His brain must be racing but I can't tell what he's thinking. Slowly he rises from his desk, walks over to the window overlooking the courtyard. Finally he says evenly, "When?"

"I don't know yet. I haven't asked her. Maybe I will next week, maybe five years from now. But I thought it best to give you a heads-up, considering the favor Bennet asked of me—and because you vouched for my character, and assured him I wouldn't have any impure designs on his daughter. But I do."

He bows his head, and his voice sounds a little choked, as if holding back a laugh when he asks, "Does that mean you intend to have relations with Mia Bennet outside the sanctity of marriage, detective?"

"Yes, sir." As often as I can.

Slowly he nods. "Well, you're right. That'll be a shit storm. But nothing this department can't weather. And it sure as hell doesn't hurt that you're the cop who took down Lowery. Bennet will have a hard time finding anyone willing to throw dirt at you."

I didn't need his approval to pursue Mia, but it feels damn good knowing he'll have my back. "Thank you, sir."

"And good luck with the asking," he says.

"I'm sure I'll need it."

Especially after last night. I haven't had a chance to see her yet today. She was gone by the time I knocked on her door this morning, and the day after any holiday is a fucking circus at the station. Add in Black Friday, and I'm just thankful I'm not in uniform and on patrol anymore.

When I get back to the bullpen, Huertas is up on his feet and hunched over his desk with his landline against his ear—I've seen him in that pose before. Barely waiting to hang up before he's ready to run out the door.

"What's happened?"

He puts down the phone and pulls on his jacket. "Word is, a certain autopsy technician eats her lunch in the courtyard every day. Even during winter."

Ah shit. "Don't you fucking jump ahead of me—"

"Sorry, brother." He snatches up the box in which Mia's serving dish and pie plate are nestled carefully against each other and padded by Sofia's best tea towels. "But I'm under orders. If I don't report back to my wife and tell her what kind of woman sends a two-thousand-dollar sterling silver serving plate to a stranger's house in a *grocery bag*, I won't ever be allowed to come home."

"I can tell you what kind of woman she is," I growl and try to head him off, but the fucker's nimble and my leg sure as hell isn't going to cooperate in a chase. "She's fucking perfect."

"That's what you said last night." Huertas spreads his arms helplessly, like this is all out of his control, and backs away. "You should have just brought her with you, let us have a look at her. Saved all this trouble. Now we get to see how fast you can run."

I can't run at all, so his slowest jog gets him beyond reach in no time. Shaking my head, I don't even try to catch him. Huertas won't screw me over. He won't ever do that. Still, by the time I've dragged on my coat, grabbed my lunch, and made my way down to the courtyard, he'll have had time to share two or three stories about my early days on the force that will be mostly true, and all stupid.

A gazebo sits in the center of the courtyard, which is probably why I missed seeing her here every damn day. From the second floor of the station, the only view is of the gazebo's roof. And if you're walking by the courtyard along the street, seeing in through the sides of the gazebo is no problem, except the same roof blocks most of the light. So you can see people sitting in there but they're shadowed. You have to actually head into the courtyard to get a good look—but I don't spend a lot of time wandering through the walkways and flowers.

Right now those walkways are shoveled clear and salted, and the flowerbeds are covered in a thick blanket of snow. I make my way to the entrance of the gazebo. Wooden benches ring the circumference of the interior, with wrought-iron café tables pulled up to the benches

to provide makeshift seating. Mia's sitting on a bench with Huertas on her right, her pale blue eyes bright and full of interest as she listens to him. A squat Thermos soup container is sealed closed on the table in front of her, along with a coffee cup from the barista's stand inside the county building.

And she *is* perfect. And utterly fucking gorgeous. A red stocking cap covers her black hair, and her cheeks and nose are pink with cold. She looks over as I climb the gazebo stairs, my steps heavy on the wooden treads, and a smile curves those full pink lips. Amusement sparkles in her eyes, and she's still listening to Huertas run his mouth as I make my way over to them.

But there's no anger when she looks at me. No accusation. So maybe she doesn't mind me knowing all of what she told me last night. Or maybe she doesn't remember telling me.

I grab one of the outdoor chairs and swing it over in front of her table. There's a break in their conversation as I ease into the seat, and now there's uncertainty and hesitancy in her smile as she regards me.

"You all right?" I ask her gruffly. "You must have left early this morning."

The pink in her cheeks deepens. "Jason dragged me to a breakfast diner. Said the best cure for a hangover is a greasy plate of bacon and eggs, followed up by pancakes."

"We can attest to that." Huertas waves a finger between him and me. "Especially in our younger days."

Yeah, she doesn't need to hear any of those stories. "Is he filling your head with his usual bullshit? You shouldn't believe anything he says."

"He was actually setting me straight." She glances over at my partner with a grin. "He was so nice, I naturally assumed that when you two did your good cop/bad cop thing, that he must play the good cop."

"I can't blame you for that assumption." I pull out one of the sandwiches Sofia sent along with Huertas this morning and unwrap it. "It's because I'm so big and strong, yeah? So I can intimidate a suspect easier than he can."

"I think she's saying you're an asshole."

Mouth full of turkey and bread, I nod. That's a fair reason to make that assumption, too.

Mia reaches for her coffee, looking over the rim at me when she takes her sip. "So you're the good cop?"

"More like 'sympathetic' cop," Huertas tells her, since I'm still chewing. "I'm the hardass, right? I play it like I don't give a shit what their problems are, all I care about is nailing their balls to the wall. But this fucker here, he'll soften up. He'll tell them some story about his dying grandma or stealing bread to feed his little sister or some old girlfriend who just kept stringing him along—so they start thinking he *understands* them, that he's just like them deep down inside, and they begin opening up. Doesn't always work, but works often enough you'd be surprised. And you'd be shocked how

many ways his old grandma has died."

She gives him a wry glance. "Probably not too surprised."

"That's right," Huertas says it like her working in the morgue had slipped his mind, and this wasn't what he was hoping to know about her from the first. "You're down there with all the grandmas. How'd you get started with that?"

Though she provided a little more insight while she was straddling my thigh last night, I expect to hear that bit about her liking puzzles. Instead she breaks out with a laugh and says, "I was trying to scare away a date."

I stop with the second turkey sandwich halfway to my face. "What now?"

"About three years ago," she says. "My family's charity foundation hosts a gala every New Year's Eve. And my mother always sets me up with some guy. Usually they're just boring, but this one was—" She screws up her face, sticks out her tongue, and shudders as if a toad just crawled into her mouth. "But Dr. Childers was at my table, and I knew who she was, so I deliberately started up a conversation about decomposition speed and maggot growth. And she picked up on what I was doing right away, trying to get rid of this guy, so she started telling us these stories… God, even *I* was grossed out. And my date had a weak stomach, so it didn't take long before he was gone. So Joan and I spent the rest of the time talking, and by the end of the night

I realized what I wanted to do."

Huertas is fucking delighted by that story. "Are you saying in that short time she convinced you to start helping her cut up dead bodies? That's some cult-like powers there."

"Ha, no." Though Mia's smiling, there's something distant and melancholy in her voice as she continues, "I was already interested in forensic pathology. What Joan told me was that she wished that she hadn't tried to do it all at once—getting married, med school and then her residency, and having kids. Said it nearly broke her. And that if she had to do it again, she'd take a slower path. A steady job in the field—such as being an autopsy technician—until her kids were older. Then go back to school when she was thirty-five or forty, so she wouldn't have missed so much of their lives."

"She's not wrong," Huertas says, suddenly solemn. "This job's got some crazy hours, but I'm lucky. I'm home most nights and weekends, spend a lot of time with my girls and my wife. I know some guys, though…they aren't ever getting those years back. Or their families back. And it's not fucking worth it."

Mia nods. "It made sense to me. And I'm fortunate that I don't have to worry about promotions or earnings, so…" She trails off with a shrug. "I don't need to rush."

"Though it sounds like you want to start a family pretty early, and I guess you need help with that," Huertas says with a subtle glance in my direction.

Yeah, real subtle. Mia's cheeks go red.

I toss my wadded sandwich wrap at him. "Get the fuck out of here."

He takes his time doing it, thanking Mia for last night's pie, saying he hopes to see her again soon. She's gracious and sweet until he actually gets going, then she bites her lip, falling quiet while regarding me from across the table, as if waiting for me to say something first.

So I do, spilling it out easily, as if the words aren't as important or as true as they are. "You want babies, I'm willing. Though not currently able."

Her answer is just as breezy. "That's okay. *In vitro* is an option."

And I can't fucking pretend anymore. "So you'll take a pass on having me inside you? You don't want me fucking you so deep and hard that you'll be feeling every inch of my cock for days? Are you in that much of a rush?"

Her pale blue eyes lock on mine, full of all the fire and need that must be burning in my own. Her response is a breathless, "I'm not in any rush."

"Good. Because if we're doing that part of it right, there shouldn't be any rushing at all." And getting pushy sure as hell didn't work out so well before. I force myself to ease up. "We'll take this thing between us one day at a time, yeah?"

Not that I can take it much faster. My cock has no

trouble getting hard—it's a goddamn stone right this instant—but I can't do much with it yet, not without a lot of pain and being a hell of a disappointment. And I'd be lying if I said that didn't bother the shit out of me. But this time I won't take that out on her. I'll heal soon enough, and there's plenty of ways to make sure she's satisfied in the meantime.

"All right." Despite that agreement, she bites her lip again, and the sudden wary light in her eyes gets my back up. Her fingers play nervously with her soup spoon as she says, "Last night, what you said to me about your first Christmas away from your father... Was that all true?"

"Because I told you I wanted into your head, you're worried I did that sympathetic good cop thing?" My gaze is rock-steady on hers as she nods, her cheeks coloring guiltily. "I'll never play that shit with you, Mia. Everything you get from me, it's real."

"Sorry. I just—"

"Don't be sorry." Trusting people can't be easy for her. But even the most trusting person might wonder, considering who I am and what I do. "Anyway, I wouldn't need to. I've known some talkative drunks, but you're in a class of your own."

Blushing and laughing, she nods again. "I really am."

Not that she told me everything. She left plenty of holes. And thinking back to what her brother filled in for me last night, tension tightens the muscles along the

back of my neck. "You said you weren't going to any more of your parents' dinners. What about that New Year's gala shit? Are you stuck doing that?"

She waves that away. "That's different. It's for the foundation, and I'll be at the head of it in a few years. So attending is part of being a Bennet. But I barely have to talk to my parents there—and I like knowing who our donors are."

Including rich donors with sons near her age? "Did your mom set you up with another useless fucker?"

"She tried to, but..." She trails off and a funny expression rolls over her face. "Remember last night, when I said you saved my life and you said I had it backwards?"

Since I was holding her close, I'm not likely to forget it. And I suppose that settles the question of whether she remembers everything we talked about. "Yeah."

Her chest lifts on a deep breath, as if she's gathering the courage to tell me what comes next. "That morning—the day Lowery showed up—that morning during breakfast, my mother asked me to confirm her plan for me to attend the gala with a date she'd picked out. I told her that I'd find my own date, instead. And she said…well, it doesn't matter what she said."

But I can imagine what it must have been. Not just sticking in the knife. Twisting it.

She continues, "So I was sitting right here eating my lunch, like I always am, and I saw you coming out of the courthouse." Her gaze turns toward the street where I'd

been that day, then she glances back at me. "I think you had just finished up in court?"

"It was my turn in the box for the Chalmers' trial, yeah." Then while walking back to the station, I saw Lowery getting out of his truck with an assault rifle. But I hadn't seen Mia sitting here.

I don't like thinking about how many times I probably walked by with her sitting here. Without any clue that everything I've ever wanted was so damn close.

"And I said to myself, I'm going to ask Detective Matthews to be my date at the gala. So I stood up"—she does now, taking a step toward me—"and Lowery started shooting."

The bottom drops out of my stomach. Because now that she's out of her seat, I see what her body was hiding—a splintered hole through the side of the gazebo wall, where a bullet had passed through. Right where her heart would have been if she'd been sitting.

Everything I'd ever wanted was so damn close…and I almost lost her before I even knew she existed.

My breath explodes from my lungs on a harsh curse. My hand snags the belt of her coat and I haul her closer, my head tipping back as I drag her mouth down to mine. She gives a welcoming assent through parted lips, her hands burying themselves in my hair, her knee braced on the seat between my legs as she bends over me, kissing me as if there's nothing else she ever wants to do.

Except there's a whole lot more we both want to do, and it's with a reluctant moan that Mia stops. Panting, she lifts her head, her lips soft and swollen and her pale blue eyes gazing down into mine. My angel, in the living flesh.

"I'll go with you to that gala," I tell her hoarsely. "If you're still asking."

Laughter brightens her expression. "I am. And I'd like that."

"I'll warn you that I'm not too good at dancing, though."

"I don't care. I'm asking because I like your face." Her cold palms frame my jaw, and she drops another soft kiss to my mouth before sighing and backing away. "I have to get back to work soon…but I've got another minute or two."

I do, too. Hopefully it'll be long enough for my cock to settle down. "You have lunch here every day?"

"Yes."

"You want company if I can get away from the desk?"

"Yes." She lifts her coffee cup and begins to lower herself onto the bench across from me.

"Oh, *fuck no*." My urgent tone freezes her in place, and she looks across the table at me in alarm. My heart's pounding a fucking mile a minute. "Don't sit there again. Christ."

Her tension vanishing, she laughs at me. "Cops are so superstitious."

"It's not superstition. It's our guts reminding us that behaviors create patterns. And patterns repeat."

"Yeah, well"—she sits—"I'm determined to break this particular pattern."

Not the bullet, I realize. She means everything leading up to it. Her mother. Her entire childhood. Her past holidays. And all those plans she has for the future that she was telling Huertas about, they're just making sure her children don't experience the same things that she did.

And put like that— "I've got a few patterns I'd like to break, too," I tell her.

She raises her coffee cup in a toast to me. "One day at a time, then?"

"Yeah," I agree. Even if taking it slow kills me.

At least it'll be a real sweet death.

MIA

MAYBE THERE'S SOME IRONY THAT, TO BREAK my own pattern, I fall into the larger one of holiday consumerism. Actually, I don't even 'fall.' That sounds like an accident, and I deliberately run toward it, embracing it with all my might. Thanksgiving was only yesterday, but I find an all-Christmas station on my car radio and turn it up, then sing along to the carols I know. I head to Home Depot and, after a workshop where I learn how to use a lathe, load up a shopping cart with decorations. Then I drive to the tree lot and pick out the tallest tree that I can drag around by myself, my heart bursting with the thrill of hope.

This year *will* be different. In every single way. Not

because of these decorations or this tree, but because I'm finally free. And I've never been this happy.

At my apartment building, I wrestle the tall pine from the top of my car, thankful the twine binding the branches didn't break on the drive home. Dragging the heavy tree across the snow and into the lobby is difficult enough. I'm out of breath by the time I reach the elevator—but still loving every second of this.

When the elevator opens on the third floor, I grip the base of the tree trunk in my gloved hands and start hauling it backwards down the hallway. My heart swells again when I hear a door swing open, then Cole's laughing, "Holy shit, angel. That thing's bigger than I am. Let me help you."

I won't say no. Especially since he shows up beside me wearing faded jeans and a T-shirt that clings to his arms and chest as if the fabric loves every inch of his skin.

But I have to warn him, "You might want to put on gloves first. I've got sap all over mine."

"I'm sure I've had stickier shit on my hands," he says dryly. "Give that over to me and go unlock your door."

I do, taking a second to catch my breath and admire the flex of his thick biceps when he begins pulling the tree toward me.

My ogling doesn't go unnoticed. "I thought it was my face you liked," he tells me.

I do. Especially the day's growth of stubble shadowing

his jaw, lending him a disheveled, dangerous air. But I'm not ashamed to admit, "I like your arms, too." And since he's coming at me backwards, "And the way your jeans fit."

"They won't fit much longer if you keep talking like that. Where do you want this?"

I haven't thought that far ahead. "Just drop it wherever. I'll be right back—I need to run down and grab the tree stand."

Along with everything else I bought. It takes four trips from my car to the elevator, and this time when I get to the third floor with my bags and boxes stacked all around me, Cole's standing right there—wearing his boots and coat.

Relief is naked on his face when he sees me. "You and I have different definitions of 'right back,' angel. And I need your damn cell number."

"Sorry. It took longer than I thought." And no one has really cared before. I flutter my eyelashes up at him. "But I'll give you my phone number if you help me carry this stuff, too?"

"Shit. You're so fucking cute," he mutters, then cups his hand behind my neck and pulls me in for a hard kiss. "Now load me up."

A six-foot-four helper makes everything easier, and four trips becomes one. It's with a huge sense of accomplishment that I dump everything I'm carrying onto the sofa, then unload Cole.

As soon as his arms are free, he cups my face and kisses me again, slower and sweeter. Then murmurs against my lips, "Let's get that tree up, then."

I'd rather continue kissing him, but the thought of putting up the tree has me bouncing with excitement. I drag off my coat and gloves, tossing them onto the pile of decorations to deal with later. "Where do you think it should go?"

He points to the bay window in the small dining area. "Maybe over there, so you can see it from the couch? Or where do you spend most of your time?"

"The kitchen. But I can see that spot from there, too." I sort through the boxes, looking for the tree stand. "Have you ever used one of these stands before? The guy at the store said it was the best one on the market but that it's always tricky getting the tree straight, no matter which one you use."

"I haven't put a tree up before. But I'm sure we'll figure it out."

I look up at him in surprise. "Never?"

He shakes his head. "I never bothered."

Uncertainty strikes me. "Is it a bother now?"

"Not a bit, angel." His lips twitch. "It's shaping up to be more fun than I expected. Though we'll probably end up with a crooked tree."

We. Just hearing him put it like that makes me so happy, I don't care if it's leaning drunkenly against the wall when we're done.

It's not. Instead it's only a *little* crooked after we get the screws into the trunk and then adjust them and unscrew the whole thing and rotate the tree and screw them in and adjust them again. Then Cole says that he's pretty damn sure the tree is just fucking with us and that it'll look less lopsided when the branches are open—so we cut the twine and it *does* look better, it looks absolutely magical, and I can only stand in front of the bare tree with my hands clasped and eyes shining.

After a long moment, I look to Cole. He's examining the tree with his arms crossed over his chest and wearing an utterly masculine expression of satisfaction—and most of his weight braced on his right leg.

"I think this calls for a celebratory drink while we sit on the sofa and look at the tree and feel proud of ourselves," I tell him.

He grins. "We should."

"Any preference in drinks?"

"I'll take a beer."

I bring him one of the bottles I keep on hand for Jason, then start making room on the big leather sofa, moving aside the bags and boxes I brought in, shifting everything to the floor.

Cole starts to help, then abruptly stops, looking into one of the plastic bags. His voice sounds tight with strain when he says, "You bought this today?"

I glance inside the bag, recognize the ice cream scoop with the wooden handle that I shaped in the lathing

workshop. "I made it, kind of."

"You *made* it?"

I narrow my eyes at him. Is it that hard to believe? "In a workshop. Not the metal scoop part, but the rest of it. I'm giving it to Dr. Childers for Christmas."

His broad shoulders start shaking and he slowly sinks onto the sofa, putting his head in his hand. "You're giving this to your boss?"

"Because she makes her own ice cream at home. I'm trying to give more personalized gifts this year."

"*Personalized?*" A deep laugh explodes from him. "I suppose it can't get more personal than this. Angel, have you *looked* at it?"

Of course I have. But I sit beside him and pull it out of the bag, turning the scoop in my hand, trying to figure out what's so hilarious. I did a good job. The wood handle is long and thick and smooth, about eight inches long and with a rounded decorative knob at the end that I'm especially proud of, considering that it was my first time using a lathe.

Catching his breath, Cole wipes his eyes. "Think dirty, Mia."

I do, and even when realization strikes…I still can't see it. "You think *this* looks like a penis?" I shake my head. "It's way too big."

His eyebrows shoot upward. "Is it?"

Bigger than most of the penises I see, though maybe they shouldn't count. Very few of those are erect. "And

it's too smooth."

"And not the kind of toy a person usually gets for Christmas."

Oh. *Ohhhh*. Suddenly mortified, I stare at it with widened eyes, unable to see anything else now that he's said *toy*. "I almost gave my boss a giant wooden dildo."

"With a handy scoop at one end. And maybe it's not such a bad gift after all. Get some ice cream on one side, pussy on the other, and a man has all the necessary food groups in one convenient meal."

Oh god. I can't stop my giggle. Then Cole reaches past me to set his beer on the coffee table, and when he gently pries the scoop from my fingers and sets it aside, too, I can barely breathe past the anticipation racing through me.

His thumb brushes my bottom lip. "So you think that was too big?"

"Bigger than anything I could ever use."

His head lowers and I close my eyes. But instead of the kiss I was expecting, he eases me down lengthwise along the sofa, with my shoulder and right side against the back of the couch. His big hand captures my wrists and pulls them over my head, pinning my arms against the leather cushion. He follows me down, lying flush against me on his side.

His free hand cups my cheek. His piercing gaze holds mine. "I swore I would never hurt you, Mia," he says in a low voice. "And I'm about to ask you a few

things—those aren't to hurt you, either. Instead it's to make sure I never do. This isn't to embarrass you or judge you. All right?"

I nod into his palm. "I wouldn't be with you if I didn't trust you."

"That's good, angel." Gravel roughens his reply. "But have you ever been with anyone else? Ever trusted them that much? Girls, boys?"

Biting my lip, I shake my head.

His body stiffens slightly. But he doesn't move, doesn't say anything in response to the discovery that he'll be my first—just stares at me, his dark eyes intense, his jaw tight. Finally he says gruffly, "You've made yourself come before, though?"

"Sure. I masturbate all the time."

Amusement flickers across his expression. His palm leaves my cheek, and I shiver as he casually flicks open the top button of my shirt. My hands are still trapped over my head, a position that subtly arches my back. Every one of my panting breaths strains the cotton over my sensitive breasts.

Until he unfastens the button in the valley between them. Then the shirt gapes open, exposing my lacy pink bra. "With just your fingers?"

"Sometimes a toy." I lift higher, encouraging his touch on my bare skin, but he simply moves down to the next button.

"But nothing like that ice cream scoop."

A breathy laugh huffs from me. "No."

"Just a vibrator? Or something inside you?" The final button gives way beneath his fingers, and he spreads the sides of my shirt. "Holy fuck, Mia. You're so damn beautiful."

The way he looks at me, I feel as if I must be. His gaze worships my belly, his callused palm sliding up over its soft swell. I arch my back again, so that he can more easily reach the clasp of my bra behind me. But his hard fingers simply grasp the lacy cups and drag them down beneath my breasts, and even though I'm lying on my back, the tension from my shoulder straps gives them a gravity-defying lift. It's like the most uncomfortable underwire ever, until he groans at the sight of me, at the sight of the lingerie plumping my breasts, my nipples hard and flushed a dark pink, and then it just feels sexy and naughty and wonderful.

"It's both," I tell him, and by the glazed look in his eyes, I realize he doesn't remember what he asked me. "The toy. You want me to bring it out here?"

His mouth curves and slowly he shakes his head. His hand slides down to the waistband of my jeans. With his gaze on mine, he pops open the snap. "Both…so it's one of those rabbit things, then? It has a dick to fill you up and little ears to tease your clit?"

"Yes." I can barely breathe or think, because he's unzipping my pants. Cole Matthews is unzipping my pants. Frantically I raise my hips, but he doesn't drag my

jeans down, or do anything except loosen them.

His head dips and it isn't until I hear his soothing, "Shh, angel. There's no rush," against my ear that I hear the urgent sounds I'm making. His mouth finds mine in a long, slow kiss—maybe in an attempt to slow all of me down, but with my hands pinned over my head and the heavy warmth of his palm resting on my lower belly and his tongue stroking against mine, there's no slowing. My heart just pounds faster and the liquid heat between my legs just gets hotter, wetter.

With a soft groan, he breaks the kiss. The ragged heave of his chest tells me that despite his words, his body isn't going any slower, either. "I need to know how much you're comfortable with, Mia," he tells me gruffly, and my breath stops when his hand slides into my panties. "And that toy is all right for you?"

"Yes," I whisper, then everything inside me clenches at the first brush of fingers over my clit.

A harsh sound rips from his chest. "*So* wet, Mia. Ah fuck. Christ."

His fingers delve deeper, slicking through my intimate folds. But not deep enough. There's no room in there with my jeans barely loosened, and rocking my hips only moves his hand with me, doesn't push his touch where I want it to go. Gritting my teeth, I moan in helpless frustration.

"That's how I feel, too, angel." With a tortured laugh, he bends his head, kisses the corner of my mouth. "Is

this all right, then?"

This is his finger pressing into me, thick and long. "Yes," I gasp. "It's *so* all right. And more."

"You can take more?"

"Please." I beg, then cry out as I'm suddenly fuller, as full as I've ever been.

"Like this—about two fingers' worth? This is how much you're used to taking?"

I can't answer, only rock my hips, riding his hand.

"You're so fucking tight," he growls against my ear. "You must have to fight to get it in every damn time."

Wildly I shake my head. "Not anymore. Not if I'm wet enough."

"You're wet enough. You're so fucking wet you could take every inch of my cock." With a harsh groan, he buries his face in my throat. His ragged breath is hot against my neck. "But not yet. So tell me what you like, angel. Tell me how you make yourself come. You fuck that toy dick in and out of your pussy? Or just let the vibrator tease your clit?"

As he asks, his thumb circles that engorged flesh. My hips jerk, a choked cry escaping me when he does it again. "That," I tell him on a strangled breath. "That."

"And what's in your head when you do? You imagining it hard and fast, or—"

"You." It's a guttural confession torn from deep within me. "I just imagine it's you. That's how I get wet enough."

His hand stills. "Me?"

"Ever since the first time I saw you."

Cole lifts his head, his gaze burning into mine. Slowly his thumb begins to circle again. "So you imagine that's my dick inside you."

Full and stretching me, like his fingers are. "Yes," I breathe.

"And when you come, it's my dick that your pussy is squeezing so tight. Do you imagine what happens after that, angel? How the feel of your hot little pussy clamping down on my cock will make me lose my fucking mind? How I'll hold you down and fuck deep and hard until I've unloaded every drop of my cum inside you?"

Oh my god. Helplessly aroused by that explicit image, I roll my hips against his hand, trying to get to that place, when everything tightens and shatters.

Relentlessly teasing my clit, he bends his head and captures my bottom lip between his teeth before releasing it to murmur, "Is what you imagine like this, angel?"

No. "This is so much better," I tell him, and he rewards me with a kiss, his tongue slicking over mine in the same slow rhythm as his fingers move inside me.

And everything within me is spiraling up, up. His fingers are patient and endless, his mouth hot as he breaks the kiss and lowers his head to my breast, latching on to my hardened nipple. The suction of his mouth begins an endless swirl of pleasure, sweeping me higher, my body rising in a taut bow—and the gentle pluck of his thumb against my clit sends me flying. I cry out, my

inner muscles clinging to his slowly thrusting fingers.

"You're so perfect, Mia," he groans against my breast, then claims my mouth in another lingering kiss as I sigh and soften against him. He releases my wrists and I hold him close, sliding my fingers into his thick hair, loving every sweet blissful moment passing between us.

But it isn't over yet. Because when he lifts his head again, his eyes are dark and intense, the need still smoldering. And his voice has a rough, primitive edge when he says, "I'm sorry to tell you, angel—what you imagined isn't anything close to what it'll be like with me."

I go still. The erection straining against his zipper is obviously much thicker and longer than his fingers were, but something in his tone tells me that's not exactly what he means. Suddenly trembling with uncertainty, I ask, "What will it be like, then?"

He doesn't tell me. Instead he pushes upright. Hard hands grip my hips. A surprised cry breaks from me when he suddenly swings my body around, so that I'm lying with my shoulders pressed up against the back of the sofa and my butt hanging over the edge of the cushions—with Cole kneeling in front of me.

Without a word, he tears off his T-shirt, revealing all that glorious muscle, the chiseled pecs and sculpted abs flexing beneath golden skin dusted with dark hair. He reaches forward and strips my jeans and panties down my hips, before rocking back to yank them completely free of my legs. Instinctively I clench my thighs together,

my hands flying down to cover that utterly vulnerable part of me that he's already touched but never seen, because this is not the sweet and gentle Cole. This is Cole, ravenous and feral and unrestrained. And I know he won't hurt me. But all that power and intensity is a little intimidating.

Tossing aside my jeans, he glances at my hands before raising his burning eyes to mine. "You don't want my mouth on your cunt?"

"I do," I whisper. "So much."

Hunger etches harsh lines beside his lips. "Then open up."

I try. I want to. But I'm so overwhelmed and so wet and so sensitive that, although I remove the shield of my hands, my legs won't follow my brain's order to unclench.

"Offer up that sweet pussy, Mia." His large palms cup my knees and his voice lowers dangerously. "Or I'll take what you're too shy to give."

Oh my god. Anchoring myself, I dig my shaking fingers into the edge of the cushions beside my hips. "Take it, then."

Primal need flares through his eyes. Roughly he shoves my knees apart, but he doesn't have to force them. At the first push of his hands, the muscles holding my thighs locked together release their tension. A growl of approval rumbles from his chest as he spreads me wide.

And takes. First with his eyes, taking a long, long look while I wait in the agonizing grip of erotic anticipation.

Then he lowers his head.

He claims my pussy in a long, hot lick from my entrance to clit that sends me reeling. Oh god. He was right. This is nothing like I imagined. Not just because the reality of his tongue is so, *so* much better than anything I dreamed. I knew it would be. And there's nothing he does that I haven't imagined. The way he kisses the sultry lips of my pussy, teasing that sensitive flesh with his teeth. The way he licks deeper, and the slow and sensual thrust of his tongue inside me. The way he pins my hips when he begins to suck on my clit, his forearm holding me in place when my body begins to writhe beneath the exquisite torment of his mouth.

But I always imagined it would be for *my* enjoyment. That it would be similar to what he did before, slowly testing my level of comfort and discovering how my body responds, so that he can bring me to a shattering orgasm. Yet from that very first lick, this hasn't been about giving me pleasure.

This is about Cole taking his.

And he told me. Told me that he'd take what I didn't give. And he does, claiming my pussy as if it's not mine but *his* to use as he pleases—and my pussy must please him, he must love it, because even after I come he doesn't ease up, but takes possession of that orgasm, too, as if my clenching flesh and the rush of wetness and even my screams are simply his due. Yet they don't satisfy his hunger, don't please him enough, because he

opens me wider and goes back for more, though *I* can't take any more, or give any more. But he's taken me over, and even as I sob in ecstasy when his lips close around my engorged clit and he sucks on that bundle of nerves while his tongue flicks and flicks, though I'm begging "I can't again, I can't," he *makes* me come again, and again, my pussy and my pleasure under his command.

I'm a shuddering, boneless mess when he finally has enough, lifting his head after a last, lingering lick. With smoldering satisfaction he looks down at me, at my legs spread wide and my knees pinned to the edge of the sofa by his hands, at the wetness glistening halfway down the length of my inner thighs. Yet he still isn't done claiming. As Cole rises over me, he doesn't allow any space between us, his hair-roughened chest gliding over all that wetness between my legs, then deliberately moves higher, allowing his abdomen to drag slowly over my over-sensitized pussy as if collecting every drop he'd wrung from me.

I'd thought he'd taken off his shirt so I could have a little eye-candy while he went down on me. But that apparently was for his own pleasure, too. So that we could be skin to skin. So that he could cover himself in my arousal. I smell myself all over his face, then taste myself when he kisses me, taking my mouth with the same hunger that he took the rest of me.

And I love the way he takes me.

Instinctively I begin to wrap my legs around his waist,

but freeze as I recall the last time I did. Cole raises his head—his eyes still burning. Because he's not boneless and limp. He's hard and big against me.

"What about you?" My throat's raw from screaming and begging. "Don't you need to come?"

"Better not." But he doesn't sound frustrated by that. Instead he sounds pleased as he slides his hands beneath my bare butt to raise me higher onto the cushion. He follows me up, lifting me and turning me before settling against him again—with Cole lying on the sofa with his head propped up on the cushy arm, me tucked against his right side with my head pillowed on his shoulder— and giving both of us a view of the Christmas tree.

But I've also got a view of his long body stretched out on the sofa, and of the way his erect cock looks like a tree trunk trapped behind the denim of his jeans. "Not even with my hand?"

"Not yet." He presses a kiss to my hair. "I tried your mitten. It was the first time I'd jacked off since getting shot, and it was going pretty damn well until I was about to come. Then you know how your body just kind of tightens up and it's like a little seizure hits?"

"Yes." That happened to me a few times today.

"It felt like I ripped my dick off."

"Ow." I cringe in sympathy. "Not good."

"You're telling me."

I lift my head. "Do you know, I've actually *seen*—"

"Nope." Laughing, he stops me. "Let that story wait

until we're eating dinner or something. Not while you're naked against me."

"Okay." With a grin, I lay my cheek on his shoulder again, then slide my hand over his chest—which is still slightly wet. "This was really dirty, rubbing yourself all over me."

"Dirty? I was cleaning you up. Your pussy juice was everywhere." He lifts his arm from around my waist and curves his hand down over my ass to slide between my legs from behind. I tremble as his callused fingers glide over my wet, swollen flesh. "I'll probably have to do it again. Maybe after we decorate the tree. Are we doing that tonight?"

"I don't know." I gaze at the tall pine. It's just a tree, the branches bare, but it makes me so happy. "I'm still basking in the glow of our success in putting it up. Maybe we can just leave it like this tonight, and do decorations tomorrow. Have you done that before?"

"Couple of times when I was a kid. You?"

"No. My mother always hired decorators to put up our trees. I wasn't allowed to touch them." I bite my lip, then ask in a rush, "Do you want to sleep here tonight?"

His arm tightens around me again. "Yeah."

Such a simple question and answer, yet my heart is knocking hard within my chest, relief rushing through me as if I just escaped some horrible fate. "Okay."

"I'll probably wake you up tomorrow morning with my face between your legs." He pauses only a moment

before adding, "No, there's no 'probably.' It'll happen."

"All right," I agree, and my voice is strained—not because of screaming or begging but because of the sweet swelling pressure within me. This moment might be the happiest I've ever been—and lying here against him is somehow even better than what he just did to me with his mouth.

But I know why. Just like the decorations will be beautiful, but the real joy of that tree is all the hope I have that everything will change, that the future will be so different from the past. Just like his fingers and tongue feel so amazing, but the real pleasure comes from the force of his need and hunger, and knowing how much he wants me.

Lying here, it's just skin against skin, and his strong arms holding me tight. That warmth and comfort aren't the reason my heart is pounding, the reason tears are stinging my eyes. Because it can never be *just* skin on skin, not with Cole Matthews—and the real terror and hope and joy is that I'm falling in love with him.

And maybe 'falling' is an accident. That doesn't mean I'll get hurt. People walk away from accidents all the time.

But I couldn't walk away from this, even if I tried.

COLE

TAKING IT ONE DAY AT A TIME IS A HELL OF A LOT easier than I expected. Maybe because I begin each day by eating an angel's pussy. Then I end most days the same way, so all the hours in between are just sweet heaven.

I've never lived with a woman before. And I can't truly say that's what I'm doing now. But except for the two nights after we painted her bedroom and moved over to my bed while waiting for the smell to dissipate, I sleep over at her place. My own apartment still gets plenty of use, though. When she's not home, I do the same stuff I did before she came into my life. And even when she is home, sometimes she needs a few hours alone, or I need

a few hours, or it just makes more sense for me to grab a shower at my place—such as those mornings when I spend a little too long between her legs and we have to hurry to get ready. I could happily spend every damn second with her, but we're not rushing this thing, and I'm pretty sure we're both being careful not to invade each other's personal space. I hear of couples that don't even bother closing the bathroom door when taking a piss. We aren't anywhere near that stage yet.

But even if I'm not living with her, my life feels wrapped up and tangled with hers. And it's a damn good feeling. We fit together so fucking easy, but with just enough friction to make it interesting.

My phone is full of the texts we send. Sometimes just asking about each other's schedules, because she's got her workshops, or meets up with Jason, and now and again she and some of her co-workers will go out for drinks. She sends links to articles she's reading, sometimes just with a laughing smiley, other times with commentary, and every time I'm struck by how damn smart she is, and how fucking curious about the world, and how opinionated she is about the way it works…yet still always willing to listen if I have a different perspective.

She doesn't always agree, but she always thinks about it. And that's a hell of a thing.

Then there's the times she'll send a link to a do-it-yourself tutorial with a *I want to do this, but I would need a little help. Would you be able to? But only if*

it's no bother.

The answer is always yes—and that it's never a bother. But the next time, she'll ask me the same way. Just like asking me if putting up the Christmas tree was a bother. Or asking me if I minded helping her move a chest of drawers she put together, though I told her that night I kissed her in the laundry room I'd be willing. Even the painting, after we went to the hardware store together and got everything we needed, before we put color down on a single wall she looked at me all hesitant and made sure I didn't mind helping her. Maybe it's just a polite reflex…or related to what Jason told me about her never being sure whether someone's going to decide she's not worth shit, or that doing anything for her is a burden or hurts them somehow. It didn't take two years for her to trust me—maybe because she's been healing like he said, and maybe because she has that near-spiritual connection to me like I do to her, thanks to Lowery's bullets. But there's still a part of her that's unsure about seeking help from anyone.

And seeking comfort? I don't know if she can. Two days that I know of, she had a rough morning at work. Because she can detach, like she says, but there's some shit you can't completely detach from. I know how it is all too well. There's been cases I've worked that will haunt me as long as I live. In December, we catch two separate cases like that. Since I'm still on light duty, I don't work them up close. But it doesn't make a difference. I still

hear about it, see the photos, and that knowing hangs like a grim pall over the whole damn station, and on those days the cheery holiday music and decorations seem like an insult.

So I know exactly what ended up in that morgue and how she must have hurt for them. But Mia's not accustomed to turning to anyone when she's hurting. Instead she withdraws, locks herself up tight where no one can get to her and maybe hurt her even worse. If it was me hurting, I have no doubt she'd be right there, holding me close. She just won't let me do the same for her yet.

Yet. Because we're taking this one day at a time. And as the month passes, there's a few small hurts between us—usually because I'm an asshole, and other times because being part of a couple is new for us both. But those hurts don't send her running and hiding. Instead she calls me a jerk, and I'll agree because she's right. And we work though the other shit because it's all easy fixes, like me promising not to lose my goddamn mind if one snowy night Mia arrives home a few hours later than usual, and her promising to remember to charge her fucking phone.

One thing's for sure, though—her hot little cunt gets even hotter when she's yelling at me. And knowing she's still mine afterward makes all those pussy juices taste even sweeter.

Hell, she's just sweet all over. And so fucking cute every day, watching holiday movies and coming up with

those personalized gifts and decorating her apartment. She's like a kid sometimes, but I can't say a damn thing, because watching her embrace it all makes me feel like a kid, too. And I know too well where it all comes from.

I don't hear a thing from John Bennet's direction. I know her parents call her sometimes, because I overhear her side of the conversation—her flat and abbreviated responses, almost always in the negative—and sometimes I see her sigh and text a short reply. Trying to convince her to stay at the mansion over Christmas, apparently. But Mia holds firm, and as the day approaches, those calls and texts come in more frequently. It's hell holding my tongue and not telling her to block them, but in the end, I don't need to. Without me saying a thing, she begins hitting *Decline* and ignoring them.

The day she starts doing that is a damn good day.

But then, every day is. The day before Christmas comes on a bright cold morning. I wake up with her snuggled against me and my dick hard as fuck, just like every morning. But I only have a few minutes to slowly wake her with my tongue before heading out alone.

Every year on this day, volunteers from the police and fire departments spend most of the day delivering toys to kids in the local hospitals—so every year, I volunteer. It's one of the few times a year I put on my uniform anymore. The kids might like the sound of a detective, but to most of them, you're not a cop unless you're dressed in blue and wearing a badge on your chest.

We finish up late in the afternoon. I know Mia's out with Jason, doing some charity thing connected to the Bennet's foundation, so afterward I join the other cops when they head out for a drink. I don't realize she's already returned home until a text comes in.

My do-it-yourself project for tonight.

She includes a link to a woman's magazine article. The site loads a picture of a banana and the headline, "Top Ten Tips to Blow Your Man's Mind During a Blow Job."

Holy fuck.

I'm still not at a hundred percent. I won't be until I get the okay to start running and adding some heavy weights to my leg exercises again. But the pain is down to the occasional twinge—not a long, agonizing twinge, but a brief, sharp twinge if I move too fast or stretch too far. Just my body telling me to slow down, but it's no longer stopping me. I haven't said as much to Mia, but she probably knows. I move around fairly easily, and I haven't broken out the crutches for about three weeks.

I'd planned to hold out until even the twinges were gone, though. Because I've jacked off in the shower a couple of times, and I'm pretty damn sure I can get through a round of sex without any real pain. But Mia is so damn worried about hurting anyone, I was afraid that even a mild flinch would make her too terrified to touch me again. But holding out for much longer might be beyond me.

I read the headline again. Yeah. Holding out is a million miles beyond me.

I'm already tossing money onto the table, getting ready to leave when the next message comes in.

Look, they have tons of tutorials on this site! Should I learn to do this? I might need help, though. Can you? Pretty please?

Not asking if it's a bother. And not YouTube this time. YouPorn. A picture comes through next—a screenshot of an actress looking up at the camera, her mouth stuffed full of cock. And Mia is on her tablet at home, looking at that. Maybe imagining that's my cock, with her pussy soaking wet.

Only by some Christmas miracle, I don't blow my load that second. *I'm on my way, angel.*

You mean you're—

She sends a picture of David Caruso putting on his sunglasses.

—COMING?

I fucking love this girl. And I'll barely last a minute after she gets her mouth on me.

Put some red lipstick on, I reply.

I'm halfway home when she sends me a selfie of her mouth, with her pink tongue flicking out to lick the tip of her middle finger and her full lips painted a dark velvety red. Holy shit. Next time I need to stroke one out, I've got a picture to help me along.

I take it as a good sign that when I don't wait for the

elevator and use the stairs, instead, my thigh doesn't give a single twinge. I text her on my way up, and a second after I pound on her door, she opens it wide—looking sexy as fuck in red heels a mile high, her dark hair loose around her shoulders, and wearing a short Santa robe in red silk edged with white fur…and probably something beneath it designed to drive me wild. Whether lingerie or her naked body, both will do the same thing.

Abruptly her eyes widen. The sultry smile she greeted me with rounds into an surprised *O*. "You're in uniform!"

"Yeah." Her hungry gaze is suddenly all over me and my dick's getting even harder. "You like that?"

Breathlessly she nods. "I didn't know how much. Oh my god." Stepping closer, she runs her fingers down the front of my uniform shirt. "I wanted this to be a Christmas fantasy for you. But it might be *my* new fantasy, instead."

"You think this doesn't fit some of my fantasies, too? I don't always play good cop." I shut the door behind me, leaning back against it. My voice is rough as I say, "You look like you're looking for trouble, ma'am. And I sure as hell would love to see you on your pretty knees in front of me, sucking me off as hard as you can."

Mia stills, her cheeks slightly flushed as she looks up at me. "Is that what you want for Christmas, detective?"

"No. Because it's only Christmas Eve, angel." I thread my fingers into the long tumble of her hair. "And unless you want to spend it handcuffed to your bed, you'd better

get on your knees."

"That's not really a threat," she whispers breathily. "It sounds like another fantasy."

Yeah, it does. How about— "I won't be in that bed with you."

Instantly she sinks to the floor, her fingers tugging at my duty belt. I catch her hand and guide it to my straining zipper, where my dick's about to bust through my uniform pants.

"Don't waste time on any of that shit. Just take out my cock and suck it, angel."

Her fingers eagerly tug down the zip. I groan as the rough slide teases my shaft, and the pressure of the zipper and fabric on my constrained dick eases.

At the sound of my groan, she pauses. "You're all right?"

"So damn right. You touching me feels so fucking good." I stroke my thumb along the bottom curve of her mouth, smoothing away her frown. "Don't you worry, Mia. I held out for a month. And if I wasn't sure of being all right, I'd hold out for another month."

She nods and focuses in on my cock again. Biting her bottom lip in concentration, she fumbles trying to work my shaft out of my briefs and through my open fly, and every moment is sweet delicious torture. Knowing she's never done this before. Seeing the flush of arousal over her skin and the hardness of her nipples beneath that red silk. Watching her mouth and her expressive

features move from frustration when she says I'm too big to drag through the opening, to concern when I help her and she seems to think my erection will break from a little rough handling, and finally triumph as the thick length juts through, curving upward like it's reaching for heaven.

Heaven reaches for my cock, instead. It's not the first time this month that Mia's seen or touched my dick, but she was always careful not to go too far and risk hurting me. She's always so damn careful with me.

This time she doesn't hesitate. Her gaze is rapt as her soft hands stroke my shaft, fingertips tracing the heavy veins, driving me to the edge in seconds.

Her red lips part on a moan when her fingers slide over the tip, slicking through a pearled bead of pre-cum. Her eyelids go heavy with need and she moves all at once, gripping my cock to hold it steady and dragging her hot pink tongue up the underside of my shaft, finishing with a languorous slide around the rim of the crown.

"Ah fuuuuuck," I groan, sagging back against the door, letting the solid wood take my weight. "No need to tease, angel. Those tips you read in that article? Just skip to the one where you're sucking. I've wanted this for so fucking long, I'm going to come real fast. But at least it'll take off the edge for what comes next."

Like a kitten she rubs her cheek against my erection, her voice husky when she asks, "What comes next?"

"Your little virgin pussy finally taking every inch of this big thick cock." Another drop of pre-cum beads at my cock slit and I almost fucking lose it when she daintily sips the drop away, then moans and goes back for another long lick. Harshly I tell her, "But only if you suck the first round of cum out of me, angel."

Her innocent mouth opens wide. Those red lips take me in, her tongue stroking the underside of my dick—and all the while she's looking up at me with those pale blue eyes.

"Mia. That's so damn good." A groan rips from my chest like a chainsaw and I battle the need to ram my cock past those fuckable lips. Where my control comes from I don't even know. "Oh Christ, yes. As deep as you can."

She draws back for a breath first, a crimson lipstick stain ringing my shaft about an inch past the thick crown. And my sweet virgin must have learned something from those videos, because she can't take much more of me on the second try, but it doesn't even matter. She gets her hands in there, squeezing and stroking, caressing every inch of my shaft while she sucks so hard on the thick head that it hurts in the best fucking way I've ever known.

"Look at me, Mia," I command hoarsely and her eyes lock on mine again. "I'm going to come. You want to back off?"

Without letting my cock slip from her mouth, she

shakes her head, and that simple answer has me groaning again, my dick about to explode.

I wrap my right hand over hers, urging a harder stroke. She breaks away and gasps for air and gets right back on there, sucking wildly, her tongue rubbing the sensitive underside of my cock's fat head like she knows just what I need to take me to the edge, but it's her soft hungry moan that sends me flying over. The fingers of my left hand tighten in her hair as I start coming, and if feels like my entire fucking soul empties into her mouth with every hot spurt of cum. She tries but can't take it all, and what she can't swallow overflows the corners of her swollen lips, and it's the hottest, sexiest thing I've ever seen.

My chest heaving, I ease out of her incredible mouth. Cupping her jaw in my palm, I swipe my thumb through the mess on her chin. "I think this is the dirtiest thing you've done now, angel."

She chokes a little, then laughs merrily. Grinning, I drag her up against my chest and kiss her, tasting me and tasting her and together it's the best flavor I've ever known. Her legs twine around my hips, and I feel her pussy against my bare cock—she's wearing panties but is so hot and wet she's scorching me right through them.

Her arms link around my neck. "And it was all right?" Her gaze searches mine. "No pain?"

"Not a bit." Which means we both know what's coming next. And I've wanted this for so damn long

that I'll be ready to come again within minutes. "I've got condoms over at my—"

Three insistent raps hit the door against my back. Mia abruptly freezes, then giggles, burying her face in my neck to muffle the sound.

Still holding her, I push away from the door. "You expecting anyone?"

"Maybe a delivery?" She slips out of my arms and puts her eye up to the peephole. Her entire body stiffens. "My father."

His assertive knock comes again.

Still whispering so that she can't be heard through the door, Mia says, "They're mad that I'm not coming tomorrow. We don't project the image of the perfect Bennet family when I don't visit during Christmas."

"Yeah, Christmas ought to be about image," I say dryly, tucking away my cock. "Go get dressed. I'll let him in. You want me to get rid of him, too?"

It doesn't surprise me when she says, "I can do it," because she never passes off her problems to anyone. She rises up on her toes and presses a kiss to my lips. "I'll be right back."

I watch her run off, then glance down to make sure I don't have cum smeared all over the front of my uniform pants. At some point, Bennet was going to find out about me and his daughter, and I suppose that now is as good a time as any. Still, what we do behind this closed door is none of his damn business.

When I open the door, Bennet's eyes widen in surprised recognition but he immediately makes the wrong assumption—though an understandable one. His gaze goes to the number on the door and back to me. "Detective Matthews! I was looking for my daughter but I must have the wrong apartment number."

"No," I tell him, swinging the door wider to invite him in. A pair of black leather gloves are clutched in his hand, and he's dressed like he's on his way to some fancy function, a nice suit with a long overcoat and gray scarf that lays perfectly around his shoulders instead of tucked inside his collar—and I never understood that shit. A scarf doesn't do any damn good unless it's around your neck. "This is Mia's place. She'll be out here in a minute."

And he's still trying to make sense of this. Maybe because I'm in uniform instead of casual clothes, so he assumes I'm on duty.

"Did something happen to Mia?" His gaze darts around the decorated apartment as if looking for signs of a break-in, his forehead lined with concern. "Is she all right? You should have informed me that she was in trouble."

"I'm not in trouble." Mia answers him as she returns along the hallway, wearing black leggings and an oversized sweatshirt. She changed out of that sexy Santa robe but must not have looked in the mirror. And one glance at her, at the long hair tangled by my hands, her

swollen lips free of lipstick but still stained red, and it's real damn clear what I was doing over here.

Bennet stiffens. His shoulders go rigid beneath that undercoat and his jaw whitens. It's with visible effort that he unclenches enough to greet her with, "Mia, there you are," followed quickly by a furious glance in my direction and an icily polite, "If you can leave us alone so that I can speak with my daughter, detective?"

"You can stay," Mia says to me. "My father won't be here long."

He doesn't like that a bit. But he's trying to hold it in—maybe because he realizes that an explosion won't help him get what he wants from her. Instead he offers, "I see you've done some decorating. Very festive."

"It is." She rises on her toes to give him a perfunctory kiss on the cheek. "Merry Christmas, Father."

He doesn't miss a beat. "My Christmas would be merrier if you were staying at home."

"It will be merry if I don't stay at home, too." She crosses her arms over her chest, not a sign of softening on her beautiful face. "And I would rather be here."

"I understand you want to run away from all the privilege you've known and pretend you're not a Bennet." The fucker could give a masterclass in guilt induction. Long-suffering exasperation and disappointment fill his reply, yet his expression maintains some stoic shit that makes him seem like a saint for putting up with Mia's nonsense. "But you have *responsibilities* as a Bennet,

Mia—"

"I spent all of today at the shelter. Jason, too. Funny we didn't see you there." She gets that dig in. "And I'll be at the New Year's gala."

"Responsibilities as a *daughter*, not to the foundation." He quickly changes course when it's clear she isn't having any of that shit. "Your mother and I allowed you to pursue your career, pointless as it is, and we supported you at every turn—"

Her incredulous laugh interrupts him. "You tried to talk me out of it at every turn! But I'm done talking. I wish you would hear that. I'm *done* trying to be the daughter you want."

He shoots a poisonous glance in my direction. "So you can be something else for *him*?"

Exactly what he means remains unspoken. But I hear the words all the same. *Slut, whore.* And I'd love to break his teeth for it. I know damn well that would only serve him, though. There's a shit storm coming for sure, and the only way to weather it is to stay squeaky clean.

So I say easily, "I'm pretty sure 'girlfriend' is the word you're looking for."

But Mia also heard what he didn't say. Bright spots of anger appear on her pale cheeks. Voice shaking with her raging emotions, she tells him, "You need to go *now*."

He opens his mouth to argue. No, none of that shit.

"I suggest you leave the premises, Mr. Bennet." I'm in uniform, so I'm real fucking polite, opening the door

and holding it wide. "I would hate to issue a trespassing citation to a pillar of the community."

The insult of me literally showing him the door paints his face a dull red. Agitatedly slapping his gloves against his palm, he stalks toward the doorway, with Mia following right behind as if to make sure he goes through it—or maybe to kick him through. She looks pissed enough that she might.

Abruptly he stops right in front of me, gets up in my face. "You think I'll let this betrayal slide? You were supposed to watch her. Not take advantage of her. You're finished, Matthews." Cold anger seethes in his quiet threat. "I'll have your goddamn badge."

I know he'll try. "You won't get shit from me."

"Why would you do anything to him?" Confusion mixes with outrage in Mia's voice, with the outrage taking over as she adds, "I'm the one telling you to go! Cole has *nothing* to do with this!"

Without taking my eyes off the fucker in front of me, I tell her, "He thinks I've been doing a favor for him."

"A favor I wouldn't have asked if I'd known the sort of man you are—promising to protect her, claiming that Jason is her only visitor, but all the while preying upon a confused and vulnerable young woman." His chin lifts, smug aggression all over his face. "Obviously you have concealed the truth about your true nature from your superiors. But I see what kind of scum you are, Detective Matthews. Soon everyone will know it."

And maybe do a lot of fucking damage with his lies. But I'm not going to smash my fist into that face and do some damage of my own. Instead I smile and aim right where it'll get me the biggest reaction. "At least I'm not the kind of scum who uses his daughter as bait when he's making a deal. Is that why you don't want anyone touching your little girl's pussy? You've got to keep it nice and fresh."

His eyes widen. Fists curling, he chokes on his rage. "I ought to—"

"Go ahead," I urge, my breath hissing through bared teeth. "Take that swing. I'd fucking *love* to haul you in for assault. It would be the best goddamn Christmas present I ever had."

Jaw clenched, Bennet stares at me for a long second before abruptly stepping back, flicking his hands down the front of his coat like we just had a brawl and he's smoothing everything back into place. "Make certain to enjoy your Christmas, Detective Matthews. Because you will not enjoy any day following it. You are finished. No one in the police department will stand by your side. By the time I'm done, you won't even find work as a security guard."

And the best response to that shit is no reaction at all. I just wait, holding the door open, as if nothing he says can touch me.

But it's not what touches me that I ought to be worried about. Because he glances back and says, "Merry

Christmas, Mia. I pray that you'll see the sort of man you're throwing your life away on—and hope to see you tomorrow."

"Just go," she says thickly.

My chest suddenly tight as fuck, I swing the door closed behind him. Because he can't do shit to me. Maybe ruin my name and take my job, but it'll be nothing. Not compared to what I'm seeing now.

Looking painfully uncertain and small, Mia stares at me, her eyes glittering, lips trembling. And she asks, "Is it true?" Her voice catches on a shuddering breath. "Did you agree watch me and report back to him?"

MIA

I KNOW THE ANSWER EVEN BEFORE COLE TELLS ME. Because his face goes white, his features suddenly taut with strain—an expression I've seen before, when he was in agonizing pain. His dark eyes search mine, like he's looking for something to say, but there's only a yes or a no.

The sour lump of betrayal lodged in my chest suddenly moves up into my throat. "You did," I whisper brokenly.

As if my devastated reply shatters the fear holding him silent, abruptly he shakes his head. "I agreed to," he says in a raw voice. "But I never intended to really do it. And I *never* followed through. I swear it, Mia—"

He reaches for me but I back away, afraid that if he touches me the brittle control I have over myself will simply splinter apart. His face goes bleak, his dark eyes suddenly empty.

His hand drops to his side, and he swallows hard, says thickly, "I swear it, angel."

I believe him. Or maybe I *want* to believe him. Because my father also said— "But you reported that Jason visited me?"

"I didn't. I never said a damn thing. I don't know how he knew." He rakes a shaking hand through his hair. "Maybe the chief told him that just to give him something. Because that's all this ever was, Mia. He went to Chief Jackson, and it was easier and smarter to let him think we were doing him a favor than to tell him to fuck off. Though that's exactly what I wanted to do."

I know my father. I know Chief Jackson. That sounds like both of them. And Cole… a 'fuck off' sounds just like him, too.

When I don't answer, despair carves austere lines into his face and he hoarsely starts again, "I swear, angel. He came to us with that bullshit, and we pretended to play along. The chief can corroborate—"

"I know," I interrupt him in a strained whisper, my entire body stiff, my arms wrapped around my stomach. "I know how my father is. And I know you wouldn't do it."

Relief passes over his face but he doesn't try to reach

for me. Instead he stares at me, his chest heaving. My posture must tell him that despite my belief, I'm still on the edge of breaking.

Utter desolation flattens his voice. "But I still made you feel like shit."

"You didn't. You didn't do anything wrong." And that's why I'm on the verge of breaking. Cole doesn't deserve any of this. Yet because of me... "He'll try to ruin you."

"He'll try, but he won't." Conviction rings through that reply. "I told the chief a month ago that I was with you. He'll have my back."

"You think my father will stop at Chief Jackson if he doesn't get his way? That's just where he'll start."

Jaw set, Cole shakes his head. "He can't touch me."

"You really think that's true?"

He knows it isn't. Because he doesn't try to keep telling me it is. Instead he says, "I'll weather it."

Tears burn my eyes. *He'll weather it.* A hurricane created by my father, simply because I refused to fall in line. A hurricane that will threaten everything Cole has fought for his entire life.

"Angel." It's soft, despite the gravel in his voice. Slowly he approaches me, as if I'm a wounded animal he fears will flee. And he's not all wrong. "When Bennet showed up that day, told me he had a daughter he wanted me to watch, I thought to myself that girl could never be worth the trouble that having her would bring down on

me. But you *are*, Mia. You're worth all the trouble in the world."

"I don't want to be trouble." I can barely speak past the constriction in my throat. "And I know how hard you've worked to get where you are. I can't bear the thought of him taking it from you."

"Maybe he won't." Gently his warm palms cup my face. "He might find that the chief and everyone in City Hall aren't so willing to kiss his ass if he tries to burn mine. But even if they did, I'd fight back. Do I seem like the type to give up?"

"No." I know he's not. He'll go down fighting. But it's the thought of him going down at all that is killing me. My breath hitches, and the swelling burn of emotion in my chest rises up, clogging my throat. "But it's because of *me*. I can't bear that he's hurting you because of me."

"I don't *care*," Cole says fiercely. "I'll take anything for you."

"But I care. Because you shouldn't *have* to take anything! Not for me. Not because of him." And I'm so close to breaking down and crying hysterically. Right in front of him, and he'd not only have to worry about his own future but worry about me, too. Frantically I shake my head, pulling away from the comfort of his hands. "I can't do this right now. I need to think."

"About *what?*" His expression hardens as his gaze sweeps my face. "Are *you* going to give up? Run back to your mansion and make a deal to save me?"

"I don't know!" I don't want to. But I would. I *would*. "I hadn't even thought of it yet!"

Lips drawn back over clenched teeth, he orders savagely, "Don't you fucking *dare* save me like that, Mia."

My tears spill over. "Then give me time to think!"

"Alone?" he challenges, and before I can draw a breath, all of the savagery leaves his expression and he says bleakly, "All right, angel. I'll give you the space you need. Just tell me you're not giving up on us."

"I'm…not…giving up." Chest hitching painfully, I try to hold it together. Just a second longer. "I'm *not*."

"I'll take that." Though he sounds as if my reply offers only the barest thread of hope. "And I'll hold you to it. Because I intend to make it as hard for you to let me go as I can, Mia. And maybe one of these days, your first instinct when you're scared and hurting won't be to slam the door in my face."

Is that what he thinks I'm doing? Shattered by the thought, I suck in a ragged breath. "I'm not. I'm just—"

"Isolating yourself so you can't be hurt or hurt anyone else. But I'm not dead, angel. And nothing hurts more than being shut out." His voice is gruff but his hands are gentle when he draws me close and presses a warm kiss to my tearstained cheek before turning toward the door. "But I understand it's what you need to do. So I'm here if you need me. And I'm here if you don't."

Cole's generosity and kindness in the face of his own pain utterly destroys me. The moment the door latches

shut behind him, I crumple to the floor, tears streaming down my face, wracked by sobs so deep it feels as if they're tearing me apart. All I wanted was a future that was different from everything I'd known. That possibility always lay ahead of me, the knowledge that if I just waited a little longer, I'd be free. But I didn't wait. Instead Lowery's bullet snapped all those chains. I broke away, tried to leave them behind—and because of that, now Cole's future is being threatened, too. And those chains are closing around me again. In a few years, I'll be free… but by then it might all be too late.

Because I want to break patterns, but my parents never will. And even if I went back home tonight on the condition that they let Cole alone, they'd still try to destroy him. Because they'd know I would eventually go back to him. And because hurting him will hurt me.

And I'll never let my parents hurt him.

Never.

That resolution echoes through me as my sobs slowly subside. Spent, I lay on the floor, feeling completely hollow, as if everything inside me has been scraped out.

Now I have to choose what to put back in.

I know what I want. It's all around me right now. Twinkling lights, the scent of pine, tinsel. Not Christmas—that will be over soon enough—but everything I felt while Cole and I put all of these decorations up. I *will* have a future that isn't dictated by my parents. It *will* be different from what I've known. I'll break that

pattern.

But I have to break a few more. Because I've pushed back quietly against my parents for years now, but it's always been by simply ignoring them. By not obeying them. Or by doing what I did when I moved into this apartment—ran away from them, avoiding any confrontation. Telling myself that there was no rush. That I would finally break those chains soon enough.

And in some parts of my life, there *is* no rush. Not in my career. And with Cole…I want everything with him, but some parts of that will come quickly and some we'll have to let grow.

But one thing that absolutely can't wait? Confronting this threat my father has made.

There might be a solution to it. It would require me to break another pattern—my resolution to never be like my parents. To never take advantage of my name. To never use it like a weapon. Maybe it's time, though. Because I've been waiting so long for armor to form around my heart, but it's never been thick enough to protect me—and it won't protect Cole. So maybe it's time to stop hiding behind a flimsy shield and start swinging a sword.

Less like a guardian angel. More like an avenging one.

But first, there's a different pattern that needs breaking. The one I didn't even realize was there.

Despite all of the resolutions that give me direction

and purpose, I still feel hollow as I silently make my way across the hall—and utterly wrung out. My eyes are swollen from crying, my nose won't stop dripping, but I don't care if I'm a horrible mess. And Cole looks as wrecked as I feel. When he opens the door, his eyes are haunted, his face drawn and pale, as if he'd spent this time suffering through hell—and his angel had abandoned him.

Never again. I can't promise heaven. But I won't ever put him through this again.

"I need you to hold me tonight," I tell him hoarsely.

He doesn't hesitate, sweeping me up to cradle me against his chest before carrying me inside. Instantly everything within me fills up, so full, all of the hollow places disappearing as my entire future slides into place. With a shuddering sigh, I bury my face in the strong warmth of his neck. "I'm not giving up. But I don't know if I can give much else until tomorrow."

In a thick voice, he says, "I don't need anything else, Mia."

Maybe not. But I'll still give him everything I can.

COLE

On Christmas morning, I don't greet the day with my face between Mia's legs. There's no Mia to greet at all. Just a handwritten note beside my pillow.

Merry Christmas!

Should be back around noon.

xoxoxo

The Avenging Angel

P.S. There are cranberry-orange muffins over at my place.

My extra key is on the counter.

I get the feeling she left that message so I wouldn't worry. But I don't know what the hell it means. Does that mean she's heading out to confront her father?

Why wouldn't she take me with her? I'd have held her through it if she needed me to. Or beat the shit out of him if necessary. And the 'avenging' part makes me real fucking uneasy. Maybe it's the job putting the worry into my head, but if Chief Jackson called me right now to say that John Bennet had just been found dead with a knife in his chest, I wouldn't be wholly surprised.

But if Mia has gone out to murder her father, she's probably already had time to do it. I don't have a clue when she left. Last night, I carried her to my bed and she was out within minutes, as if the emotional turmoil had sucked her dry. I was feeling pretty fucking drained myself. But I held her all night with my head racing and my chest aching, and it was around five in the morning before I finally slept.

Which must be why I didn't wake up when she slipped out of bed. That could have been any time between five and eleven, which was when I began stirring. And the only good thing about sleeping that late is it gives me less time to go out of my goddamn mind.

I send her a text. The message never gets marked 'delivered.' As if her battery is dead again. Or she's turned off her phone. Maybe because she doesn't want anyone tracking her device.

If she killed her dad…fuck, I'll help her cover it up. I'll say I was screwing her all morning. And spent the entire night filling her up with my cum. Though I probably won't need to say anything. After a jury hears

what sort of man John Bennet is, she'll be acquitted. God knows real murderers have been let go for flimsier reasons. And with the kind of lawyer she could afford, shit. Opinion will spin so far in her direction that the city will be throwing her a parade afterward.

And maybe if I tell Mia the kind of bullshit that goes on in my head when I don't know where she is, she'll never forget to charge her phone again. But that's all part of hooking up with a cop.

So is this. After a shower, I drag on a T-shirt and jeans, then grab her key off the counter. I let myself into her apartment, find the muffins—and 'just science' my ass, this woman can bake—and wander my way into her bedroom. The leggings and sweatshirt she was wearing are in her hamper. So is a damp towel, but the tile in the shower is already completely dry. So she changed and bathed pretty damn early. Her long winter coat is gone—the classy trench, not the puffy one—and I'm pretty damn sure her tall black boots are gone, too.

So she dressed up before heading out real early on Christmas morning. Aside from the Bennet mansion, there's not many places I can imagine her going to. At least no knives are missing from the block in her kitchen. Because she obviously had a purpose. But stabbing her dad wasn't it.

I'm working on my third muffin and feeling a bit more at ease when I head back to my apartment at eleven forty-five. *Around noon* could be any time now.

And it is.

My phone buzzes when I'm still in the hallway. A text from Mia.

Sorry! I turned off my phone. I'm almost there.

Thank fucking Christ. But she turned off her phone? *Do you need an alibi?*

How about Paul Espinoza?

The mayor? That could only be about one thing: John Bennet's promise to ruin me.

How'd that go?

Easier to explain when I get there.

Which looks like it might be right about now. The elevator dings and opens, then for a moment I think my eyes are completely fucked, like maybe the bullet that grazed my skull finally started to mess up some shit in my brain. Then I realize who I'm seeing.

Your mom's here.

Oh god. Run for your life. And don't listen to anything she says.

Yeah, I'm not running. I tuck the phone into my back pocket.

Patricia Bennet is a few inches shorter and a bit thinner than Mia, but there's no doubt where her daughter got her looks. God knows where Mia got her warmth, though. Her mother smiles when she sees me, a curve of lips so similar to Mia's, but the pale blue of her eyes remains sheer ice. Her black hair is smoothed back into an elegant roll, and she wears a long coat in winter

cream. Her black heels don't show off her legs as much as they just scream class and 'no one's good enough to touch this shit.' She carries a black leather handbag in a firm grip, and her hands are covered in kidskin gloves the same creamy color as her coat.

Her piercing gaze sizes me up as she comes down the hall, and there's a moment—probably around the time when she realizes that I really am this damn big— when there's the same flicker of unease in her eyes that I've seen flicker in other women's. It's the flicker that makes them veer over to the edge of the sidewalk, carrying their keys with the pointed ends sticking out between their fingers. A flicker that says my size isn't a sexy turn-on, like it is for Mia. It's just intimidating in a certain, terrifying way.

And I'll use my size to deliberately intimidate a lot of people. But women? Especially if I've seen that flicker? Fuck no.

Not that Patricia veers anywhere. Instead her chin comes up a bit—and that smile never falters. Her voice is smooth as glass, without Mia's rusty edge. "You must be Detective Matthews!"

"That's me." I gesture to Mia's door. "I'm afraid your daughter isn't home."

And even though I have the key, there's no damn way I'm letting her in there to lie in wait.

"That's all right." She reaches out a gloved hand. "It is you who I've come to see, detective. I've heard about you

from my husband, of course."

I grasp her surprisingly warm hand—there's life beneath those soft kidskin gloves—and say dryly, "So it's your turn to tag-team me, then?"

She probably doesn't know a thing about wrestling but has no trouble parsing my meaning. Chuckling softly, she shakes her head, and reaches into her handbag for a square of thick white cardstock. "I'm afraid that my reaction to the news of our daughter's interest in you wasn't exactly the same as his. Instead I have come to extend a personal invitation to the New Years' gala."

"That's kind of you. But Mia already invited me." I open the door to my apartment. "You're welcome to wait for her here."

"Thank you, detective." She sweeps past me on a subtle wave of perfume, her heels tapping on the hardwood floor. "As for the invitation, I would like to make it an official one. In hindsight, I can't believe it was overlooked, regardless of your relationship with Mia. Our little city might have been the site of yet another mass shooting, its name synonymous with tragedy. You prevented that."

"Just doing my job, ma'am." I take a few steps into my living room and stand with my hands tucked into my jeans' pockets—and where I'm still easily visible from the hallway. I leave my apartment door wide open, because there's no fucking way I'll let this visit turn into a smear on my name.

Though that's probably not Patricia Bennet's style. A false accusation would be more up her husband's alley, I bet. Because Mia said her mother doesn't like to be humiliated, and suggesting a big brute like me touched her would likely qualify as humiliating.

"Well, the foundation would like to officially recognize you for doing that job." In the middle of the living room, Patricia swings around to face me again, her gaze assessing as it runs down my length. "Have you had the opportunity to be fitted for a proper suit or tuxedo? A man of your size, I imagine it's not easy to find one that you can borrow."

Was that a jab at my bank account? That's amateur hour. "I'll manage."

I've already managed. Back when Huertas got married and I stood up as his best man, I had a formal suit made then. That was eight years ago but my size is pretty much the same. So after Mia invited me to this thing, I dug it out of the closet and sent it to the cleaners.

Apparently intending to stay for a few minutes, she begins pulling off her gloves, tugging at the tip of each finger to loosen them from the close-fitting leather. The only gleam of color I've seen so far glitters in the huge sapphire gracing the middle finger of her right hand, and the matching stones dangling from her ears.

"I understand you are still on restricted duty, detective?" Her gaze sweeps the apartment the same way it swept over me—assessing it all without any visible

reaction yet still giving off an air of faint distaste.

So it's not a mansion. But it's not a leaking shack. And it's clean. Considering what I came from, there's no chance I'll ever feel ashamed of my home now. "I am."

"You seemed to have healed well thus far." She's wearing a sympathetic expression when her gaze returns to me. "But it must be worrisome, not knowing your future, or being certain you will ever fully recover."

Is she talking about my health or her husband's threats? Either way, it's still nothing. "I know my future pretty well."

And that future is coming up right behind me.

"Mother?"

Flushed and panting a little, as if she ran up the three flights of stairs and down the hall, Mia comes straight in, her pale eyes running over me as if she's looking for signs of blood. And she's so damn beautiful, her hair in a thick wave down her back, that coat as sexy as fuck. When she sees that I'm unscathed, she shakes her head and turns toward her mother—and walks past her toward the kitchen, where she sets a bag full of takeout boxes on the counter.

"Well," Patricia says lightly. "Now that I see what fine cuisine you have available, it is quite apparent why you wouldn't want to return home for a traditional Christmas dinner prepared by our chef."

"And that dinner will soon start, so why aren't you there?" Mia regards her mother unsmilingly. "Are you

here to threaten Cole, too?"

"Of course not." Brows rising, as if she's surprised by that accusation, Patricia glances toward me again—then reaches into her bag. "Actually, I have a Christmas gift for him…though, ultimately, it is for you. But just a little something to help you both along."

"No, no, no. We don't need—"

"Nonsense, Mia." She pulls out a small jewelry box topped by a festive bow. "Go on, then."

Shit. Mia's looking at the box that her mother places in my palm like it's got a bomb in it. But it's not a bomb.

It's a fucking giant diamond ring. A huge stone is surrounded by smaller stones, and they're all twinkling brighter than a strand of Christmas lights.

Patricia regards it with a small, wistful smile. "It was my own mother's engagement ring. So of course it should one day belong to my daughter."

It seems like a nice, if overly generous, gift. And a little premature—because although there's nothing I want more than to marry Mia, her parents only discovered we were together yesterday. And the only word tossed out was 'girlfriend.' Yet Mia's still eyeing the ring like she's waiting for it to explode.

"Mother," she says warily. "This really wasn't necessary."

"Of course it is." Patricia's pale gaze rises to meet mine. "I understand the common trend among young couples is for the groom to spend a few months' salary on an engagement ring. You could still do that, detective,

and perhaps come up with a pretty little bauble. But wouldn't you rather be able to give Mia a ring worthy of gracing her finger?"

Holy shit. I knew what Patricia was, knew that she liked to stick in the knife. So I was looking out for it. But even watching for it, she still slides that blade right between my ribs. Because I'm suddenly staring at the ring with my heart feeling tight and sick, thinking that *this* is what Mia deserves and thinking how I could *never* afford it. I couldn't. Not even if I busted my ass on the job for twenty years and didn't have any expenses. And it's just a fucking *ring*. Yet when I ask her to marry me now, this fucking thing will *always* be in the back of my mind, and there's not a goddamn thing I'll be able to give my angel that won't seem like shit in comparison.

That's not amateur hour. She stabbed deep. And it'll leave a scar.

Yet she gave me a taste of what Mia's known her whole damn life. And maybe because Patricia did it to me this time—or maybe because after a life of it, this was one time too many—but either way, if you push something hard enough, it'll break.

And Mia fucking snaps. Eyes glittering with fury, she snatches the box out of my hand and slaps it into her mother's palm, then grabs the other woman's wrist and steers her toward the door. "I tried to just walk away, Mother," she seethes through gritted teeth. "To just leave and forget everything you ever said to me. And I never

said a damn thing in return because I didn't want to hurt you like you hurt me. But I shouldn't have worried. You can't be hurt because you don't feel anything. You're a cold, heartless *monster* and you will *never* be welcome anywhere I am, not ever again."

She shoves her mother through the door and into the hallway, where Patricia spins around to face her, chin high, mouth tight.

"I don't deserve this from you, Mia. I have *always* looked out for you."

"No, you have not."

"I have! You're too trusting. Even this *man*"—she spits the word—"he's just another corrupt police officer. I asked a friend to look at him, and she found a sealed record in his criminal history. When the truth of that comes out, do you want to be married to a criminal? Do you know anything of his father and how many times he's been in and out of prison?"

"Everything I know about his father tells me that he's just like you. The only difference is that you have money." A dangerous note hardens Mia's voice. "But not for long, Mother. Because I have a Christmas present for Cole, too. He said that he'd love nothing better than to see my father hauled off to jail. And I'm doing my best to be Santa."

I can think of a few things I want more, but I'd take that. I just don't know how the hell she'd do it. "What do you mean by that, angel?"

She answers me but her gaze never leaves her mother. "It means that first thing tomorrow, I'm hiring a forensic accountant. Because some people don't break their patterns—and last night I realized that my father thinks that he's not only better than everyone else, but that he can also get away with whatever he wants. And he'll use whatever methods he has to in order to secure his business deals. So it made me wonder if he was using the foundation's money or the Bennet family trust in addition to his private funds. I guess we'll find out."

"Mia!" Her mother stares at her in horror. "You can't do that. If even the suggestion of such a thing got out—"

"I *can* do it. It's entirely within my rights as a Bennet and as a member of the board, and I'll pay for the financial review out of my own pocket. So what do you think, Mother? You think he's capable of it?"

Her icy blue gaze darts from Mia's face to mine, then to her daughter's again. "I don't… You can't do this."

"I can. I *am*. And if I find what I think I will, I intend to take everything. I'll ruin him. So if want to spare yourself that humiliation, I suggest you divorce him and run far away. Or I'll pull you down with him. Then I'll crush you both and I won't even look down when I scrape you off my shoe."

Offended pride and anger lifts her chin higher. "And you'll do this for him? Betray your family for *him*? Your father was right, this man needs to be put in his place. We'll find a judge to open that sealed record and you'll

see who he is. The whole city will."

Fingers curling into claws, Mia lurches forward. "Don't you even—"

I catch her around the waist, drag her raging form back against my chest. In a soothing tone, I tell her, "Easy, bad cop. I don't care if it comes out. You want to know what's in there?" I ask Patricia, and wait until her gaze meets mine. "I was fourteen years old when my dad pimped me out. So you want to open that up? You want to talk about how it feels to be betrayed by someone who's supposed to care for you? About how it feels to end up in some sick bastard's bed because your old man needs to make a deal? I got a feeling you know a little something about that."

Spots of color appear high in her suddenly pale cheeks. "You know *nothing* about me."

"Maybe not. But I know people you can talk to." I use my kind and gentle voice. "You probably should."

She stares at me, her mouth tight, before abruptly shaking her head and turning on her heel.

Mia watches her stalk toward the elevator in stunned silence—and her body tense, wary, as if she doesn't believe it's really over. Only after the elevator doors close on her mother's rigid face does her body relax against mine. "You ran her off," she says in awe. "And she didn't say anything while going. She *always* gets the last word."

"I guess she's not ready to talk about this."

Mia doesn't say anything for a long breath, then

hesitantly asks, "You really think… You think my father… did that to her?"

"Yeah."

Her mouth pulls into a frown and she stares down the hallway for another long second. "I don't know how to feel. About her, I mean. If it's true, it's horrifying."

So is what her mother did to her all these years. "I feel like you don't owe her anything. But that's me. You can take your time to work it out for yourself. There's no rush."

She nods and her hand comes up to clasp my forearm, still wrapped around her waist. "What you said to her… that was you playing good cop, right? It wasn't true?"

"It wasn't. All that my juvenile record will show is that I tried to shoplift some food from a grocery store."

"But if that record was unsealed…can it hurt you?"

"Nah. The man who arrested me is sitting in the chief's chair. And the only thing I've stolen since is a pair of your panties."

She giggles and turns within the circle of my arms, looking up at me. Then her smile fades and she bites her lip before saying, "The size of a ring doesn't matter to me."

Ah shit. There goes the sick clench of my heart again. But I don't let a bit of it show or bleed into my voice when I tell her, "I know it doesn't."

Her face softens like she saw and heard it anyway. "That doesn't mean it doesn't eat at your pride. Like not

being able to have sex with me did."

Goddammit. I thought I'd hidden that pretty well, too. "You could tell?"

Deliberately she arches an eyebrow and purses her lips, as if to say it was obvious as hell, then she smiles and lifts her hand to cup my jaw. "I'm the queen of 'Just because it shouldn't bother you, doesn't mean it won't.' So when what my mother did gets to you, whether it's about a ring or anything else, just remember that I've already had everything money can buy. But I wanted something *more*…and you've given me that. I just hope that what I give back is enough."

This time the clenching ache within my chest is sweet. "It is, angel. Anything you give." I push my fingers into her thick hair, my gaze searching her face. Beautiful, so beautiful—but with a few shadows amid all the brightness. "You all right? That's a lot of shit that came at you in a short time."

"Yes." Her voice thickens, and regret darkens her face. "And I'm sorry I shut you out last night. I just…don't have a lot of armor around my heart."

"I'll protect it for you."

She gives a short, watery laugh, her eyes suddenly glistening. "You're the biggest danger to it, Cole Matthews."

Just as she is to mine. Gruffly I tell her, "I should have done better. You took a hit yesterday because of me, when you found out about your dad asking me to watch

you. I should have prepared you for it, told you about it. It just wasn't anything that was ever serious to me."

But I should have realized it would be serious to her.

"I know. And it's okay." She draws a shuddering breath. "That wasn't what hit me so hard, not after you told me what happened. It was just *them*. I was just so tired of them. I wanted to leave them behind and they won't let me. I'm sorry she came at you today."

"I'll survive." And I'm not sorry the way it played out. Seeing Mia catch fire and hearing how she plans to burn her parents down was fucking amazing. But maybe not for her. "Are you okay? Do you need space again for a while?"

"No. I just need you." But even as my heart swells up, she hesitates before adding, "Do you want to come over to my place, since the tree and everything is over there? We never explicitly discussed our plans for Christmas Day. But maybe I should have, instead of assuming that you want to spend it with me."

Still uncertain that she's worth everything that she is. Gently I push her toward her own door. "I'm coming over for *you*, not for the tree. I'll grab that takeout bag and be right there. I also have a present for you. And a box of rubbers"—realizing I'm doing my own assuming, I tack on—"if you want me to bring them."

Clicking open her deadbolt, she tells me, "Just leave them there."

That ache goes real tight and painful again. Except

the interpretation I put on her words doesn't match the breathless way she said them. So instead of assuming one more time, I ask her in a raw voice, "Are you saying you don't want me to fuck you? Or that we don't need them?"

Mia's head whips around. She sees my face and I must look like I'm in hell because she quickly shakes her head and reassures me, "We don't need them."

Fuck yes. And fuck the food. I'm about to eat something else.

Swinging the door to my apartment shut, I slowly stalk across the hall, my cock trying to bust through my jeans and lead the way. "Just let me make sure of what you're saying. You want me to come inside you?"

Cheeks flushed, she nods.

"You on birth control?" I'm pretty damn sure she's not.

"No," she whispers.

That breathy answer has pre-cum spilling from the tip of my dick, my body preparing to fill her up in every possible way. "So if this means that I knock you up, you'll want our baby as much as I do?"

Hope gleams in her eyes as she answers, "Maybe even more than you do."

Not possible. "I thought you weren't in a rush?"

Head tipping back as I move in closer, she rises up on her toes. "I'm not. But there's no reason to wait, either. Is there?"

I can't think of a single one.

So like a starving beast I claim her mouth, loving her sweet taste, the hungry whimper that comes from her throat as she returns the kiss. Slowly I back her into the apartment, my hands buried in her hair and holding her steady while she tears at her belt, then at the buttons of her long coat, our shuffling steps punctuated by her soft little moans.

We're on a straight line for the bedroom but I can't wait that long to get a deeper taste of her. We've only made it as far as the Christmas tree when her coat hits the floor. I drop to my knees a second later, then have to groan at the pure perfection on display before me.

"This fucking dress." I've never seen her in it before, but it's sexy as sin—thin shoulder straps that seem barely strong enough to hold up the fabric cupping her beautiful tits, crimson silk that hugs every curve and flirts with her knees. "I'll take it off you later, but right now I'm going to—"

Get my head under that skirt. Except as soon as I lift that flirty hem, sweet Jesus. I'm struck dumb by the sight of what she'd hidden away for me to find. She's wearing those tall boots that I've loved forever but even those didn't prepare me for the black stockings and suspenders decorating her sleek thighs…or her bare, glistening pussy. Not a panty in sight.

"Is this all for me?" I ask hoarsely.

"All for you," is her husky confirmation. She widens

her stance and pulls the skirt from my frozen hand, lifting it higher. Her voice lowers to a whisper like she's sharing a secret. "And you want to know the best part? I ended up going to church like this."

Oh my dirty little virgin. This Christmas just keeps getting better.

Groaning, I palm her ass and haul her hips forward, aiming that sweet pussy at my mouth. Her delicious musky flavor explodes across my tongue. She cries out, her hands fisting in my hair, holding on tight for balance when I tease her hot little clit with side-to-side licks, the kind I know drive her so damn wild and get her so fucking wet.

And I'm rushing. Rushing too damn fast. Except it doesn't feel like that. Because this has been more than a month coming, every day like endless foreplay, and Mia's a virgin but she's not shy or scared or innocent— and she doesn't have a cherry left, because if anything remained after she used her toy then my fingers and tongue took care of the rest. And this part, with me on my knees worshipping at the shrine of her cunt, this we've done slow and fast and all the speeds in between.

It'll just be getting my cock inside her that's new. And that's when I'll take it slow and easy.

And I need take it slower now, now. Oh fuck. This is the moment when her legs start trembling and her head rolls back and she digs her teeth into her bottom lip, but can't stop those helpless moans. This is the moment

when she starts riding my face and her juices are dripping down my chin and coating the inside of her thighs, and that's usually when I work three fingers into her tight channel, fucking her with them deep and hard, sucking on her clit until her entire body seizes up and her pussy clamps down on my fingers like it'll never let them go.

But this time I don't have any fingers to offer. I've got a good grip on her ass but my other hand is frantically tearing at the fastening of my jeans. Because I thought a ripped-up muscle hurt but real pain is what my dick's suffering now, knowing I'm so damn close to pushing my way past her tiny entrance, into that cunt that's never been opened up by a real cock, and it's agony having anything standing between me and her pussy now.

So I need to slow it down, because I don't have enough hands holding her up, and I know that just before she comes her knees will give out. But her pussy tastes so good, so fucking good. And her engorged clit is so damn hot, and every time I flick my tongue and suck a little harder her moans and her gyrations get more erratic, because she's about to come and no fucking way am I slowing down.

Then her knees go. But I don't let her fall, instead wrapping my arm around her hips and pulling her against my face to steady her, slowly easing her down to the floor and sucking on her clit all the way.

The orgasm hits her just before she's all the way

down. Her fingers about rip out my hair, but I barely notice because when she comes all that juicy wetness intensifies into a liquid rush. And usually I'll lick it all up, or rub it all over my face and chest, but right now she's so wet and ripe for fucking that I can't think of anything but getting that syrupy sweetness all over my dick.

Not fucking her yet. Just giving my cock a little taste. Just easing this pain.

Because she's so beautiful. So fuckable. She's half-lying on the Christmassy quilted rug she bought for the base of the tree, her hair spilling around her head in a tangled black halo. Her red lips are parted as she pants, her skin glistening with sweat. One of the silk straps holding up her dress has slipped down over her right shoulder, exposing the perfect scoop of her breast and a cherry-red nipple. That flirty skirt's up around her waist, and her legs are splayed in that boneless way she has when she's recovering from an orgasm. And everything else on display, Jesus. The lacy lingerie belt, those suspenders and her pale thighs with the soft inner skin reddened from the stubble on my jaw, the stockings—all of it frames her pussy, turning the slit flushed a deep pink and dripping with her juices into a work of art.

My head's pounding in unison with the veins in my cock as I move over her, holding up my upper body with one stiff arm braced beside her shoulder, taking the rest of my weight on my knees. I fist my ironhard shaft in

a hand that shakes with need. With me hovering over her like this, the difference in our sizes is so goddamn stark. I'm a huge fucking brute. She's tall and curvy, but compared to my bulk she's just a little thing. And comparing the tiny entrance of her pussy to the thick head of my cock?

I've got to take this so slow. And easy.

"Not going to fuck you yet, angel." Each harshly grated word is a necessary reminder of what I'm doing— and I'm *not* fucking her. "Not until we're in a bed. I just need to feel all those hot pussy juices against my dick. Not going to take you yet."

"But I want you to," she breathes and the rusty edge of her voice threatens to scrape away my control. Her thighs come up and grip my sides, and the movement unfurls the petals of her pussy. "I love it when you take what's yours."

Mine. And she's offering it up. Right here. Though she ought to be in a soft bed. And I ought to treat her right. So I'm *not* going to fuck her here.

But I can't stop myself from moving closer and sliding the ruddy crown of my dick up and down that juicy slit. My breath hisses through my teeth as her plump pussy lips part around my cock's head, enfolding it in their scalding embrace.

Trying to regain my sanity, I slick the tip upwards and tease her clit, but can't resist another pass through the drenched heart of her. Mia's thighs grip me ever

tighter, her hands moving restlessly up and down her silk-covered belly like she wants to grab hold of me, or touch herself—and she does, sliding her hand up to cup her breast and pinch her ruby nipple, then making a soft urgent sound before her hips begin rolling as if she's trying to push me inside her.

"Angel." I growl like a savage beast when I feel that taut little pussy stretching, giving. *"Not yet."*

"I can't wait, I can't." She's gasping, shaking. "Just do it here. Take me here."

Gritting my teeth, I fight the need to slam deep. We ought to be in a bed. I need to go slow and easy. It's her first time. *Our* first time. But how the fuck can I go slow? Her pussy's so hot and wet and tight that it's just sucking me in. Or that's Mia, shoving me in deeper with each rock of her hips, her legs wrapping around my back and trying to pull me closer. And she's begging for more of my cock, her desperate "please, Cole, please" ringing sweetly in my ears.

And as for the bed... *Fuck.* It's Christmas. I should give her what she wants.

With a tortured groan, I slam my hips forward and bury the full length of my cock inside a paradise of wet heat, bottoming out at the end of that long, hard stroke. Her strangled gasp stops me for an instant, her body in a stiff bow beneath mine and her luscious cunt holding me in the sweetest, tightest heaven I've ever known. *So fucking tight.* But if I'm too big and too deep, then she's

loving that, too, because that gasp melts into a thick moan, her head rolling bonelessly to the side and her back arching. And after all the waiting and the pain, I'm finally inside my angel. So goddamn deep inside her. I gave her want she wanted. *Now* I'll take it slow. I'll pull out and pick her up and carry her to the bed and finish this there.

Sweat dripping into my eyes, I ease back until just the head of my cock's inside her, but her cunt's so swollen with her arousal that her inner walls clutch me even tighter. Goddammit. Grunting with each stroke, I fuck my way back in, all the way into the greedy little pussy that won't let me go, won't let me treat my angel like I should. And doesn't this pussy know it's *mine*?

Mia does. Her fingernails are scratching the fuck out of my back as my big cock takes control of every inch of her cunt. I use the fat head and thick curving shaft to rub up against that sweet spot inside her that makes her start to sob and whine and writhe. I bottom out again and ruthlessly grind against her clit, until her inner walls are even hotter and tighter but she's so slippery wet that I can't stop pumping into her, into this incredible hot pussy that's being good for me now, so damn good, *too* damn good because Mia's starting to tremble and if she comes now, with me inside her, if I feel her cunt squeezing me like it'll never let me go, I'll lose my goddamn head and fuck her straight through this floor.

But I can't stop. Can't stop can't stop can't stop.

Because I'm about to make my angel come and I'd rather take another bullet than abandon her pussy now.

She starts moaning then, helplessly moaning my name, her head thrashing from side to side, her hands clutching at my shoulders as if trying to anchor herself. Her hips arch up off the floor, making the thrust of my cock strike up higher and deeper inside her. Then her whole spine is arching up, her boot heels digging into my ass, and that sultry cunt grips me so goddamn tight just before her head tips back and she screams. Her inner muscles start convulsing and her orgasm brings the rush of wet that makes every hammering stroke into the slick grasp of her pussy a million times better than the one before.

Everything's better than it's ever been before, better than everything I imagined. The way she falls boneless again, and how I follow her down, gathering her close as I continue to thrust inside her. Now it's slow. So slow, savoring her kiss and the shining light of her eyes. The soft bounce of her tits. Her husky voice moaning that I feel so big and so good inside her. So now I take my time, loving everything she is, because it's not my mind that I've lost, but my heart.

And it's not her pussy that finally pulls me over. It's her trusting arms twining around my shoulders. It's her legs holding me tight. It's her soft cries muffled against my throat, and her frantic

—*I love you, I love you*—

Giving me everything, after everything she already let me take. My whole goddamn world boils up and through my cock, filling her with my seed, my future, my heart. Everything I have to give in return.

Then I fuck her through the floor.

MIA

THE TREE IS DEFINITELY CROOKED NOW, LEANING forward at a forty-five degree angle. I don't know how it's still standing at all. And I'm not sure at what point Cole and I knocked it so far off-kilter. But at least it didn't fall on us while we were beneath it.

Though I'm also not sure we'd have noticed if it did.

And I'm not sure if Cole has noticed that there isn't anything else beneath the tree, either. Just a quilted tree skirt. Not a single gift for him. And not for lack of money or time. I either made or bought something for almost everyone else I know. But for the one person who matters most? Nothing.

Which means I've completely failed at Christmas.

I should have just gotten him a mattress. Or a dining set. Or a washer and dryer. But I want him sleeping *here*, eating *here*…and making out with me in the laundry room while we wait for our clothes to dry. Just like he has been all this past month.

This would have all been a lot easier if he'd just told me what he wanted for Christmas. What he *really* wanted. Sending my father to jail doesn't count. That won't happen for months…maybe years. And only if there's anything in the financials to find. I truly think there will be. But, still. That doesn't help me today.

An otherwise completely wonderful, incredible day. Except that now I might ruin it.

My shame spikes when Cole comes back from his place, carrying the bag of takeout and holding a brightly wrapped box. He's so wonderful. Everything about him. I don't deserve this much happiness. But I'll take it. And do better next year, I swear.

He stops in his tracks, staring at the tree. "How is it still up?"

"A Christmas miracle?"

His grin flashes. "Sounds about right."

Though I've taken off my stockings and boots, I'm still in my Christmas dress, and his eyes hungrily sweep up and down my length as he comes closer. He drops a kiss to my mouth as he sets the takeout on the kitchen counter, then lays the present on the breakfast bar. It looks professionally wrapped in red-and-silver striped

paper—as if he went out, took the time to select a gift, and picked out the wrapping, making certain to choose red. Because he knows I love red. And he loves red on me.

And I didn't get him anything.

"Hey." Hard fingers grip my chin and bring my gaze up to his. Concern darkens his eyes. "You all right?"

"Yes." Though my voice is thick.

"Angel." He says my name like a gruff admonishment for lying, and he sighs. "You must be disappointed. You've got a refrigerator full of groceries and I know you meant to be cooking all morning. Not eating takeout for Christmas."

"Oh. No." That doesn't bother me at all. We both like this restaurant and have ordered from it before, which is why I stopped there on the way home. I untie the plastic bag, begin pulling out cartons. "I actually thought it would be kind of nice just to sit on the couch and be lazy and stuff ourselves full of Peking duck. I can make all that other stuff later."

"Your plans did get pretty fucked this morning, though."

I giggle. "Yeah. Really well."

"Shit." He comes up behind me, his mouth on my neck and his hands on my waist, pulling me back against the hard wedge of his erection behind his zipper. Instantly I'm wet, remembering the unbridled ecstasy of his thick cock pounding inside me, all that hunger and

strength unleashed. "So why don't you finally tell me what you really did, then I'm going to fuck you again. How the hell did you end up at church?"

"Because I went to see Paul at his house, and found out that's where he was." Clenching my thighs to ease the ache building between them, I ask breathlessly, "Can you hand me a couple of those bowls?"

"You know you can just microwave the cartons." But since he knows I won't, Cole lets me go and reaches for the serving bowls. "So you hunted the mayor down?"

"Right after Mass was over. It wasn't weird. I know his family really well."

"Apparently, since you went without panties." His voice is teasing.

My face heats. "I didn't think that through. I just intended to come straight back to your place and… wake you up."

"Next year," he suggests and kisses me again, then helps me empty the takeout cartons into the bowls. "So what did you say to the mayor?"

"Mostly we had a conversation about all the things I'd like to do when I take over the Bennet Foundation in a few years."

His eyebrows shoot upwards. "You told him you're sending your dad to jail?"

"No, I…" I had no idea he didn't know this. "It'll all come to me when I'm thirty years old, regardless. When my great-grandfather created the foundation and

family trust, he wrote in a provision that the heir can take control of both when they reach thirty. He said the future belongs to the younger generation, so they should be making the decisions. And we all have our own personal money—and I'll inherit a lot more when I hit thirty—but the bulk of the fortune itself, the mansion… it's all a big Bennet machine. I just get to decide how to run that machine." I sigh and glance at Cole. "Why else would my parents have treated me the way they did? My father wants to control me when I take over, and my mother wants me to feel so incompetent that I'll never claim that position."

"I just figured they were selfish pieces of shit."

"Maybe that, too." Not that it matters much anymore. "But no matter what happens after that financial review, I intend to take over and push them both out—then hire Jason on, since it should all be partially his, too. So I'll pay him an obscene amount to run everything, because I'd rather keep pursuing the career I am now. But Jason's interested in it. That's why he went to law school, and why he's doing all that work for those nonprofits now."

"So you've been planning this for a while."

"Yep. And my father has his own money, just like I do, and I can't kick him out of the mansion because that belongs to the family…but everything else, I'll take from him. He won't have the Bennet power behind him. And he won't have any influence in this city after that. So this morning, I reminded Paul that staying on good

terms with me will be far better in the long run than helping my father cause trouble for anyone I've taken a romantic interest in."

Cole boils it down in that blunt way of his. "So you strong-armed the mayor."

"*Nicely.* I brought a gift for his family. And I don't think Paul really likes my father, either, so…" I shrug. "Convincing him to tell my father to go fuck himself if he makes any attempt to ruin you wasn't difficult."

"So you saved me again, angel." His voice is pure gravel as Cole cups my face in his big hands. His dark eyes seem to worship my every feature as he looks down at me. "I don't fucking deserve you."

"You do," I tell him. Lifting my chin stubbornly, I add with fire, "Don't *ever* let me hear you say that again."

My vehemence seems to amuse him. "Deserve or not, I'm sure as fuck never letting you go." He claims my mouth with a soft, lingering kiss. "Now go open up your present, and I'll start warming up these bowls. You'll need a lot of fuel for what I'll be doing to you later."

Happiness and guilt war within me as I carefully unwrap the box. Both emotions melt away into sheer pleasure when I move aside delicate tissue paper to reveal a gorgeous cashmere sweater.

"Oh…It's the *same* one."

"Because you said that shrunken one was your favorite."

"This one is now." Heart so full, I slide my fingers

over the soft fabric. "But how did you find it? I got the other one two years ago. It's not still available in the stores."

"I had that mitten, which told me the size and the brand. The rest took a only a bit of tracking down online. I thought you might have done the same, but after snooping around in your closet, I knew you hadn't bought a new one."

"I felt like I didn't deserve to. Not after ruining the first one by being so careless and stupid." And I'm so glad I didn't now. Knowing Cole hunted down a replacement because he knew me, knew it was my favorite... I never knew my heart could feel so full.

"That's just bullshit." Though bluntly said, his voice is gentle. "Look at what you did, Mia. You got away from your parents and fought for a new life for yourself—and you could have taken it so damn easy. No one would have blamed you if you did. But instead you went out and put that life together with your own two hands. Did you fuck up sometimes? Shrink a sweater? Sure. But that little mitten isn't a failure. It just shows how strong you are, because even after a setback, you didn't give up. You kept on doing your laundry every damn week—along with everything else you kept working on. Ah, shit. Don't cry."

But I am. Because he sees *me*. And he sees me in the very best way—and far more generously than I see myself. Hot tears spill down my cheeks and I leap for

him.

"I love you." Wrapping my arms around his neck, my legs around his waist, I press wet and salty kisses to his mouth, his jaw, everywhere. "I love you."

"Mia." Hoarsely he stops me, his dark gaze filled with raw emotion. "Everything I am belongs to you. That's been true since the day I first looked up at you. I didn't know who the hell you were, but I do now. And I love you so fucking much. Everything about you."

My tears fall harder. "I love everything about you." A sob rips through me and I bury my face in his neck. "But I didn't get you a gift. I'm sorry. I'm so sorry."

"For what now? Mia." Frowning, he forces me to look at him again. "What are you sorry for?"

"I tried to find something perfect. And personal. Like all the others. Gifts were *never* personal before. Just something my mom hired someone to get. But it didn't matter if it was something I wanted or needed."

Understanding and amusement soften his face. "That's why you made stuff like that ice cream scoop."

Choking on the lump of tears in my throat, I nod. Brokenly I tell him, "Even if it wasn't perfect, I wanted them to know that they mattered. On a personal level. But I couldn't find anything perfect for you. Something that was…good enough. And every time I asked what you wanted for Christmas, it was like you didn't want anything."

His callused thumbs gently swipe the tears from my

cheeks. "Angel," he says softly. "The only thing I want, you've already given. Every day for a month. Yesterday, today, tomorrow. Because you're here with me. And you're everything I could ever want, on Christmas or any other day. For the rest of my life."

A shuddering breath rips through me. "That's all I want, too."

"Then next year's gifts are going to be real easy." His gaze filling with heat, he lifts me onto the edge of the counter, hitching up my skirt. He groans when his fingers find me hot and wet, and in the next moment his thick cock fills me up with a long, delicious stroke that leaves no room for anything inside me except for Cole—in my body, in my heart, in my soul. His body taut with strain, he roughly commands, "Now tell me what you want for Christmas, Mia."

Breathlessly, I whisper against his lips, "Just you."

"And what do you *need*, Mia?"

The answer will always be the same. "Just you."

And he sweetly, sweetly gives me both.

COLE

THREE YEARS LATER

MIA FREEZES AT THE TOP OF THE STAIRS when she sees me, her pale blue eyes widening and her red lips rounding. "Ohhhhh," she says in that voice that tells me her pussy is warming up and a new fantasy is playing out in her head. "I always forget how *amazing* you look in a tux. You should really wear one more often."

"You don't forget how I look," I tell her gruffly. "It's just that after watching you slink around in gowns like that every New Year's Eve, I'm so goddamn hard for you by the end of the night that I fuck the memory out of

your head."

And the gown she has this year…Christ. It's a shimmering silver that covers everything from her diamond-encircled throat to her pretty little feet, but clings so close to every inch in-between that it doesn't conceal a damn thing. Not the perfect roundness of her tits. Not the hot curve of her ass. Not the swollen mound of her belly.

"I remember *exactly* what we did last year," she purrs in that husky voice as she gracefully descends the stairs.

So do I. And just like last year, there's a good chance that the first time I take her won't be *after* the gala. More likely I'll just fuck her at the bottom of these stairs.

Or maybe not. Because the soft patter of little feet announces the waddling arrival of our son, clad only in a diaper. My heart swells up at the sight of him, just like it does every time. Little Nicholas has Mia's black hair and pale blue eyes, and owns my heart as completely as his mother does. He's drooling and chewing on his fist, but his beautiful little face breaks into a smile when he sees me. His single tooth gleams as he laughs and lifts his chubby arms toward me in a silent demand as irresistible as it is cute.

"Come here, you little bug." I sweep his cuddly little body up against my chest, and when I glance up at Mia she's doing that *Oooooh* thing with her velvet red lips again. A big man in a tux holding a baby is pushing all her fantasy buttons. But then, she seems to make that

face whenever I hold the baby, which is pretty damn often. "Give us a kiss goodnight."

He lands a wet smack on my chin, then on Mia's cheek. And she's smiling, but I see the moment of indecision and regret flash through her eyes when I hand little Nick over to Carol, who's been helping us out around the house ever since he was born. Because Mia would like to do it all—and she *could* do it all—but after the forensic accountant she hired a few years back found exactly what Mia expected him to find, to the tune of millions of dollars of embezzled funds, suddenly a heap of new responsibilities landed on her shoulders. Even after delegating and sharing that burden with Jason, simply being *the* Bennet in this city carries a lot of weight and obligation. So I've tried to lighten her load as much as I can—which included persuading her to hire Carol, who eases the burden here at home.

A burden that had increased now that we're living in this big house. With the baby coming and with a new role for Mia to play, we both realized we needed something larger than our apartments. Did it grate on my pride when Mia outright bought a house that I could never afford?

Not a damn bit. Because it was what she needed. So it was what *we* needed. And together we've spent two and a half years making it our home. And that's what this place is really worth to me. Not the price tag, but the life we've built here together.

For the same reason, she'll probably never return to the Bennet mansion. Because the life she lived there isn't one that she ever wants to revisit. Instead Jason resides in the mansion, since he's the heart of the Bennet Foundation right now and that location is convenient for everyone involved, and that seems to please Mia. Partially because he loves living in that mansion, and she loves knowing he's happy. Partially because it's a slap in her father's face.

No surprise, John Bennet didn't end up serving much jail time. Fuckers like him almost never do. But he'll never be much of anything in this town again.

And Patricia, she followed Mia's advice and divorced his ass just before the shit hit the fan, then got the hell out of town. I don't know where she is now. Don't care, either.

The only thing I care about is right here. "He'll be all right," I tell Mia.

"I know," she sighs. "I just hate leaving him."

Every time. Me, too.

Softly I kiss her, then reach for our coats. The limo's waiting outside, and Mia holds my hand as we walk down the front steps to the circular driveway. The front of our big house still blazes with colorful Christmas lights—though this year, I didn't let Mia help, except to tell me which decorations she wanted where. I barely survived multiple heart attacks last year, coming home to find her on a ladder, fastening a string of lights to the

eaves on the third floor. Trying to do it six months pregnant? No fucking way was I going to let that happen. Which means we might soon become one of those families that leaves their holiday lights up all year.

A flash of long leg peeks through the shimmering silver as Mia steps into the car. I slide into the soft leather seat across from her, because I fucking love looking at my wife.

She loves looking back. "I still like your face," she says huskily, then pushes the button to close the privacy screen.

We've gotten real familiar with the locations of those buttons.

And even with that swollen belly she's so damn graceful, hiking up her dress and straddling me in a smooth movement. It's pure sweet torture when she does this. Because she's got her hair done up and her lipstick perfect, and the drive to the gala doesn't take too long—not long enough to fix them up again. And it's no one's goddamn business if I'm fucking my wife in the limo. So I don't like to mess her all up.

Her arms link around my neck and her mouth is so close to mine, teasing with every warm breath. "I've figured out a plan for our empty-nest years."

After the babies are grown up. After she's gone back to med school and become a medical examiner.

"What's the plan?" I hope it involves a lot of fucking.

"Well…" She reaches between us and slowly unzips

my trousers. "I think we should become a crime-solving duo."

I let out a quiet grunt of pleasure as her soft hand grips my length. The past years, she's gotten a whole lot better at getting my big cock out of my pants just by dragging it through the zipper opening.

"What about Huertas?"

"He can still be your partner when you're on-duty," she says, and her hot tongue flicks out to tease my bottom lip. Groaning, I chase her mouth but she leans back, denying me. "But this will be when you're off-duty. Like if someone ever gets stabbed while we're at the gala, but there are no witnesses. I'll examine the body and tell you what kind of person must have done it—how tall, how strong. Whether they're right-handed or left-handed. And you'll use your deductive skills to solve the crime. Then we'll find a private room and celebrate our victory when you bend me over a table."

My breath hisses through my teeth when she drags the tip of my dick through the scalding wetness of her cunt. "This is a damn good plan."

"I know." Her head falls back as she sinks down, burying half my cock within the tight clasp of her pussy. "Oh god. That feels *so* good."

And even after three years, I barely have any goddamn control. My hands clamp over her hips and I ram up between her thighs, forcing myself deeper on a hard stroke. Mia cries out, her fingers gripping the lapels of

my coat, then rides me back down.

"Fuck, angel," I groan against her exposed throat. "Your pussy takes my cock so good. Every goddamn time."

Every time. Every way. Every day. I fuck her hard but it could be slow and be just as perfect, and just being with her will always be the best part of it all. I take her now and love her more with every thrust, waiting until she trembles and screams, then empty my entire heart and soul into her pussy when I come.

She falls against me, her chest heaving, the belly rounded with our baby pressing against my stomach. "This is the dirtiest thing we've ever done," she claims, panting.

Not even close. "Pretty damn sure we did this last year. And the year before."

"Yes." Lightly she kisses my mouth. "But we cleaned up. And this time, I'll be walking around all night with your cum between my legs, while I'm all knocked up with your baby."

Holy fuck. My spent dick jerks inside her, as if trying to squeeze out a few more drops.

She laughs merrily, looking down into my eyes. And this moment, fuck. It's like my heart just tries to burst through my chest. Because she's my angel. Always my angel.

And every single day with her is heaven.

❋ END ❋

FIND KATI WILDE
Website: www.katiwilde.com
Email: kati@katiwilde.com
Twitter: @katiwilde
Facebook: authorkatiwilde
Instagram: authorkatiwilde

ABOUT KATI WILDE

Kati Wilde is a tight-lipped, loose-hipped woman of indeterminate age and low breeding. She loves to write about strong heroines, obsessed alpha heroes, and happily ever afters.

You've reached the end of *Secret Santa*, but Christmas isn't over yet! Flip this book over to enjoy Kati Wilde's second holiday romance, *All He Wants For Christmas*.

You've reached the end of *All He Wants For Christmas*, but the sexy holiday fun isn't over yet! Flip this book over to enjoy Kati Wilde's first Christmas romance, *Secret Santa*.

the man who loves you feels like he's got big fucking holes in his chest when you're not cuddled up next to him. So he might come looking for you."

"That would be bad," she whispers. "If he came in and Santa was giving me a really big Christmas tree."

I can't stop my laugh. Christ, I love this woman. So much.

Her breath shudders as my fingers slick between her thighs. She's already so hot and wet, I'll be able to slide into her so fucking easy. But that's not the plan.

Not yet.

"Your pussy's begging for my thick cock, baby. But before I give it to you, you've got one more present to open."

This time when she turns onto her side, I let her. Her brown eyes narrow at me. "What is it?"

Just a small gift. But I've had it for a year. Now it's in the palm of my hand, ready to slip onto her finger.

But first, I give her a note. Her gaze widens as she begins to read.

> **Open the box.**
> **Put on the ring.**
> **Say you'll marry me.**
> **LOGAN**

She looks up with me, eyes shining with tears of joy and hope.

And with a single word — *YES* — she gives me everything.

✳ END ✳